the face
of the
deep

A Novel
by Michael Mitton

Part 1 of the Dorchadas Trilogy

An Amazon self-published book
© Michael Mitton 2019

ISBN: 9781672264013
Imprint: Independently published

First published December 2019

The very best novels set the mind racing whilst pulling on the strings of the heart. This novel does exactly that, whilst simultaneously inviting the soul to come out of hiding. I loved (and needed) every single second I spent reading this book.   So, do your soul a favour and get a copy

Pete Hughes   KXC London

In the beginning you weep.
The starting point for many things is grief,
at the place where endings seem so absolute.
One would think that it should be otherwise,
but the pain of closing is antecedent
to every new opening in our lives.

Belden C Lane
The Solace of Fierce Landscapes

Do not forget to entertain strangers:
For thereby some have entertained angels unawares.
The Letter to the Hebrews

CHAPTER 1

As the Reverend Douglas Romer approached his pulpit, he knew that this, almost certainly, would be his last sermon at St.Philip's. That morning he had nicked himself with his razor as he shaved away several days' stubble, and he felt the wound throb as he approached the ancient oak steps that rose up to the pulpit. The meagre congregation strained at the hymn. The organist fumbled the final notes, and it was an awkward chord that hovered for a while in the medieval rafters before the building fell into an anxious silence, save for the creak, creak of the Vicar's ascent of the pulpit steps.

He felt faint as he entered the cramped octagonal space and instinctively touched the cut on his neck. His finger felt moist and for a moment he held it in front of him pondering this release of lifeblood. For the briefest moment he thought of the young men of the first World War trenches, whose names would be read out at next month's Remembrance Sunday. He winced as he thought of the violence of warfare. He turned on the failing pulpit light that reluctantly flickered into action. The congregation looked hard at their dimly-lit Vicar, and some noticed the rose red stain on his bleached clerical collar. But Douglas did not dare look back at any of these faces. He had lost courage for such things weeks ago.

'In the n.. n.. name....', he started, and then paused. He breathed in, feeling the air cold in his lungs. The congregation was still standing. It always remained standing until that final 'Holy Spirit', which was the cue to sit down. But those words never came on this Sunday. Instead the congregation looked up to a pathetic figure, a shadow of the keen young Vicar who had arrived ten years earlier to this suburban Sheffield parish with such life and promise. But now they beheld a very different minister, one who was approaching his fiftieth birthday, and yet who now seemed so much older. The sound of coughing stirred Douglas, and he looked out at the nervous congregation beneath him, and he spied Mavis, his faithful, loyal and supremely understanding friend. He watched her mouth trembling as she stared up at him. He quickly looked away and down to the cold stone floor of the nave, over which for centuries the faithful had shuffled to collect their bread and wine from the altar. But it was also on that very same cold stone floor that he stood, shaking in an agony of grief, as he gripped the side of the wicker coffin that enclosed the precious mortal remains of his beloved Saoirse, whose soul he commended to the mercy of God - the God who had violently snatched her from him a week before their second wedding anniversary. That was more than two long, long years ago now. Then as now, his stammer had got the better of him, and he failed to deliver one word of his carefully prepared eulogy.

Once again, he took a long, deep breath, feeling the cool air finally clearing his head. He completed his acknowledgement to the Holy Trinity without stammer, and the pews creaked and groaned as the congregation yielded their mortal frames to the dark wood. He then prepared to embark on a sermon that he had only prepared in his head, for the whisky had prevailed over duty the night before, and this morning the iPad document, that should have been gleaming with a nicely tuned sermon, revealed nothing more than the date. He would be on his own today.

'My friends, if God.. ' he started, with a husky, trembling voice, 'if there is a God…' And that was it. It was it, because Gerald Bentley OBE had had enough. He stepped out of his pew and, grasping tightly the lapels of his tweed jacket, he stood in the aisle and addressed the congregation in a tone that he had used many a time at the Church Council meetings, a tone that he used to remind the congregation just who really was in charge of this church.

'Come on. Someone's got to say it, and I don't mind being the one to do it.' The congregation, who until two years ago had known nothing but proper Sunday services with good evangelical preaching, had learned to navigate the last two difficult years reasonably well. But never had someone interrupted a sermon before. Not even Gerald Bentley. Something had to be very seriously wrong. Every face looked at the man standing in the aisle whom few loved, all feared, and with whom most found themselves agreeing, even when they knew it was against their better nature.

'This has frankly gone on long enough. I've not spent seventy-one years of my life coming to this church only to be told by the man who should be leading us that God no longer exists. I'm sorry, but this has got to stop. I'm sorry, Vicar,' he said, without any sign of sorrow in his face, 'I'm very sorry for your loss, but we don't like how it's affected you, and we don't want any more of this mumbo jumbo, New Age, Buddhist nonsense you've been dishing up these past few months. Frankly, you

5

need to… well, you know.. I'll say it straight - it's time you stood down. I'm sorry, someone has got to say this. Don't you agree, Peter?' he said, looking hard at the very frail former warden, Peter Stackpole, who was busy fiddling with his hearing aid and was struggling to work out quite what was going on.

While Gerald Bentley regaled the congregation with further evidence for his argument, Douglas watched as if from another world. He heard very little of what Gerald said but simply looked at him with a lost and vacant expression on this face. His reddened finger was running itself up and down the pulpit edge. He watched while Gerald made his speech, and he watched while someone else said something, and he watched little conversations breaking out in the pews and many anxious glances being thrown at him. He instinctively looked to find Mavis, but only saw the back of her bent figure sniffing its way out of church.

And then he saw Saoirse, sitting alone in the front row, dressed in the bright cerise top that he had bought her for her last birthday on earth. She smiled up at him and lifted her hand and wiggled her slender fingers as a reassuring wave. Her head leaned kindly to one side, and her dark Irish hair fell across her mouth. She gently brushed it out of the way and then blew him a kiss.

There was a hand on his arm. It belonged to Glenda, the church warden. 'Come on, Douglas. We can see you are not well. I'll help you to the vestry'. It was the only act of kindness he experienced that morning, his last morning at St.Philips for a long time.

*

It was that image of Saoirse in the front pew that occupied Douglas' mind as his plane took off on a damp October morning from Birmingham Airport. With his knees pressed hard against the back of the seat in front of him, and a corpulent passenger squeezing him from the adjacent seat, he was glad the flight would not be a long one. He stared out of the window at the wisps of cloud speeding past him. He was remembering the very first time he met the girl who was to become his bride. As chair of Governors of St.Philip's Primary School, he was leading the interviews for the new teacher.

The moment Saoirse walked into the room he loved her. There was something delightfully coquettish about her, and within minutes she had all the interviewing team laughing. Having only seen her Irish name on paper, she quizzed them about how to pronounce her name and, as she suspected, none of the interviewers knew. Douglas made a stammered attempt, and her laugh in response filled the room with sunshine. 'No,' she said in mock rebuke, as if he were one of her pupils. 'It is not pronounced "Saucy", Reverend Romer, 'It is pronounced "Seersha". The name means "freedom" in the Irish language. I am sorry to present you with such a challenging name.' And her sunny smile felt to him to be the kind of smile for which he had been searching all his long years of singleness. Whatever came of this moment, he knew that this would be a name, and hers would be a face that he would remember all of his days. The plane emerged from the clouds and the bright sun dazzled through the windows, causing some of the passengers to pull down their blinds. Douglas closed only the blinds of his eyes and soaked in the brightness of the rising sun and the bitter sweetness of the memory.

The Governors were unanimous about appointing this excellent, if unconventional and not altogether respectful candidate. It was Douglas' happy job to phone her and tell her the good news. She whooped with delight on the phone and then, most unlike him, Douglas found himself asking her out to dinner that Saturday. He supposed she would never accept an invitation from a shy cleric, ten years her senior, whose stammer had got the better of him in one or two of his questions at the interview. But she did accept, without any hesitation. She arrived at his Vicarage in tight blue washed denims, and a cream Kashmir top. Her dark hair glistened hints of red in the evening light. He had never seen anything so beautiful, and he had to fight hard to stop himself weeping like a child. He stood in the doorway and muttered something fairly nonsensical until she eventually put him out of his misery and teasingly asked if unbelievers were allowed in the Vicarage. He apologised nervously, and invited her in and made her a cup of tea. She sat at the kitchen table as he made the tea, and straight away they were talking together as if they had been friends all their lives. After the first few minutes, his stammer had sunk without trace and in all the precious days of their life together, it never re-emerged.

So much was shared that first evening over dinner in a small French bistro. Douglas was amazed by how much he disclosed about his family, for he found Saoirse to be a wonderful listener. Every time he touched on a tender piece of his family story, she would pause from her meal, with fork hovering mid-air, and would listen intently, with her head at a slight angle. He told of his pain over his alcoholic and overbearing father, the reason, so he supposed, for Douglas' shyness and his stammer. He spoke of his nervy mother who was an excellent art historian by trade, and a lover of poetry by nature, whose anxieties were no doubt exacerbated by her husband's addiction. Saoirse in turn spoke about her family, a passionate Republican family from the South of Ireland. She admired their passion, yet recoiled from her father's anger and, as she saw it, an obsessive Republicanism with strong anti-Protestant and anti-British prejudices. In her home, it was her mother who was the more fond of the liquor, but although she harboured similar prejudices, she had a gentle and sensitive side to her nature, and she resorted to poetry for comfort.

They both chose the creme brûlée for dessert, and as they both tapped into the hard sugar topping, they got on to the subject of faith. Saoirse reacted strongly against the dominating religious atmosphere in her home and so fled to England to, as she put it, 'breathe in some strong Protestant fresh air for a change.' But generally she avoided religion altogether, and she soon preferred the world of drugs to religion and she coyly told Douglas of her early troubled years in the UK. In turn, Douglas told of his more conventional life - of how he was converted to Christianity at Oxford University and how this seemed to lead naturally to ordination. They laughed as they realised what different lives each had led, and yet somehow they seemed to have so much in common. That evening Douglas laughed so much that his jaw was aching by the time they were drinking their coffee. And, much to his surprise, he found himself at one moment weeping - something he had never done in the company of anyone in his adult years.

It was approaching midnight as the taxi drove them back, and as he was about to step out of the taxi, Saoirse took hold of him by the hand and kissed him on his cheek and in her teacher voice told him to be a good boy and get to bed soon. He watched the taxi depart from his drive taking her off to her flat, and then he went into his unlit kitchen, dropped to his knees, and sobbed his thanks to Almighty God, the God in whom she did not believe, yet the one he firmly believed had brought them together. He knew without any doubt that this sweet and fiery Irish girl, whose name was freedom, was to be his wife. He had never felt so alive, and so free.

8

As they met together in the following weeks, they often talked about religion and beliefs, she venturing her well-established atheistic convictions and her commitment to pacifism, and he explaining his firm evangelical faith and the upholding of biblical values. Normally when faced with the stern challenge of a convinced atheist, he would rise to the challenge with evangelistic zeal. But there was something about the peace of her spirit that softened the zeal, and much to his surprise, he found himself more concerned to understand her convictions than to seek to change them. He envied the freedom he saw in her. She was certainly well named. At the same time she envied the sturdy faith she saw in him. She had always admired the life and teachings of Christ, but just simply could not believe in the religion that had caused so much pain in her family and her people. As far as he was concerned, Saoirse was so loving, so good, so passionate about justice issues, that he felt she was much closer to God than he ever was. As far as she was concerned, Douglas was such a handsome, sensitive and kind man of real integrity that she never had any difficulty in accepting and respecting his faith.

The plane banked away from the sun and Douglas opened his eyes and rubbed away the tears that at one time had been such strangers to him and yet for the last two years were his almost daily companions. He gazed at the blue, empty distance in front of him, and felt a sense of relief that he was journeying a long way from his parish.

'Got business in Cork, have yer?' asked the corpulent passenger next to him, in a voice that Douglas imagined even the pilot could hear. He had finished reading his paper and was attempting to stuff it in the pocket in front of him, which was already under considerable pressure from his plump knees.

'Er, not business... family,' said Douglas, not in the least wanting to engage in conversation. His companion on the other hand, was not in the least wanting to travel *without* some conversation.

'Oh aye, you Irish then?' he asked. 'Not that I've got anything against the Irish, might I say - just in case you are. We got some Irish in our road as it happens. Keep themselves to themselves, like. Very pleasant. Any road, I'm doing business with the Irish in Cork, so I've got to get on with them, haven't I?' He laughed causing his whole massive frame to shake violently.

Douglas could see that this could be a very tiresome conversation, and the rudeness that had become fairly customary for him these last few months rose up in him as he said, 'I'm visiting an aunt of my deceased wife, if you must know. Do you mind if I have a look at your paper?' His neighbour was somewhat taken aback, and he reluctantly passed his paper to Douglas. 'You won't find much to humour you in there,' he said. Douglas buried his head in the paper pretending to be absorbed in an article about the torrid love life of an American celebrity of whom he had never heard. To keep his fellow passenger quiet, he read it avidly, as if he were the celebrity's greatest fan, but his thoughts were a long way away from American celebrities. There had only ever been one celebrity in Douglas' life.

Saoirse's family had lived in the city of Cork for many generations. She was an only child and had very few relatives, so once she moved to England she seldom returned to Ireland. She lived what she called her 'dangerous years' in London for a time and, after a particularly painful break-up with a Spanish dance instructor, she moved north and decided to train as a teacher. Much to her surprise she discovered she had a good brain, and gained a First Class degree at Sheffield and, following her PGSE course, she embarked on a very promising teaching career. She avoided all close relationships in these years, but when she met Douglas she knew she had found a heart in which she could finally rest. Though he was a decade older than her, she felt utterly at one with him.

It was a miracle that either of her parents made it to their wedding due to their horror at her marrying a 'Proddy', as they called him, and a Proddy minister at that. They managed to get through the wedding with minimal conversation with Douglas. And, for reasons Douglas never understood, two years later they blamed him for Saoirse's death, as if she had received a terrible divine punishment for marrying a British Protestant. So they, and many of the family, had cut him off completely.

Douglas' parents were shocked when he told them that finally, after many years of singleness, he was getting married. He was in his mid 40's and his mother confided with him that she had assumed he was gay. It took her quite a while to adjust to viewing her son as straight again. Neither parent were very sure about his young Irish bride, but they could not deny that she made their son very happy. When Saoirse died, Douglas' father said very little and returned to the bottle big time. His mother became even more nervy than usual, and Douglas found it easiest to keep clear of both his parents as neither could comfort him. His mother continued to phone regularly however, and just recently, she hooked naked anger in him when she suggested he should be 'over his grief' by now and looking for someone else. More than once he had slammed the phone down on her and then suffered pangs of guilt for days after.

These were times when he would have loved the comfort and friendship of parents who understood him, but the world he now inhabited seemed to contain neither friend nor family who could offer him such comfort. There was Frank, the American priest who was working for a time in his deanery, who had been a wonderful support to him, even leading the main part of the funeral, but he had now returned to California. Douglas came to the lonely realisation that Saoirse was the only person who ever really understood him, and she was now a pile of ashes in a box beneath the damp, cold soil in the sprawling graveyard of his church. Frequently he would be found kneeling in the grass by the blue pearl granite stone that marked the site of her grave. There he would speak with her, imagining her soft, lilting voice replying with her usual mixture of humour and common sense. He dreaded forgetting the sound of that sweet voice.

A reverberating snore interrupted Douglas' thoughts. His fellow passenger had fallen asleep. Douglas felt relieved and put down the paper with its lurid news and peered down at the soft strips of cotton wool cloud that floated between him and the Irish Sea beneath him. He remembered how he and Saoirse often talked about visiting her homeland, but as fate would have it…. *Fate*. That is what his once strong evangelical religion had now come down to: Fate - the very thing his religion was opposed to. He had tried, God knows he had: desperately praying at her bedside as he stroked her bandaged and cruelly injured head, longing for her to open her gorgeous, mahogany eyes and smile that beguiling smile at him. He prayed with an intensity he did not know was possible. In his desperation he bargained with God, attempted to bribe him, even threatened him. But despite his desperate prayers, she slipped from him. God remained stubbornly reluctant to perform the miracle which he so willingly performed on human lives that Douglas regarded as far less deserving.

As a faithful Vicar, Douglas had preached many a sermon about God's protection, but when Saoirse needed it, it was nowhere to be seen. 'He will give his angels charge over thee', so the scripture said, but no angel flew down in that dreadful moment when his beloved needed the shield of a mighty wing. He had preached with conviction and excitement about divine healing, but when his darling Saoirse needed it, God had either forgotten how to do it, or he had decided she did not qualify for such treatment. Presumably it was her atheism that meant she was so coldly disregarded. The only thing God did on that terrible day was to take from him his most precious treasure and leave him to tough it out on earth for the rest of his days, having tantalised him for two short years with such exquisite love and happiness.

He was so lost in his thoughts, that it shocked Douglas when he felt a thud beneath him as the plane landed at Cork Airport. It slowly taxied to the terminal and while it trundled along, Douglas turned his mind for the first time to the practicalities of this visit. He was getting away from the parish on the advice of his bishop. The wardens had contacted her after the disastrous sermon (or non-sermon) on Sunday, and in response she had phoned Douglas that evening. She had a reputation in the diocese for being somewhat cold and efficient, and yet Douglas had found her to be a very compassionate support these past two years, so it did not surprise him that when she called him, her tone was one of kindness and concern. She urged him to get a sick note from his doctor and take a few days break from the parish, especially to get away from the Vicarage to protect himself from the well-meaning and the not-so-well-meaning visitors. She would speak to her secretary to arrange an appointment for him to come and meet with her.

So he had to think of somewhere to go, and he hit on the idea of making a visit to Saoirse's homeland. He knew he had to steer well clear of her parents, but she had always spoken with great fondness of one of her aunts called Ruby, who apparently held none of the prejudices of the rest of her family. Saoirse had often said that Ruby would love to meet Douglas. She had intended to come to the wedding, but at the last minute sent a message saying she was prevented by a bad bout of 'flu. Having missed her at the wedding, they had always intended to take a trip to the south of Ireland to visit her.

Such was his troubled state of mind that Douglas had booked the flight and was on the plane without ever giving thought as to what he would do once he arrived in Cork. All he knew about Aunt Ruby was that she lived in the little coastal town of Dingle. Saoirse had always said jokingly, 'Dougie, darling, if you ever find yourself on your own and adrift in the Republic, just make your way to the wee town of Dingle, and ask for Aunty Ruby Kennedy - they all know her there and you'll soon find her. Go and knock on that large black door of hers and she'll be thrilled to see you.'

Douglas heard Saoirse's smiling voice in his mind as he drove away from Cork in his hire car, and headed for the Dingle peninsula. A sense of hope rose in him with the thought of meeting one of his beloved's relatives. It would be a connecting point with her - he would hear more of her childhood, and the life she led as she grew up in this south west tip of Ireland. She might help him to understand Saoirse's parents a bit better. Maybe Ruby would somehow help him to turn a corner in his grief, help him to find a purpose to live again. This aunt felt to be a last hope in his world where hope had been in such short supply in the last couple of years. But the welcome visit of hope to Douglas' heart was to be short-lived, for yet another disappointment was awaiting him.

CHAPTER 2

Douglas chose to take the route to Dingle via the Connor Pass. It was at its most majestic as Douglas drove his car up to the summit of the mountain and he was pleased to discover a parking area where he pulled in. Driving the last mile or so demanded full concentration as he negotiated the sharp twists and bends of the narrow road, and he needed to stop for his nerves to recover and so he could absorb the surrounding scenery. As he got out of his car, a fierce wind buffeted him, but holding fast to a railing, he gazed over the glaciated landscape of sunlit mountain, corrie lakes and brooding, sweeping valleys either side of the brow. On one side he could see the great Mount Brandon, and below it Brandon Bay. He recalled an ancient story he had heard of a Brendan of old who, with a group of friends, sailed the Atlantic ocean in a tiny boat trusting the hand of God to keep them safe on the wild ocean waves.

Douglas chose not to dwell on the apparent random protection of God for his humans in this turbulent world, so he walked to the other side of the car park and there he looked down to the little town of Dingle. He admired the clear outline of the seaboard, and across the blue water he could make out the coastline of the Ring of Kerry. For the first time in many months he felt a sense of contentment. For two years nothing had appeared beautiful to him. This scene did. And somewhere down there in that little town there was someone who might be able to help him. He was about to meet some flesh and blood of Saoirse's who didn't treat him with suspicion. He trusted Saoirse's word, that Aunt Ruby was made of different stuff. He almost felt excitement as he got back in his car and drove down the winding road to the little coastal town.

Once in Dingle, he parked the car, and entering one of the many bars in the town, he was pleased to discover they were still serving lunch. It was a genial landlord who served him, so Douglas lost no time in asking about Saoirse's Aunt Ruby Kennedy. Sure enough, the landlord had known Ruby, but, as he put it in a rather hushed voice, 'She passed over, sad to say. Not so long ago, it was. God rest her soul.' He completed filling a glass of Guinness as Douglas stood rigid, stunned by this news.

The barman placed the partly filled glass on the counter, waiting for it to settle then called to an elderly lady sitting by the smouldering peat fire, 'How long ago was it that Ruby passed from us?'

'Oh, it would be just before Christmas, Tommy. Just before Christmas, it was. A sad loss so it was. She was a dear soul was Ruby, but it was the drink that got the better of her in the end, so it did now. Fond of the wine she was. Bit too fond, you'd say. Aye, God rest her.' She grasped a poker and prodded some of the peat in the fire.

'Aye - sad loss indeed,' said the barman as he filled the final portion of the glass and placed it carefully in front of Douglas. 'That will be fifteen euros in total for the lunch and Guinness please. She lived just up the road, she did. Did you know her well, now?'

Douglas was struggling to come to terms with this dreadful news and only managed a mumbled, 'Er, no .. she was a relative of... a very good friend.'

'Yes, well, many people knew poor Ruby. As I say, a great loss. Sit yourself at a table there. The food won't be long now.'

Douglas grasped the cold glass and made his way to the table. He sat and looked at the dark liquid in utter dismay. Ruby was his last hope of finding a place of warmth and healing. He should have made enquires before he came. He should have checked. He should have done so many things. He slumped wearily in the chair which creaked in protest. He had no energy to even think about what to do next. He sipped at the beer which provided little comfort.

When the Landlord brought the steak and ale pie (for which Douglas now had no appetite), he said, 'If you are looking for a bed for the night, there's St.Raphael's Guest House just two doors down. Elsie O'Connell runs it. She's got vacancies - I just checked. Just say Tommy sent you. Enjoy your pie now. It will do you a power of good, it will.' Douglas doubted if anything could do him good just now.

Apart from the the elderly lady by the fire, Douglas was the only customer in the bar. He was grateful for the quiet as he eventually made his way through most of the pie. He tried to think what to do with himself. He knew he should start making plans about a flight home, but felt too weary to do anything. In the old days, he would have said a prayer and would have expected an exciting little miracle to help him out. But for Douglas, those days of straightforward answers to prayers were well over. Still, he needed to do something, so he made his way out of the bar. As he left, the barman reiterated, 'Elsie O'Connell's - just a couple of doors down. You can't miss it. Good luck.' He stepped into the street where he was greeted by a cold drizzle.

Sure enough, two doors down a rather antiquated sign advertised 'St.Raphael's Guest House. Superb rooms at affordable prices. Vacancies.' The door was ajar and Douglas made his way into a rather cramped hallway that was lit by an antiquated lamp perched awkwardly on a table littered with leaflets advertising the many delights of the Dingle Peninsula. Douglas sighed and, as he was starting to look for a bell to ring, he heard the sound of someone limping down the staircase.

'Will you be the gentleman from England looking for a room then?' asked the voice as it made its way down the staircase.

'Yes, please', replied Douglas looking up the dark staircase.

'I'm on my way,' said the voice, and Douglas saw eventually that it belonged to a small woman who clearly struggled with pain in her left leg as she manoeuvred it down the final bend of the staircase. As she arrived in the hall, Douglas saw that she was wearing vintage cat eye glasses with brightly decorated edges, and above the glasses rose an impressive, if somewhat unkempt, 1960's beehive hair style that was reddish in colour, though revealing at the roots a rather more natural grey. As she arrived a little breathlessly in the hall, she peered up at her new guest. Douglas looked down at a kindly face that was decorated in different colours radiating from the Tiffany lamp on the small hall table.

'How long will be you staying now?' she asked as she delved into the pile of leaflets and pulled out a diary.

The question took Douglas aback, as he had really not given thought to this. And with no Aunt Ruby, he guessed he would be returning home soon, so he said, 'Just a night or two please.'

'Hm,' said Mrs O'Connell, 'You'll need longer than that if you are to see our beautiful peninsula. The air will do you good, especially if you come from the city, which it looks like you do. You been before?'

'No.. My wife has… had an aunt..'

'Oh aye, Aunt Ruby Kennedy was it? Tommy mentioned it.'

'That's the one - yes'.

'Ah poor soul, God rest her. Here, let me take you to your room. Your case is in the car is it? You can pick it up later and you can park your car in the yard just behind us. Now your room is this way.' She commenced the journey one stair at a time to the first floor.

'Ruby was a great lass, but a poor soul, so she was,' she wheezed, as she paused half way up the gloomy staircase. 'She was well known around here – a nice lady, but fond of that red wine, don't you know. Merlot was her downfall. God knows why, but it always had to be the

Merlot. Maybe something to do with her name - Ruby. My God, you should've seen her go at it. You used to see it all round her lips, for God's sakes. Made her look like that Lady Lala. She never was a beauty, mind.'

'Gaga, I think…' said Douglas, as he followed the proprietor to the top of the winding stairs feeling obliged to correct her.

'Aye, she did get that way a bit, poor soul. The wine did her brain no good at all, it didn't. Now here's your room.' He followed her into a small room. Hardly 'superb', but perfectly acceptable, he thought. 'Number 4. Cleaned it his morning. Your en suite is here. Tea and coffee on the window sill. This key for the front door, this for the room. Breakfast from eight to nine. Let me know if you want the full Irish.'

As she started to leave the room she added, 'Now there's plenty of pubs in town where you can get a nice meal tonight. No need to book at this time of year.'

'Ah, yes, that will be very nice. Thank you.'

She closed the door and Douglas sat on his bed feeling most desperately alone. It was now raining hard against the window that overlooked a street lined with colourful shops, houses and pubs. He lay on the bed, closed his eyes and listened to the spatter of the rain on the window. Even the sky was now weeping, and oddly it felt comforting. It understood, and it was the rain that nursed him into a quiet sleep that was blessed with no dreams.

When he woke after a couple of hours, it took him some time to work out where he was. The rain had stopped and the light was fading into a sullen gloom. He went and collected his car and his case. It did not take him long to unpack, but the unpacking was full of aching memories. Saoirse used to pack his case. A few weeks after their wedding he had to go off for a clergy conference, and he took this same suitcase. When he arrived at his room at the conference centre, he opened the case, and he found his clothes beautifully packed. Such care had been taken with each item, and on top was a bar of chocolate and a little note full of affection and humour.

He also remembered her packing her case before that fateful journey. She was so excited, but also so sad to be leaving him for those few days. She kept asking him what to take. She wasn't used to a hot climate. Together they worked out each item of clothing and he remembered watching her delicate hands carefully folding and placing each item in the case. He hated the thought of her being away, but they both knew she had to go. She owed it to her Egyptian friend, Lolly, who had been such a good friend to her at University and she had long wanted to visit her country.

They wept so much at the airport. As she squeezed him tight at the departure gate and whispered 'pray for me, my precious darling', did she have a premonition that this was to be their last moment together in this world? As her friends speeded ahead of her at the security gate, she turned and waved so hard. He knew she was trying to make him laugh to distract him, but did her beautiful face, reddened by grief, betray any sign of what was to come? That this was her last day on this earth? It was the only time she asked him to pray for her. And he did pray, more to comfort himself in her absence rather than pray for her to have a great time with her friends in Egypt. He should have prayed so much more for her protection. What was he thinking of? He had failed her - failed to pray for her; failed to protect her. He had failed to convince her about God. If she had believed would she have been saved? God - protection - salvation: what use was all that now?

In those few moments, as he stood there, haunted by memories, little did he realise that in the days to come, in a way he could never remotely have imagined, he would finally begin to make some sense of the bewildering questions of life and death, light and dark, that besieged him through every moment of the last two torturous years. And he certainly could never have imagined who was to become a guide for him in this curious pilgrimage upon which he had unwittingly embarked.

CHAPTER 3

<u>Journal 8 October</u>

It's a while since I've written in this pathetic book. There has been nothing to write - only misery. Anyway, I've now arrived in Ireland. <u>Her</u> land. So sad we never came here together. She loved it so much. We just thought we had so much time ahead of us. Came over here to meet her Aunt Ruby who she used to speak about so affectionately. Turns out her wonderful aunt was over fond of the Merlot and it killed her. So much for my brilliant plans.

It was terrible unpacking the case. Brought back so many memories. I love them and I hate them. They bring me close to her again, and yet they remind me of the bitter reality of her loss.

What the hell am I doing here? I'm sitting in a little room in a place called Dingle, in the far south of Ireland. I'll go out in a minute and see what the place is like. Don't really feel like it, but can't sit here all night. Feels like it gets dark a bit earlier here. Dark - it's so dark. Everything is so dark.

Church was dreadful on Sunday - can't write about it. But I think that's the end of it. Will have to find another job. I really loved them when I first went there - she even loved it on the times she came. Should I have got her to come more? They all started to disapprove of her not coming. What nosey people church people can be. What business is it of theirs anyway? Mavis was wonderful of course. Came and saw me after the service. She just loved Saoirse and was quite happy with the way she was. Saoirse loved her.

Look at me - my mind dancing around all over the place. I just don't know what to write, what to think, what to pray. Not prayed for several weeks now - months really. Told Mavis she needed to do the praying now. I noticed it made her cry and I rather wish I hadn't said it. I suppose one day I'll accept it - all this God stuff just doesn't work. Can't quite let go of it all, life's lonely enough as it is. Time for a Guinness. Had one at lunch and even though I was so depressed, it tasted good. It's right what they say - it does taste better in Ireland.

*

The rain had returned when Douglas made his way out on to the streets of Dingle, so he made his way into the first bar he came to which happily served dinner. As he paid the bill, the waitress said to him, 'You looking for live music tonight?'

'No,' he said as he received his receipt.

'All visitors like the live music!' said the waitress and as she smiled, Douglas realised that she was genuinely trying to be kind and he felt he couldn't disappoint her.

'So where do I go?' he said.

She looked delighted, and responded, 'They've got live music up at *The Angel's Rest* tonight. Just left out the door, down the road for forty yards, and then turn left again. It's down the alley. You can't miss it. You'll love it, you will. It's music all year round there.' The waitress continued, 'Some of the other pubs only have music in the summer season. The Americans love it, they do. Stuffed with Americans the town is in the summer. They're all searching for their ancestors. God knows why. But it's good business for us, so I won't complain.'

Douglas rather liked the thought of bright-faced Americans prowling around the tombstones spotting the names of their Irish relatives and then descending on the bars to celebrate. 'I'm sure they find comfort in it,' he said as he put on his jacket.

'Well, that they might,' said the waitress. 'But you have to watch the dead - they can play a few tricks on you, if you're not careful!' She laughed as she handed Douglas the receipt and then added, 'Enjoy the music.'

Douglas stepped out of the warm pub into a blustery and wet night. He momentarily had second thoughts about the music, but then decided he couldn't let down the cheerful waitress so he followed her directions which led him to a small white painted building. Above the door in a Celtic script was written *'The Angel's Rest'*. There were two signs by the bright red door, one boasting that the bar provided live music every night of the week all year round. The other announced that the bar offered excellent facilities for funeral wakes. Undaunted, Douglas ventured in and found the place was full of life. As he waited by the bar he looked around at this rather curious venue. The walls were decorated with a bizarre selection of musical instruments, stuffed dolls, a stained Victorian painting of a rather severe angel with huge wings and not looking at all restful. There were old press cuttings mounted in black

20

frames, and also, somewhat surprisingly, the mainframe of an old cycle hung randomly from the ceiling. Ivy had crept into the building from the roof and covered the upper part of the back wall, which was still yellow-stained with tobacco smoke from days gone by.

The bar was about half full, and groups of people were either gathered at the bar, or around the small tables that were scattered around the room. Douglas joined a small queue of people waiting to be served at the bar. A bearded man was sitting in the corner strumming a guitar. A young woman with a rather mournful face sat next to him. After he had played a few chords the young woman sang liltingly in such a way that Douglas felt both sadness and contentment at the same moment. One or two people in the bar sang softly with her, but most were in animated conversation and allowed the song to skim over their chatter.

Something about the place felt curiously welcoming, and Douglas was surprised to find himself feeling quite at home as he clutched his €10 note and lent against the bar waiting to be served. Before he had time to place his order, a glass of Guinness was placed firmly in front of him. The hand that held it was slim, well weathered, with prominent blue veins. It belonged to a man who smiled at him and said 'Welcome stranger.' He laughed a kind laugh, and then said 'Sláinte – your good health, son. And when I say "good" I really mean it.'

Douglas was a little taken aback. 'Thank you,' he said awkwardly, accepting the glass. The donor of the drink continued to look at him as if he were greeting a long lost friend. Douglas took a sip, which left him with a cream moustache and he asked, 'I'm sorry – I think you must be mistaking me for someone else. We haven't met have we? My memory…'

'Well, in a manner of speaking we have met. It's lashing it down outside, and I wondered if you'd make it. I'm so pleased you have. Shall we?' His own glass was half drunk and with it he pointed to an empty table. The man seemed genial enough, so Douglas agreed. As they settled at the table, Douglas took a longer look at him and noticed the man's strong wavy hair surrounding a kindly, bearded and rugged face.

As they settled at the table, the stranger took a sip from his glass, looked at Douglas and said, 'How's it going then?' He spoke with the Irish lilt in a strong yet gentle voice.

'I'm sorry,' apologised Douglas for the second time. 'You say we have met, but I'm afraid I can't recall your name.'

'Yes, of course, Douglas. My name's Dorchadas – nice seeing you again. Though, if I may say so my friend, you are looking a wee bit weary just now.' He reached out his hand, which Douglas shook with some uncertainty.

Douglas had never heard this name before. It was very unnerving to hear this stranger use his name so confidently. He was a newcomer to Ireland and had only just arrived in Dingle. Had Tommy or Mrs O'Connell been chatting about him? That must be it. He assumed the whole town gossiped about new arrivals. But yes, this Mr Dorchadas was right, Douglas was feeling a bit weary. Without a doubt he was.

The girl finished her song, and after a short applause a middle-aged, fair-haired woman at the back of the pub struck up with another song about a girl called Mary. Her voice was beautiful. No sooner had she started than the guitarist joined her. It was clearly a song he knew well.

Dorchadas leaned over to Douglas and said in a confidential tone, 'That's Shelagh singing – she lost her daughter last year, you know. So sad. So, so sad. Terrible dangerous things, the roads are for young people. Terrible thing.' His voice stuttered and he sipped his Guinness. 'But listen how she sings! Imagine singing like that twelve months on from losing a child? There's something admirable in that woman.' Both men knew they had touched a sorrow that was well beyond discussing. Neither of them spoke while Shelagh sang her song, for the whole pub had fallen silent. Douglas felt they had somehow entered a holy shrine and any conversation would have been sacrilege. He couldn't see her clearly as there was a group of people in front of her, but he heard the words clearly. She sang a song of homesickness, of a longing for a land where the Mountains of Mourne sweep down to the sea. Douglas thought of the raw grief that would still be in her heart as the sea of death had parted her from her daughter with such severity. It was a sea that Douglas knew so well and hated with a deep loathing.

To distract him from this sorrow, Douglas look a closer look at the motionless Dorchadas whose eyes were closed. He might have been sixty. But there again he could have been ten years either side of that. His skin was dark and had lines and creases around his eyes that gave his face warmth and tenderness. His hair was a mix of grey and tan but his bushy eyebrows were an entertaining mix of white and ginger. His short beard was mostly grey. His was the kind of face that made you want to smile. Even with his eyes closed, he looked like he was just about to tell a joke. Or was it rather a face that was about to burst into tears? It was hard to tell.

Mary finished her song, and there was warm applause from all in the pub. There was a break from the music and conversations around the tables quickly took its place.

Dorchadas opened his eyes and looked back at Douglas. 'So, how are you finding it here in the Emerald Isle?' he asked with an endearing smile. They talked for a little while about Douglas' trip from the UK and his abortive attempt to meet an Aunt who was now deceased.

'Ah, Aunt Ruby?' said Dorchadas. 'Fancy you being related to old Ruby. She was a lass, she was. My, we had some great conversations. I'm so sorry you never got to meet her - you would have loved her, you would. She was a natural story-teller.'

'And she liked the wine, I hear.'

'Ah, poor soul, that she did. But it wasn't the drinking that killed her. That's what she wanted people to think. Actually it was the cancer. The drink helped with the pain. She didn't want to bother people with her sorrows and pains. She was a valiant soul, was Ruby.' Dorchadas looked genuinely very sad as he took a sip of his ale.

Then Douglas asked, 'I didn't quite catch your name - Dor...?'

'Dorchadas – no, it's not a common name. It's Gaelic for "darkness" as it happens.'

'Oh dear,' said Douglas smiling teasingly. 'Your mother can't have liked the look of you!' He quickly felt anxious that his humour might have misfired. Saoirse loved his humour, but did tell him more than once that people didn't always get it.

'Ah, well now, the mention of parents takes us to the point, Douglas.' He lowered his voice and looked from side to side. 'You see, Douglas, I have none. Now, hold tight, this is always the difficult bit of the conversation, but I'll give it to you straight. I don't have parents as you understand it.'

Douglas looked concerned, 'You mean your parents abandoned you?'

'No, Douglas. I never had any parents. I wasn't born, if you get my meaning.'

Douglas started to feel uncomfortable - he had liked this man up til now, but something now felt a bit spooky. But Dorchadas leaned forward and said quietly, 'Well now, you are familiar with the concept of the angels, are you not?'

'I am'

'You ever met one?'

'No, I can't say I have.'

'Well - you have now. How do you do,' and with that Dorchadas put out his hand which Douglas limply shook. 'Fancy another pint of the dark stuff?' he said, holding up his glass which was nearly empty.

CHAPTER 4

Douglas felt his heart sink. For a few moments he thought this stranger might turn out to be a new and interesting friend, but instead he had managed to find the company of a crackpot who would now, no doubt, be trailing him around town. He would soon be asking him for money. Douglas would quickly need to devise an escape plan.

He started to stand, saying, 'I think I'll need to be going, but thanks very much for the drink and it's been good to meet you.'

Dorchadas put a firm hand on his arm and looked intently at him. 'Douglas, you don't have to believe this. It really doesn't matter to me, but won't you at least let me tell you a little of my story. It's not nine o'clock yet. But I promise if I get boring, you can leave. Sure I may be a little crazy, Doug, but don't you think it's the crazy ones who often have the wisdom?' He emphasized the word 'crazy' and raised an enquiring eyebrow as he said it.

Douglas slipped slowly back on to this seat. 'Crazy' was one of Saoirse's favourite words. She had actually said more than once that Douglas needed to be crazier in life - in her view, he was inclined to take life far too seriously.

'How did you know…?' he asked Dorchadas cautiously.

'I know a few things, Doug. Only a few things. It comes from being around a long time. And it comes from listening to many stories.'

'You'll forgive me for not buying into this angel thing immediately, but go on, tell me a bit more about yourself.' Douglas took a swig of his Guinness and then opened his hands towards Dorchadas, as if inviting him to take to the stage.

Dorchadas drained his glass and held it for a while to his lips to gather the last drops of the foam. 'You can't beat it, can you?' He smiled almost like a child as he put the glass down, and then his face became serious. 'I'll give it to you straight, Douglas, because it is no use trying to faff around with this. I'm what you would call a retired angel. I mean, I see them angels in the shops - you know those cute ones with wings and the like. Or that one on the wall there with ridiculous wings! Very humorous they are. Well, I can assure you I never looked like that. When I was a proper angel, if you like, I could actually look like anything I wanted. I did try the wings a few times and they were fun. I found they tended to frighten the humans though.' He looked thoughtful for a moment and scratched his bearded chin. He then pushed his lower lip up and turned to Douglas and said, 'We never wanted to frighten any of you, you know. We only ever wanted to be kind.' Douglas was taken aback to notice a tear edge its way into the corner of his eye.

'Ok,' said Douglas looking quickly away. 'I have read the bible a fair bit and I have read that it is possible to entertain angels without realising it. But if I'm honest, I'm not really sure nowadays about angels and demons and all that sort of thing. Sorry if I'm offending you.'

'Douglas, listen.' Dorchadas put his weathered hand over Douglas' and squeezed it with a gentle strength. 'Listen, Douglas – listen to the truth. Give that busy brain of yours a bit of a break. It's time to use your heart for a change. I know just a little of what you've gone through. But it is time to open that wounded heart of yours again. It's been closed for too long.'

He kept holding his hand in his tight grip, and it was the grip that curiously suggested that he might actually have been telling the truth, ludicrous though such a notion was. Douglas had mixed feelings however about this so-called angel lecturing him about opening up his heart – it had endured far too much of a battering in the last two years for him to open it up to a complete stranger, angel or no. And he felt distinctly uncomfortable with Dorchadas apparently knowing so much about him.

'OK – can I go at this steadily?' said Douglas, pulling his hand away. 'I'm sitting in a pub in a small town in Ireland, sipping a Guinness and chatting to an angel with an Irish accent, who claims he's retired.'

'Yep, that's about the sum of it, Douglas. As I'm retired from my, well… normal duties, shall we say, I'm allowed to do this kind of roaming around in human form.'

'So what's this retirement business? I have never heard of angels retiring. I thought they lived forever. And I've never heard of them being Irish either for that matter. Is that in the book of Revelation somewhere?' Douglas was aware of the sarcasm in his voice, but it did not seem to put Dorchadas off.

'Ah, well, yes, the retiring bit is a little tricky,' he said, and ran his finger up and down his empty glass. 'There, I must confess, it is not all a pretty story, Douglas.' He looked down and Douglas was aware that Dorchadas did not look at him as he said this. 'But that part of it you don't need to hear about just now.'

He looked back up at Douglas. 'As for the Irish bit, why shouldn't you have Irish angels?' His smile returned. A man at the table near them started up another song that immediately had those around him chuckling. The guitarist struck up again, and a young woman with a fiddle joined in.

The strangeness of the conversation meant that Douglas kept taking gulps from his glass so it wasn't long before it was empty. 'Ok, well can we go back to your name? You told me that your name is Gaelic for darkness. I mean that has to be nonsense if you don't mind me saying so. In my studying about angels, I understood them to be quite the opposite - full of light. Unless...' Douglas felt a jab of anxiety in his stomach as a very uncomfortable thought came into his mind. 'Unless you.. are more demon than angel?'

The hand returned to Douglas' arm and gripped it tight. 'Look at me.' Douglas looked up at him. His was without doubt a face of great kindness. His rich brown eyes were deeply set and sat comfortably under the bright bushy eyebrows. They were dark, but a comforting dark, not sinister. Though the rest of his body looked older, his eyes were somehow those of a child. They looked intently at Douglas as he said almost in a whisper, 'Have you never heard of the darkness of God, Douglas?' Laughter resonated around the pub as the song continued. It was in marked contrast to the mood Douglas saw in his new friend's face.

'Yes,' Douglas answered with some hesitation.

'My calling, Douglas, has been to serve as a messenger of the dark things of God. We don't get a choice in these things.' He released Douglas' arm and sat back and sighed. He looked ahead of him and said, 'I don't mind saying, I envied my brother and sister angels whose job it was to do the lovely things like bringing about his great healings, and getting people out of jail, and helping them silly humans out of the fixes they get themselves into. And I envied those whose job it was to go to some poor unsuspecting soul and bring them some good news. They always brought back funny stories! I don't mind telling you, Douglas, there's been many a day when I would have gladly swopped places with any of them. And I can tell you this, Douglas, many of them angels aren't always what they are cut out to be, if you know what I mean. They take a lot for granted. But look now, your glass is empty, let me fetch you another.'

'Oh, it's my turn – please let me'

27

'Right you are, Douglas, I won't say no. Fetch us another pint, and I'll need to be off to the jacks. That's the problem with being sent in human form. I thought we'd be spared all this part of your humanity. Ah, but no. He says it's all or nothing - fully human and that's the deal. Well it seems to me that I got given one of the weaker bladders and I'm minded to put in for a complaint, I am! Anyway, you be a good lad and get the Guinness now – we'll leave the Jameson's til later. We need a clear head just at the minute.' As he stood up from the table, Douglas realised how very tall this new companion was.

He slipped out of the tight corner where they were sitting and on his way to the toilet he made a comment to the man with the guitar and the whole corner erupted in laughter.

In a state of some bewilderment Douglas ordered the Guinness. 'You friends with old Dorch, then?' said the young barman while he waited for the first pour of the Guinness to settle.

'I just met him for the first time this evening,' Douglas said cautiously.

'Ah, well, you'll not go wrong there then. He's a good man is Dorch. The whole world loves him.'

'Has he lived in this town long?' Douglas asked, trying to get some clue as to the true nature of this new acquaintance.

'Ah well, he's not that kind of fellow – if you know what I mean. He comes and goes. We're glad when he comes and we miss him when he's gone. That's about the sum of it. Most reckon he does far more good than harm. That'll be seven euros twenty please.'

Douglas wound his way back to his table, nursing the two full glasses carefully. Obviously this Dorchadas wasn't an angel, yet why would he spin this yarn? But then Saoirse did say her countryfolk did like their storytelling, and maybe this was how they did it. Douglas decided that another Guinness would give him the courage to listen further to this curious man. Even if he was a little crazy, there really seemed no real harm in the guy. And there was that reference to 'crazy'. Did he know Saoirse? Douglas felt he had little to lose by spending the rest of the evening with him.

When Dorchadas returned he looked a good deal more serious. He settled back into his seat and thanked Douglas for the drink. The fiddle player and the guitarist were playing a beautiful ballad.

'Now tell me, Douglas, you are a priest are you not?'

What was it about clergy that they somehow managed to look like clergy even when they weren't wearing their dog collars? It annoyed Douglas intensely. He had hoped that he had successfully disguised this fact but clearly not. 'Yes...' he admitted after a pause. 'But a very bad one at the moment.'

'Well, I know priests are not perfect, but for goodness sakes, you have all given up a lot to serve God. But the thing that annoys me, Douglas, is this. So many of you do the worthy work: you turn up on Sundays and deliver the goods; you run your church meetings; you go visiting the sick; you sit on this committee and that doing loads of good, and you chair school governors meetings, God bless them. But the thing is you never really get to *know* this God you work so hard to serve. It doesn't make sense to me, Douglas.' He looked at Douglas with his kind eyes, in such a way that Douglas felt uncomfortable. Dorchadas was touching one of his many raw nerves, and Douglas did not want any old stranger in a pub prodding at them. He looked down at his beer mat.

Dorchadas leaned forward in a confidential way, and placed an elbow on the table. He drew his face close to Douglas and said in a soft voice, 'Douglas, how *well* do you know Him?' He then leant back and kept his eyes fixed on his new friend, waiting for an answer.

Douglas was not at all happy with this conversation. His faith was a wreck and he wanted no one to inspect it. In time he would give it a decent burial and do the equivalent of 'coming out', but only when he was emotionally strong enough. So rather limply he replied to the question, ''I suppose the answer is not well enough.'

'Mmm – that sounds like a technically correct answer, Douglas. I have to be honest with you I get pissed off with the way you priests get so professional about your faith. And I have never liked 'supposes'. They don't work for me.'

He noticed Douglas raise his eyebrow at 'pissed off' and said, 'Don't worry about my language Douglas. You see I'm a *retired* angel, so I don't have to be as correct as the others. Now, back to the point – how close have you got to this God you have spent plenty of years serving as a priest.' He looked at him intently again.

Rather than answering, Douglas sipped his beer and then said, 'Tell me what you see, Dorch, as you apparently know so much about me?'

Dorchadas leaned back in his seat and grinned. 'You calling me 'Dorch' now are you, Doug?' Douglas couldn't help but laugh with him. 'I am a bit of a 'dork' too, you know. So the name works well.

Anyway,' he leaned forward again and raised his eyebrows, and patted Douglas' hand with his finger that was damp from the cold glass. 'I do know a bit about you, Douglas, but *only* a little and some time I'll tell you how I know, but don't let it worry you just now. But even if I knew nothing about you, I'd read a lot from your poor face, you know. I can tell you have had a rough time of it, and I feel so bad for you son, that I do. But the thing is this - you are not alone, you know. What I mean is, you have friends that you have read about, but have never met, and they have much to tell you. You should really meet them.'

Douglas felt a genuine curiosity as he asked, 'Such as who?'

'For a start, the guy you preached about in your last sermon. It was Jacob if I recall. I hear it wasn't a bad sermon, Douglas. Oh yes, a couple of angel mates of mine were there and they told me they quite enjoyed it. They loved the joke about the parachute at the beginning! They've been telling it to quite a few others...' He smiled broadly and took a sip of his drink.

The conversation was now becoming frightening. Had someone been spying on Douglas? He started to suspect Gerald Bentley. 'Just a minute, Dorch – I can't quite cope with this. Are you telling me that a couple of angels turned up at my church the Sunday before last and listened in to my sermon, then went back up to heaven and shared one of my jokes with a few other angels on their way?'

'That's about the sum of it, Douglas,' said Dorchadas pulling the glass to his mouth with care. 'We do have a sense of humour, you know. I think you'd enjoy some of our jokes. But let's get back to the point – you preached about Jacob. Well that's all very well, but the thing is, you've never *met* him, have you?'

Douglas' anxiety about how Dorchadas knew so much about him, was making him irritable, so he answered sharply, 'No, of course I've never met him! There is the small matter of the fact that he lived several thousand years ago! Time travelling was not a grace that was bestowed with holy orders, you know.' Douglas took a sip from his glass and was beginning to wonder quite where this conversation was heading.

'Ah, Douglas. You know this is where I really miss the days when we used to smoke in the pubs. Because in a moment like this, I would take a long drag from the ciggie, and then slowly and dramatically breathe out the smoke, shaking my head and look quizzically through the smoke at you and calmly fill you in about time travel. I have to confess,

Douglas, we angels do love a bit of theatre. Oh, my, we do!' He chuckled as he reflected on past conversations.

Douglas was wondering whether to start a discussion about angels smoking, when Dorchadas returned from his revelry and said, 'No, the thing is Douglas, it's not quite like that. Of course, you can't catch a TARDIS - oh yes, I do watch that too! It's not bad, actually. I like the new Doctor.' He chuckled again, 'And time travelling is rare, I agree. But there is more than one way to travel through time. You see, you can't approach this with that tight brain of yours. You need to use your *heart*.' Here he knocked at Douglas' heart, which was near disastrous as Douglas was just returning his glass to the mat. 'Your heart Doug, is the heart of a poet, but you won't acknowledge it. Now listen, were you or were you not made in God's image?'

'Yes, I believe humans are created in God's image,' said Douglas as if he were back in one of his bible study groups again. A loud applause interrupted them for a short moment as a song came to an end. Dorchadas turned round and clapped and made a comment to the musicians who acknowledged him with smiles. 'That's such a beautiful song, don't you think?' Anyway, how's your glass doing?' He checked Douglas' glass, and as it was well supplied, he continued.

'So you are created in God's image – I'm assuming you are a human, Douglas, unless you're another angel in disguise doing a good job of deceiving me!'

Douglas smiled. Despite the fact that so much about the present conversation was making him deeply anxious, he couldn't help warming to this curious Irishman. The beer was lowering his resistance, and he decided just to go with it now.

'Ok, this is the thing Douglas. Think of that word – "image": it is connected, is it not, to the word 'imagination'. The images of God were made to imagine. It's obvious isn't it?' He took a couple of sips from his Guinness, and leant forward confidentially again. 'Now Douglas, you have seldom used your imagination. Except when you go to your poetry. You like the poetry, don't you?'

How Dorchadas should know of his love for poetry was another disturbing mystery. But he was right. 'Yes,' he confessed somewhat nervously. 'My mother gave me a deep love for it.'

'I know son. She gave you much. Well then, remember that young Emily Brontë? She wrote a special poem *To imagination*. Dorchadas then breathed in and closed his eyes, and began:

'But thou art ever there, to bring
The hovering vision back, and breathe
New glories o'er the blighted spring,
And call a lovelier Life from Death.
And whisper, with a voice divine,
Of real worlds, as bright as thine.'

Douglas was completely taken aback by this sudden recital of a poem that had been one of his favourites for a long time. It was a poem that both he and his mother had learned by heart, and when he was a child they would often recite it together. Douglas couldn't deny that Dorchadas recited the verse beautifully, but he was so thrilled to hear it, that he put a hand on Dorchadas' arm and said, 'Let me continue…

'I trust not to thy phantom bliss,
Yet, still, in evening's quiet hour,
With never-failing thankfulness,
I welcome thee, Benignant Power;
Sure solacer of human cares,
And sweeter hope, when hope despairs!'

They were both silent for a short while, until Dorchadas said 'Well, there you are, Douglas. Look what imagination gave to that dear, poor lovely soul. She was my favourite of the three sisters, though I only ever got to speak with her once - up on the moors it was. She wasn't frightened of me you know - she had such a wild spirit, and oh, her imagination! But do you know, she discovered *real* hope through that gift, that benignant power. I saw it. She was a true traveller of both heart and mind she was. So much happens when humans really get to work on their imaginations. And, among other things that's what we angels are here for, Doug. I mean you need a certain amount of that Benignant Power to cotton on to the fact that we exist, don't you now!' He laughed his endearing laugh again.

A man shuffled past their table on his way to the bar. 'Good on you, Dorch. How you doing?' he asked. 'Your glass need a refill, does it?'

"I'm doing just fine thanks Fin, and my glass is fine. Rhona doing well, is she?'

'Oh that she is now, Dorch. Much better. She thanks you again for your visit.'

'Any time, Fin. Any time.' Fin completed his unsteady journey to the bar.

'Now Doug, where were we?'

'Imagination, Dorch. Benignant Power. And Emily Brontë.'

'So we were, Doug. So we were,' said Dorchadas and then looked hard down at the table. He then looked up at Douglas and continued, 'Doug, there's so much I want to talk to you about. I really believe you are here in this wee town for a reason. I can see there's a terrible rupture in your heart, and the problem with being me is... well, is that I get to feel something of that rupture myself, I surely do.' He looked at Douglas with such an expression of raw sorrow, that it took Douglas aback.

Over the past two years Douglas had many expressions of sympathy offered to him, but something about Dorchadas' response felt like it had a different quality. It felt to Douglas that Dorchadas must have experienced some similar trauma in his life. And yet it was not just that. It was like he had some true understanding of the wound in Douglas' heart. He had only known such a level of understanding from one other person in his life. Whilst this was unusually comforting for Douglas, it also had the effect of drawing up from his soul those strong feelings of grief that he had worked so hard to keep buried. He therefore quickly drained his glass and said, 'Dorchadas, it has been very good to meet you, but I have had a long day it's time for me to get to my bed.'

'Aye, lad, yes you have had a long day, and I won't be keeping you up. But remember what we talked about - that benignant power. And I'll be here tomorrow night if you want to continue our conversation. I can't tell you how good it is to see you here in Dingle. You sleep well now.'

Douglas rose from the table. He shook Dorchadas' hand as he left and because the emotion was still strong in him, he said nothing, but he smiled at his new friend and made his way to the door. As he made his way out, he heard a man's voice call out, 'Dorch for God's sake, your glass is empty...'

The rain had stopped and for a few moments Douglas stood outside the pub and breathed in the night air. It held the scent of rain mixed with the beery smell coming from the pub door. A young couple were walking on the other side of the road. They were clutching each other tight and giggling together. Douglas simply watched them make their happy way down the road as tired tears made their well worn way once again down his face. He turned and walked back to his Guest House. Little did he know that he had just had one of the most significant meetings of his life.

CHAPTER 5

When Douglas awoke the next morning in St.Raphael's Guest House he momentarily wondered where he was. But the events of the previous evening soon came back to him, and as he got up and shaved he heard the sound of Dorchadas' voice as clearly as if he was still back in the pub. He ran the razor around his chin, careful this time not to cut himself. 'Doug, there's so much I want to talk to you about. I really believe you are here in this wee town for a reason. I can see there's a terrible rupture in your heart..' He remembered these words so clearly, and many of the other words that Dorchadas had spoken to him. He felt so puzzled. Just who was this guy? What was all this angel business? And how did he apparently know so much about Douglas? Who had been talking to him?

As he showered, it was the latter line of enquiry he pursued. Who could have been talking to Dorchadas? It seemed that someone had filled him in on his story. But then no-one knew he was in Ireland. As he explored possible explanations, he was left with the uncomfortable conclusion that Dorchadas was in some way psychic, a power of which he had never been that fond. And what was all this imagination business?

Such questions were still buzzing in his head as he made his way down to breakfast. The dining room was a small room next to the hallway and had four tables laid and prepared for breakfast. A selection of cereals and fresh fruit was on the sideboard. As he settled himself at the table by the window, he heard the voice of Mrs O'Connell calling out from the kitchen, 'Sit yourself anywhere and help yourself to the cereal and fruit. I'll bring your breakfast in a few minutes. Do you like the black pudding?'

'Yes, I do, please,' called back Douglas and went to help himself to some cereal. He returned to the table and looked out of the window at a pleasantly bright morning, with wispy clouds skimming high over the streets of the town that were shining bright with the rain from the previous day. He was just wondering whether he was the only person staying in the Guest House when he heard sounds of movement in the room above him.

After a short while, Mrs O'Connell bustled into the dining room with a plate that certainly did justice to the term 'Full Irish Breakfast'. Anything fuller was hard to imagine. 'Well now, this will do you good, that it will,' she said as she placed the plate in front of him. She stepped back and made an attempt to settle in place the tower of hair above her head, which was clearly contending with her this morning. 'You'll have to forgive my appearance, Douglas, I'm long overdue at the hairdressers, I surely am. And I woke late.'

'You look just fine,' said Douglas who was warming to the proprietor of his Guest House.

'So, did you get a good meal last night?' she asked as she made some attempt to bring order to her hair.

'Yes, and I went for a drink at *The Angels Rest* too.'

'Oh, did you now. Lovely music there. I go and sing there myself when I get the chance. Wonderful landlord there, bless him.'

'I met an interesting character,' said Douglas, cutting into his sausage. 'Said his name was Dorchadas - you met him?'

'Oh yes, everyone knows old Dorch,' she said, finally giving up on her attempts to tame her hair. 'He tells a tale or two, that he does!' she chuckled. 'We take him with a pinch of salt, we do, but you can't help loving the man. Now, how's the breakfast? I hope to God I've given you enough. I'll fetch you the coffee.' With that she bustled out of the room back to the kitchen. Douglas was pleased that at least he had established that his recollection of the previous night was an actual meeting with this curious gentleman, not an hallucination brought about by his state of mind.

As Mrs O'Connell returned with a large coffee pot, a couple of guests made their way down the stairs and entered the dining room. The man was wearing a well-faded Stetson, checked shirt and blue jeans and said in a Southern States American drawl that yielded little to his attempt at an Irish accent, 'Top of the mornin' to you, Elsie,' and he roared with laughter.

'Och, you'll be learning the Gaelic next,' said Mrs O'Connell.

'Sláinte!' said the man, horribly mispronouncing the Gaelic.

'I should stick to the American!' said Mrs O'Connell, and they all laughed. The couple engaged in an animated conversation with Mrs O'Connell about places they could visit that day. Douglas hurriedly finished his breakfast as he had no interest in joining their conversation.

After breakfast he made his way out into a street brilliantly lit by October sunshine. He decided to explore the town and felt a sense of contentment as he wandered the streets, dropping in to the occasional shop and an art gallery, where he spent some time admiring striking paintings of the Atlantic Ocean and talking with the artist about her work. Something about her perceptive spirit reminded him of Saoirse and for those few moments he felt comforted by her company. He then found a bookshop which also served coffee. He pulled off the shelf a collection of Irish poetry, and then settled into a welcoming sofa. He was brought a welcome mug of coffee which he sipped thoughtfully as he browsed the pages of the book. He was familiar with the likes of Yeats, Moore and Swift but then he came across a couple of poems by Padraig Pearse, one of the young men executed by the British after the 1916 Rising. He felt sad to think of this young life so full of passion and poetry, extinguished far too soon by the violence of the bullet.

Thus, as he sat in that bookshop armchair with the autumn sun beaming on him through the window, his mind turned back, as it so often did, to his beloved Saoirse. She often spoke of the Easter Rising and how it was *the* story told in her childhood home. He remembered one warm, summer afternoon they sat under the shade of a tree in one of their favourite Derbyshire pubs, she told him about her family and their ties with the Republican movement going back several generations.

'You don't know what it's like to grow up with hatred all around you, Dougie,' she said, and Douglas found it impossible to imagine how such a loving soul could have had any encounter with hatred in her life.

'I could see it in both my parents,' she said, as she cupped her slender hands around a glass of her favourite pear cider. 'They could be such good people at times, but then I would see the hatred rise up in them. It was a terrible thing to see, sure it was. It frightened me, but, in a way, it also excited me. I mean, I hated the violence I could see in them, but what I loved was their passion, Doug. They were both so passionate. They hated injustice of any kind.'

Douglas remembered those moments so well. He recalled how the sunlight sparkled through the leaves of the tree and seemed to ignite her for a few moments. It was in that balmy afternoon conversation that she told of her own passion for justice and peace in the world, her hatred for the powers that bind and afflict people. She was so eloquent. More than anything she hated firearms. Her father was clearly familiar with them and he had even shown Saoirse the couple that he possessed illegally. She hated their being in the same house as her and several times pleaded with her father to get rid of them. He would always assure her that he would, but she suspected he never did. She impressed Douglas with her knowledge of the arms trade and her various attempts over the years to write to politicians and join protests. Douglas told her that it was a world he knew nothing about, and did not particularly want to know about.

'Why are we talking about these terrible things?' she asked as the breeze ruffled her beautiful hair. She leaned over the rustic table and clutched Douglas' hand. 'I'm now with you, Dougie. You are my family now and I look at you, my darling, and there is no violence in you. It's your world I want, my precious. You and I - we can live in peace, can't we?'

'Yes, my sweet. You will always be safe here,' he replied, and immediately moved round to her bench and wrapped his arms around her tightly.

'Can I be getting you another coffee? Looks like you are well stuck into the book there.' It was the voice of the shop assistant.

Douglas could not speak but just shook his head. Such memories were among his greatest treasures, yet were also the source of his deepest pain.

He turned back to his book, to Pearse's poem *The Mother*. The final lines touched him:

Lord, thou art hard on mothers:
We suffer in their coming and their going;
And tho' I grudge them not, I weary, weary
Of the long sorrow - And yet I have my joy:
My sons were faithful and they fought.

Douglas closed his eyes again and thought, 'Lord, thou art hard on husbands, too. I too weary, weary of the long sorrow...' He thought how Saoirse would have fought for peace if she had had more time. She hated war and violence, and often talked about doing more to make the world a more peaceful place. So much she could have done. So much....

After such a large breakfast, he skipped lunch and carried on his wander around the town. He came to the church which presented an immediate conflict in his soul - this was the symbol of the very thing that was the focus of his current downfall. Only a few days ago (it seemed like months ago) did he ascend those pulpit steps and publicly 'break down', as the wardens had put it. He had served the church for many years, yet now every church building was a stone-cold reminder to him of his failure. However, some old instinct gave him the confidence to enter. It was quite different from St.Philip's, which was a cold and dull South Yorkshire building. This Irish building was somehow much warmer, even though it was larger. It felt full of life and colour. As far as he could make out, he was the only person in the building, so he took advantage of the quiet and settled himself in one of the pews at the back.

Sitting there, and feeling a stranger in this church building, reminded him of Saoirse's first visit to St.Philip's. They became engaged very soon after that first wonderful evening at the French Restaurant and only then did Douglas risk being public about the relationship. He was very wary of gossip in the parish, and hated people asking intrusive questions. Only Mavis knew, and she did well to keep their secret. But once Douglas announced the engagement in one morning service, the whole world knew. Saoirse came to church that Sunday - her first time - and it was the first time the congregation set eyes on her. Every person there was completely taken by surprise. Some were even shocked, especially when Douglas announced they were getting married in four months' time. Saoirse teased the church wardens by saying how dismayed she was Douglas had not asked the Church Council's permission for making such a significant change to the Vicar's status! She stayed to the after-service coffee and endeared herself to many of the congregation that day, though some discovered that she was not a church-goer, and this seriously disturbed them. However, thankfully, they did not convey that displeasure to her on that particular day.

When everyone had left, only Douglas and Saoirse were left in the building and they both sat in a pew and chatted together about the response of the congregation. Saoirse told Douglas that she immediately loved the building which surprised Douglas, as he had no particular fondness for it. She then turned to him and asked, 'Dougie, is your God male or female?'

Although Douglas was used to her direct talking, he was rather taken aback by this question. He knew the official evangelical answer, but he knew her well enough to know that official answers never worked. Despite that, he started, 'Well, my love, the bible says...'

'Now, now, Dougie,' said Saoirse with just a hint of her teacher voice. 'I don't want you quoting the bible at me, so let me ask it differently. Do *you* think of God as male or female? What do *you* think?'

Douglas had not given this subject much thought, but he looked at Saoirse and said, 'Saoirse, I think I have always thought of him as 'him'...'

'And...' she said, smiling winsomely.

'And... then I met you,' he said and intended to continue, but her soft smile completely overwhelmed him and the conversation was temporarily halted by a long kiss.

'Excuse me, Reverend Romer,' said Saoirse pulling herself away and adopting a serious expression. 'I hardly think that carrying on like this with a member of your congregation is appropriate. I will be reporting this to the bishop straight away.' She was unable to hold her serious face for long, and they both laughed out loud, a laughter that was seldom heard in the ancient building.

'I think the problem is,' said Douglas returning to her question and holding her hand tightly, 'I follow God, I preach about him - yes, 'him'; I have spent countless hours learning about 'him', but I suspect if I really got to know - I mean properly know - this God of mine, I may well discover there is as much 'her' there as 'him'. Saoirse smiled kindly at him as he tried to explain thoughts that struggled to emerge as words. 'Sometimes....' he continued. 'Oh, I don't know. It's just, I've met you, and in you I feel I have met real love. I now know what real love is. I know God loves me, and I love him - technically.'

'Technically?' asked Saoirse leaning back in shock. 'Is it possible to love technically?'

'I'm afraid it is - but it's not real love, is it? And I have found real love in you - a most wonderful woman. So, of course, there has to be female in God's love. What do you think, Saoirse? Help me out!'

'Dougie, I have seen what men do with a very male God and I don't like it. I have a feeling that if your church discovered that the one up there is just as much mother as father, the church would be a much healthier place.'

Douglas looked at the young woman sitting next to him who was supposed to be an atheist, yet was already teaching him things about his faith that he had never considered. He felt so excited about the road ahead of him. He knew this would mean he would change, but he welcomed it. And, miracle of miracles, she had agreed to be his wife. He grabbed her to himself and held her tight. She never saw the tears that time but she had a suspicion they were there. She knew she was holding a man of faith, yet a man who also had his doubts. The last thing she wanted to do was to damage his faith, so as she hugged him, she whispered in his ear, 'Dougie, I love your love for God. Don't ever lose it.'

There was a noise behind him and Douglas was suddenly back in the Dingle church. It was a priest, dressed in his long black robe.

'I'm so sorry, I didn't mean to disturb you,' he said almost in a whisper and proceeded down the aisle to the east end of the church. Only when he was out of earshot did Douglas reply, 'Don't worry, I was disturbed long before you came in.' What was disturbing him now was the thought of how sad Saoirse would be to know of his loss of faith. How sad she would be to see him like this. How sad. This was the point his life had reached - a full stop of sadness. He was more sure than ever there was nothing in this world now that could cure such sorrow. But this was only his second day in this little town and it was a town that was most definitely going to surprise him in ways he could never have imagined.

CHAPTER 6

His recollections of Saoirse in the church had left Douglas feeling exhausted, so he returned to the Guest House and slept for an hour or so. It was evening when he woke and he felt much more at peace in himself, and ready for a meal. On his way downstairs, he heard Mrs O'Connell in the kitchen.

'Is that you, Douglas?' she called out.

'Yes, Mrs O'Connell, I'm just off for a meal.' Mrs O'Connell appeared in the hallway wiping her hands on her apron. Her hair had finally succumbed to a form of discipline, and Douglas suspected it had been brought into line by a skilful hairdresser during the day.

'Now, I'm thinking you are going to be here for more than a couple of days,' she said, reaching for her appointments diary. Douglas realised that he had given no thought at all to how long he was intending to stay in Dingle, so was a little unsure how to answer. It then became apparent that Mrs O'Connell was not asking a question, but making a statement.

'So, I'm booking you in for the week,' she added, writing in her diary with a pen that she constantly cursed as it failed to write fluently.

'Thank you,' said Douglas still very unsure quite how long he would be staying here, but could find no reason to contradict her.

'Oh, damn this infernal thing,' she said as she cajoled the reluctant pen to enter the booking in the diary. She slammed the book and pen back on the hall table and then asked, 'So will you be seeing that Dorchadas again this evening?'

'Er... yes, I think I might,' said Douglas. He had not made up his mind whether or not to return to *The Angels Rest.*

'Well, if you don't mind me saying so, Douglas, few people regret their conversations with Dorch. I know he's a bit... you know.' She tapped her head. 'But we are all a bit like that here in the South. Don't write any of us off. But he's a good lad, he is, and he's not always here, so it's as well to see him while you can. He could be gone tomorrow. He comes and goes, he does. Now, you have a good evening, I've got a cake in that oven which, if I don't get it out in the next few seconds, will be cremated. You have a good evening.' With that she hustled back into the kitchen, and as Douglas left the house he smiled as he heard the lament from the kitchen, 'Oh, holy mother of God, what has been going on in that there oven?'

He enjoyed a fish supper down near the waterfront and then felt decidedly unsure about whether to venture back to *The Angels Rest* again. Despite so many memories flooding back to him during the day, he was feeling quite peaceful and he did not want a weird ex-angel messing with his head. However, though he hardly knew her, he found he did trust Mrs O'Connell, and it was because of her that he found himself ducking under the low doorway of *The Angels Rest* and returning once again into the music-filled pub and making his way to the bar to order his Guinness.

As he ordered his drink he was a little disconcerted to see no sign of Dorchadas. He was not quite sure whether to feel disappointed or relieved. He asked the barman, 'Have you seen Dorchadas this evening?'

'Dorch?', said the barman as he waited for the ale to settle in the glass, 'No, not seen him yet this evening. You can never tell with Dorch. Know him well, do you?'

'No,' said Douglas. 'Met him for the first time last night. He told me to come back tonight and meet him.'

'Oh, he'll be in then - take a seat and he'll be here soon, sure he will.' Douglas took his drink. The pub was fairly full and the only seat available was at a small table at which sat Shelagh, the woman who had sung in the pub the night before. He asked if he might sit at her table, and she was very welcoming. He recalled how Dorch had told him about the terrible loss of her daughter in a car accident just a year ago.'

'You visiting Dingle?' she asked as he settled at the table.

'Yes, just here on holiday for a few days. I heard you singing last night - it was beautiful.'

'Och, I've not got much of a voice, but I've got a soul and you have to let your soul sing from time to time, that you do. It's one of its ways of healing. Did I see you talking with Dorchadas last night?'

'Yes, that's right.'

'Well, he's been a wonderful help to me.' Her glass was empty, and Douglas offered to get her a drink, but she declined, saying, 'No, you're all right, I'll be up singing again in a minute, then I'll get something after that.' She then tilted her head and looked at Douglas. 'What did you say your name was?

'Oh, sorry - I'm Douglas.'

'Well, pleased to meet you Douglas. I hope you don't mind me saying so, but I think you've known a similar wound to mine. Don't worry, I won't poke my nose in. It's just - it can be a comfort to know that others understand.' She paused and Douglas remained silent. 'It was our Claire - coming up to her twenty-first she was.' She nodded.

'Please, you don't need to...'

'No, no - sure to God I'm not going to bore you with the whole story, Douglas. It's just - I wanted you to know how Dorchadas was such a help to my Sammy and me. He's got - well - shall we say unusual ways about him. He introduced me to one or two people I thought I'd never meet in this life and they did me a power of good, they did. So, don't you go getting worried about Dorch. He's a man to trust, that's all I want to say.'

The suspicious bit of Douglas began to wonder if Dorchadas had skilfully set Shelagh up as a softening up operation, but just as he was thinking it, Shelagh said, 'Now don't go thinking Dorch has got me to speak to you, he hasn't. Anyhow, it's time for me to have my ciggie outside, and then I'll come have a sing. Hope you enjoy our beautiful town and the weather's kind to you. It can get awful rough at this time of year. Now drink your beer, son. It'll do you a power of good.' And with that she slipped away from the table and headed outside clutching her pack of cigarettes.

Just as she was making her way out of the door, Dorchadas came in and looked around the pub. When he saw Douglas, his eyes lit up and he came straight over and shook Doug by the hand.

'So sorry to keep you, Douglas. I was with Father Julian who's been going through a bit of a tough time of late and he's not, shall we say, short on vocabulary. But a fine priest, that he is. Now, looks like you hardly started your glass, let me get mine and we'll get chatting.' With that he made his way to the bar and with the usual laughter his glass was filled and he was soon back at the table.

'So, how's your day been, Doug?' asked Dorchadas as he settled his long legs behind the small table.

For a time, the two men talked together mostly about the town of Dingle and the surrounding area. Dorchadas gave Douglas a quick summary of the places he could visit around the town and the peninsula while he was here. They stopped talking while Shelagh sang a couple of songs. After her songs, Dorchadas turned to Douglas and with an enquiring, even probing, look in his eye, he asked, 'So Douglas, have you thought more about the benignant power - the wonderful gift of imagination - that we spoke about last night.'

'I'm not sure I have,' replied Douglas honestly.

'Well, I've been thinking about this today, Doug, and I'd like to make a suggestion.'

'Ok, Dorch - go ahead,' said Douglas, intrigued.

Dorchadas paused with his brows furrowed and then looked up at Douglas and said, 'Last night we talked about how you preached on Jacob, and I said it was no good preaching on the man until you met him. You remember?'

'Yes,' said Douglas with some hesitation. 'And I did say, if I recall, I was not into time travelling.'

'That you did,' smiled Dorchadas. 'And then we got talking about the imagination. And that's the clue, you see, Doug. That's the clue. And I can see you have got a wonderful heart and mind, and it is not difficult for you to see with the eyes of the heart.' Dorchadas was now looking intently at Douglas.

'Isn't it?' asked Douglas. 'I'm not so sure.'

'Well, I suggest we give it a go,' said Dorchadas, smiling again.

'Give it a go?'

'Yes - let's meet Jacob. Are you willing to trust me?'

Douglas took a long draft from his glass, then sat back with a look of puzzlement on his face. Why should he trust a man he had only just met, and moreover a man who purported to be an angel? And what on earth could he mean by 'let's meet Jacob', when the Jacob in question happened to be a character who lived over three thousand years ago. But Douglas was always fascinated by the power of the imagination, and it was that fascination plus the strengthening confidence provided by the glass of Guinness that caused him to turn to Dorchadas and say, 'Yes, Dorch. I trust you.'

Dorchadas smiled a reassuring smile and said, 'Close your eyes now.' And before Douglas had the chance to feel awkward or embarrassed, Dorchadas clutched his hands and said, 'Now open that heart of yours, Doug, and tell me what you see.' Douglas dutifully closed his eyes and did his best to open his heart. Nothing could have prepared him for what he was about to experience, and though his eyes were closed in this world, some different eyes within him opened to a world that he never thought he would catch sight of, let alone enter.

In days to come, Douglas found several ways of trying to explain what happened to him next. Hypnosis was his preferred explanation. He did also wonder if Dorchadas had slipped a hallucinogenic drug into his Guinness. Whatever the cause of it, for a period of time, whilst his body remained firmly seated at a table in an Irish pub, his spirit entered a quite different world, and a very ancient world at that. In the world he stepped into, it was no longer night time, and he was no longer indoors. Douglas found himself standing somewhat unsteadily on a dusty path, and Dorchadas was next to him holding his elbow. The sun was shining warm upon them, and judging from its angle, Douglas guessed it to be late afternoon. To their left long grasses whispered in the light wind, and to their right there was a bank of swaying reeds. Douglas had no idea where they were, but, despite the utter bizarre nature of this sudden transportation, he recalled afterwards that at the time, arriving in this totally different environment seemed the most normal thing in the world.

'Can you see him, Douglas?' said Dorchadas.

The path on which they were standing led to a beautiful gathering of palm trees, and there in their midst, was an elderly man sitting in their shade on a beautiful chair that might have come right out of Tutankhamen's tomb. Just beyond him was the bank of a great river.

Douglas was still feeling very unsteady, and despite the impossibility of the situation, he nonetheless guessed where they were: 'Dorch - this... this river, is the Nile, isn't it?'

'That it is, Doug. Beautiful, is in not? And there's your man. He's mighty near the end of his days now. He's a grand age and he's ready for off. But there's nothing wrong with his mind, and he'd like to meet you.'

'You mean...'

'Yes, I mean Jacob. The fella you preached on, remember?'

Douglas did not want to be reminded of that sermon, and so quickly whispered, 'Have you met him before?'

'No need to whisper, Doug. His hearing's not great. Oh yes, I met him a few times – officially and unofficially, if you know what I mean. In my reckoning, he's one of the best. I mean, there has to be something about a guy whose story takes up a fair chunk of the first book of the bible now, don't you think?' He laughed out loud, but still the old man didn't stir from his deep slumber by the quiet, flowing Nile. A bowl of dates lay on a small table by his seat.

'He loves this chair, Douglas. I've been to see him here once before. It's in his favourite spot – but no use when the old Nile floods mind you.

He loves the sound of the wind whispering through the rushes. He knows all those water fowl by name now – Egyptian names, of course. You know he's not that bad at Egyptian.' Dorchadas put his large hand on Douglas' back and slowly walked to the seated man. 'His days are short though, Douglas, so we mustn't keep him too long. But let's go and see what he's dreaming about.'

Douglas was completely overwhelmed – he was about to be introduced to none other than the great Jacob of the bible – Israel, the founder of the nation, one of the great revered patriarchs studied by humans for thousands of years! And yet, as with a dream, the absurd felt normal, and he now rather looked forward to engaging the old Patriarch in conversation. Dorchadas walked right up behind him and cheekily tweaked a bit of the old man's dull white hair and said in a loud voice, 'Wake up, you old dreamer!'

Jacob woke with a start and tried as best he could to look behind him. He grinned. 'Dorchadas, you fool. I might have guessed you would turn up now. Is it my time? Have they sent you to escort me to my fathers?'

Dorchadas looked at Douglas. 'You notice the man speaks English, Douglas! It's the imagination doing it, you see – far better than one of your google translators! And the old Hebrew and Egyptian is a might too hard even for an old angel like me.'

'What are you saying, Dorch, and who are you speaking to? Jacob protested. 'I can't hear you. Come round where I can see you with my poor old eyes.'

Dorchadas and Douglas moved round to the front of the chair, and smiling broadly, Dorchadas leaned down and hugged Jacob. 'Let me introduce you to a new friend of mine - meet Douglas.'

And so Douglas set his eyes on this old man of destiny. Son of the great Isaac who in turn was the son of the even greater Abraham. It was clear this elderly man would soon be in their esteemed company for he looked frail and deeply weary. And yet Douglas could see a great dignity in the old man who now lifted his head and squinted his eyes in an attempt to see his two visitors. Ancient skin hung from his jowls. His mouth was slightly open and his lower jaw had a tremor. 'Not as tall as you, Dorchadas, but then few are. Is he a good friend?' His voice was weak and husky, yet confident.

'Oh aye, a good friend, Jacob. How's it going for you today?'

'Let me get you a drink and something to eat,' Jacob said, and clapped his hands loudly. They heard movement from a small building nearby, whose reed canopy Douglas could see just over the papyrus leaves. 'The Egyptian wine this year is out of the world, Dorch – you've got to try it. And the girl will bring you some of my favourite sesame and honey cakes – you'll love them. There are a couple of stools over there, I think. Pull them up and settle yourselves. I'm ready for a conversation. I've had a busy morning thinking. I'm so old now you know. So very old. And there's a lot to think about when you are old.'

Douglas pulled up a stool and Jacob looked at him, his poor eyesight causing him to frown severely. 'When I last met this angel, I asked him to tell me what the afterlife is like, but he refused to tell me, and he said he's retired now – whatever that means – so apparently he's not qualified to speak about such things. I ask you, I've met a few angels in my time, but this one is a bit of a handful!' His trembling mouth widened into a broad smile, which became a laugh which then produced a coughing fit. The two guests watched the old man struggle out his cough, and then settle back in the chair, red faced and tired from the exertion.

'Ah here she is,' said Jacob, and from a narrow trail through the papyrus came a young Egyptian serving girl carrying a tray of wine and food. Douglas had seen her image on many an Egyptian painting and tomb wall. She placed the tray on the small table next to Jacob, and said, 'Your food and wine, Master Israel.'

'Thank you, my dear,' said Jacob. She smiled at him, and then swiftly departed.

'You serve it out, Dorch', said Jacob, and Dorchadas got to work on filling three goblets with wine, and handed out the honey cakes.

'I'll get to the point of our visit, Jacob,' said Dorchadas with his mouth full of sesame seeds, some of which sprayed out as he spoke. 'Pardon the spitting if you will. You just can't stop eating these delicious things. I do like being in human form when these are on the menu! Anyway, as I was saying, I'll get to the point...'

'Yes', said Jacob, 'please *do* get to the point – I know what you can be like, Dorchadas.'

Dorchadas, quite unfazed, continued, 'Douglas has been travelling a very rough road of late, and it's caused him to ask a few questions about this God of ours. Well, you're a man whose had a few knocks in your time, so this is the thing. Your man Douglas here is a mighty fine man and he's trying his best to do the work of God in his world, but if the truth be told, the man hardly knows God at all. So over to you, old man. Tell him how you got to know the Almighty.'

Douglas immediately felt very indignant at this highly inaccurate assessment of his spiritual state. He didn't recall saying anything of this to Dorchadas and he felt rather exposed and a bit let down by his new friend. He tried to protest, but Jacob was too deaf to hear his mutterings and leaned back in his chair and proceeded to brush crumbs and seeds from his chest and then licked honey noisily from his fingers. Thus, the great Jacob of old began to tell his story.

CHAPTER 7

'I thought I knew him when I was a young man,' Jacob said and he leant forward to take a sip of wine. 'Go on - do try this wine. As I said, an excellent year.' Both Douglas and Dorchadas instinctively pulled their goblets to their lips and Douglas had to admit that this was a wine of which any vintner would be proud.

'See those buildings over there?' Jacob waved his hand to the other side of the river. Douglas peered over the wide river and saw dust rising from the desert beyond the fertile fields and could make out a vast building being erected. 'I can't see it now, of course, but I know Pharaoh is constructing one of his ridiculous buildings – don't tell him I call them that. He's very touchy about them. He wants them to last thousands of years. I doubt they will. I realise they are great – astonishing they are. But what use are such buildings? It's what happens in here that counts,' he said tapping his heart with his thumb, 'not trying to impress people with grand buildings, or with wealth or power. All that nonsense fades away.'

Jacob continued, 'I tried it, you see. 'Not great buildings. But I longed to be admired - to impress people.'

He paused and looked mournful for a while, and then added, 'I did actually love my brother, you know – sorry, what is your name again?'

Douglas spoke his name loudly.

'Ugas? That's not a name I know. Anyway, no need to shout - I'm not deaf.' Dorchadas looked at Douglas and winked.

'I loved him, you know. And I hated him. You can love and hate at the same time I discovered. We were twins and mother told us that when we were born, he came out first all covered in red hair and I was grabbing hold of his heel with my little hand, and that's how we got our names. His name means 'Hairy' and mine 'Deceiver'. They reckoned that even then I was trying to cheat - to deceive them into thinking I was the eldest. Fancy being called those names!' Jacob chuckled. 'Trouble was, Ugas, I *was* a deceiver you see…My name was exactly right for me. I certainly always wanted to get one up on Esau. But not just Esau - everyone!' Here he coughed again and grasped his goblet of wine, spilling part of it on his robe in his haste to get it to his lips. Dorchadas rose from his stool momentarily but realised the old man didn't need assistance, so he settled back.

Jacob breathed in a long breath through his nose, pursing his wine-stained lips. A tear had formed in his right eye and sparkled in the sunlight. 'I never really wanted to deceive anyone, but it became a way of life. And do you know who I deceived?' He leant forward in his chair, 'My own father as well as my brother!' and he thumped his ancient hand on the side of the chair with some force. 'My God, I had to get out of town then. Esau had wild blood in him, and I knew that when he found out I'd robbed him of his birthright and blessing, he would not hesitate to batter every last drop of life out of my deceiving body.

'So I fled – and I was miserable. What's the use of a blessing if you feel cursed? I ended up at my uncle's place who turned out to be a bit of a kindred spirit – another deceiver! Hm!' He smiled an uncertain smile. 'But then something extraordinary happened. Just when I thought I had put myself out of the reach of God's love, I was given the sweetest gift imaginable.' He sat back and the sunlight flickered through the palm leaves over his face which made it full of colour and life. His cheeks were moist and he impatiently wiped his hand over them to dry them.

'Refill the goblets if you will please, Dorchadas'. Douglas had hardly taken a drop for he was so taken up in hearing this famous patriarch tell his story. Dorchadas refilled Jacob's who took a sip from the reloaded cup and continued.

'I was by the well, you see Ugas. It was a really hot day and the air was still and heavy.' He breathed in deeply and closed his eyes and raised his head to the sky. He paused for a moment savouring this ancient memory. He opened his eyes and looked at Douglas. 'Someone had put a little wooden seat next to the well and I sat on it sipping the cool water and pouring it over my head. Then I heard the most beautiful singing.' He placed a hand around his ear and looked into the distance, acting out again the scene he loved so dearly. 'There were various people around the place and I looked round to see who it was, and then I saw her – you wouldn't believe her beauty, Ugas!'

'Douglas!' said Douglas abruptly in a loud voice, feeling it was time Jacob got his name right.

'What?' Jacob paused, looking a little startled and squinted roughly in Douglas' direction.

'My name's Douglas – not Ugas,' he shouted.

'Douglas?' Jacob attempted to pronounce the name, but struggled. 'I don't know that name either. Never mind. Where was I? Ah yes, her hair…'

'Excuse me, old friend, we need to keep it moving,' said Dorchadas who knew the old man's tendencies to get stuck on his stories of his much beloved Rachel.

'Yes, Dorch of course… Well, she made her way up to the well, and one of those nearby told me it was Laban's daughter called Rachel. Well, do you know what I did, Douglas?' The old man leaned forward and looked hard at his guest through his hazy yet bright eyes, 'I kissed her!' Jacob laughed his wheezy laugh with delight and clapped, and Douglas smiled.

'To me she got lovelier and lovelier every day.' His smile changed to a frown. 'I said Laban was made of the same stuff as me. Well, he did a damn good job of deceiving me on our wedding day. For who should be under that veil – *after* we had made our vows mind you – but her sister Leah! Can you imagine! Married to the wrong woman! Dear God, I could have gladly strangled Laban there and then. But, you know, Leah was actually quite sweet - but nothing like my Rachel. Well, the day I eventually did marry my beloved, my, my, my… But alas she wasn't with me for long – died birthing our dear Benjamin. She came and she went, but this life would have been worth living had she only been with me for but one day. She was my precious gift from heaven.' He sighed and rested back in his chair and his mouth contorted and quivered as he tried to master his emotion. He looked up at the palm leaves.

Dorchadas looked at Douglas and knew what he was thinking. He leaned forward and placed his hand on Douglas' and said quietly, 'I know. I know.' As it happened, Douglas found some comfort as he thought of this old man going down a similar road of grief to his own. He was also made aware of something he had long suspected - that even if he lived into great old age, he would still be tipped over into tears at a memory of his days with Saoirse.

Jacob recovered himself and said, 'How could that be, Douglas?' he said shaking his head and finally getting Douglas' name right. 'An old swindler like me, given the most beautiful girl in the world! Why should God do that? I had been nothing but trouble to him from the moment I was born. But despite his kindness to me, I still didn't *know* him Douglas,' he said frowning. 'That came later. More cake, dear friend?'

He raised his eyebrows and Douglas saw the teary eyes trying to focus on him.

'No thanks,' he said, 'but it is most delicious.' He loved being called 'dear friend' by this Patriarch.

'Mmm – not as good as usual I think.' He looked sad and munched his biscuit slowly, and there was no conversation for a while and they listened to the sighing of the Egyptian wind in the reeds that seemed to bow reverently towards the elderly man in his riverside chair.

It was Dorchadas who broke the silence – 'Tell him, old man, tell him.'

'What? Yes, yes.' He brushed away the latest collection of crumbs from his lap. 'I still don't find it an easy story to tell, you know. Well, before my beloved Rachel left us, we were on the run again. I was fleeing from Laban who was furious with me. But worse than that, Esau was hell-bent on destroying me - or so I feared. Never judge life by what you fear, Douglas. But I did, and I was pretty sure my days were numbered. We came to a little river – a stream really – called Jabbok – sounds a bit like Jacob doesn't it?" He paused for a moment thoughtfully, his misty eyes moving to and fro.

'News came through that Esau was on his way to meet us – with four hundred men. Literally, four hundred! Well that was it – there was no chance of escape. I sent Rachel and all the household and belongings over the river. I didn't want any of them hurt because of my silly foolish family battles. I watched them go wading over that river. Rachel was on one of our donkeys – her favourite – she called him 'Faithful', and he was. She was the last to go over – I kept hurrying her on. "Go on, go on," I kept saying to her, worried that Esau would come around the corner any moment. She was so strong, but I could see the distress in her eyes. She thought she would never see me again. I still see her now - smiling so kindly at me, and then turning her head and riding like a noble queen across that river, her head held high and the bright sunlight catching her long brown hair. I watched her ride over the hill and then I sat on the bank of that stream in the afternoon sun. I never realised a man could feel so lonely. It was a very depressing moment. All kinds of things go through your mind at that time. You ever faced death, Douglas?'

'Not mine,' said Douglas coldly, not wanting to disclose or discuss his own story.

53

'I hope you never have to until it is your time – it doesn't feel good. Especially not if you haven't lived a good life. I felt a great sense of waste. Jacob the deceiver, the heel-grasper, was now going to get what he deserved. By some grand mistake in the heavens he had been granted great wealth and the most beautiful wife, but inside he was no better than a wretched pauper. He had connived his father into gaining a blessing, but he lived the life of the damned.

'The dark came quickly that night – we have spoken of that darkness, have we not Dorchadas?'

'That we have, sir', said Dorchadas who was listening as intently as Douglas.

'It was a terrible dark. Thick cloud hovered in the heavens so there was no light by moon or stars. I tried to sleep but it was no use, I was too restless. I yearned for the night to end. Then, in the early hours, I heard footsteps coming fast towards me. I stood up and shouted, "Who is there?" It had to be either Esau or one of his four hundred men. It was so dark I could not see the shape of the person until they were as near as you two are to me now. He pounced on me and I fell to the ground. I was a strong man then, so I immediately fought back and locked my opponent in a tight grip, but he soon escaped. He was not my brother or anyone I knew, even though there was something oddly familiar about him. He was a man of a similar build to me. He did not speak a word – I kept asking, "Who are you?" But he would not answer. He came back at me again, and on and on we wrestled with the sweat from our bodies making it harder to grip. It was a fight to the death, and I was determined not to be the one to die. Get me some ale, would you Dorchadas? Good as it is, this wine's not helping my throat.' He leant back and tried to clear his throat. He looked to the sky and drew in deep breaths of the warm air. His chest rattled as he breathed out.

Dorchadas was up immediately and called out a message to the serving girl who returned hurriedly with a flagon of ale, and poured some into Jacob's goblet. He immediately drank about half of it, then wiped his glistening mouth with the back of his hand. He placed the goblet carefully on the table beside him.

'My God it was a tough fight. It felt like this fight that was the sum of all my life's battles. My energy and fight were all but gone when the dawn light started to break, and for the first time I began to make out the features of the man I was wrestling. Just as I tried to get a good look at his face, he walloped me right here in the hip.' He lifted his left hip in his chair and tapped it. 'Been hard to walk with it ever since.' He coughed and reached for his ale again and sat back in the chair and closed his eyes.

Douglas listened intently as he continued, the patriarch's voice now so quiet he had to strain to hear his words above the sound of the swaying reeds and grasses.

'I fell back with the pain of it and lay on the ground. He stood there heaving, catching his breath. I waited for the deathblow, but it never came. I remember his hands fell to his side and they twitched from the exertion of the fight. I lay in the dust – blood was in my mouth and pain in my hip. But I wasn't going to let him go, so with one last burst of strength I got up and threw myself at him and he fell to the ground hauling me down on top of him. And then, he pulled my head to his and at last he spoke.

'In between his deep breaths, he said, "Let me go, for the day is breaking." Don't ask me how I knew, but at that point I knew it was no human that I was fighting.'

Jacob looked up at Douglas. He grasped tightly the arms of the chair and pulled himself forward. 'I don't expect you to believe this, dear friend, but I can tell you, at that moment I was in no doubt at all that, all through that night, I had been fighting none other than God himself, the great *El Shaddai*, who had come to me as a night-time fighter. In all my years on this earth, I had never imagined such a thing could happen. And there we were, limp, exhausted, bruised and hurting, sprawled in the dust that was sprinkled with our sweat, spit and blood. And he asked me to let him go for I was still clutching his robe with my aching hand.'

'And so, did you?' asked Douglas. It was a story he knew well - he had even preached on it recently - but he had never heard it like this before.

'I'm not sure what possessed me, but I heard myself say, "Not until you bless me". Do you see what happened, Douglas in that dark night?' He was still bent forward and with his elbows propped on the sides of his chair, his left hand was wringing his right. His lips trembled as he spoke. 'All those years I had been running - not from Esau. Not from Laban. Not even from myself. I had been running from *God*. And why? Because from my earliest years I believed that Almighty God would *never* want to bless one like me. Why should he bless a man who was a conniving deceiver from the moment of his birth? Surely, he would take one look at me, and what would he see? A whole, rancid dung heap of sin. But I was wrong. You see, Douglas, I had quite the wrong view of him. I discovered that he was one, who, far from being put off by all my wrongdoings, yearned so deeply for me to see sense that he was willing to fight me tooth and nail in that dark night by the river, and wrestle flesh to flesh until I got the message. So, I had to know - I had to know, and I asked him, "*Can* you - *will* you bless me?" Could the Holy One bless a wretched man like me who had spent most of his pathetic life deceiving his family, his God and himself?'

'So, did he?' blurted out Douglas.

Jacob dropped his hands to his lap and then said, 'No... Hm – no.' He chuckled and reached for his cup of ale and sipped it slowly and then chuckled again.

'Well come on, put him out of his misery, old man. Tell him what happened.' Dorchadas was as keen as Douglas was to hear the end of this story.

'I'm about to, Dorch. Patience, patience. I realised just how long I yearned for that blessing.' He put the cup back on the table and continued, 'Do you know, I think every man, woman and child has a longing deep down in their hearts, and it is a longing to know that when God Almighty looks upon them, he likes what he sees. For some reason, most of us assume he looks upon us with dismay and disappointment. Well, when I asked God to bless me, it was that longing that was crying out. I just needed to know that God would somehow...' he paused, and looked a little vulnerable, 'Well, *approve* of me. I knew he couldn't like me, not with the life I had lived, but I just felt somehow, he might be able to reach out beyond his disappointment in me and – well, *bless* me. Yes, bless old Jacob. But he looked hard at me and he said he would *not* bless me. Oh, for a brief moment I felt utter dejection and despair filling my weary soul. But he went on, and I remember it so well, Douglas.'

The old man leaned to his right, leaning on the arm of the seat, and with his left hand he pointed to the sky. 'The sun was coming up now and my wrestling partner still looked a battered specimen after that fight. I released my grip on him and I sat back in the dust. He shifted his body and he came and knelt right next to me. He lifted his head and his long damp hair fell around his face. I stared at him, and do you know what I saw?' Jacob dropped his arm and rested it on the chair arm. 'I saw utter goodness, Douglas. I mean *utter* goodness - and total authority. Though he was kneeling there on the dirty ground with dust and sand and blood all over him, a glory blazed from within him. There was no doubting he was God. And then, would you believe this? He straightened his arms and leaned on them, and he was like a lion on all fours. He leant over to me so that his face was as near as this.' Jacob pulled his left hand up close to his face. 'He did not bless me, but he asked me a terrible question. He asked me, "What is your name?" It was the worst question he could have asked me.'

'Why was it the worst question?' Douglas asked, totally absorbed in the story.

Jacob dropped his hand to his lap. 'Why, don't you see, Douglas? My name means 'deceiver', 'con-artist', 'fraud'. It is a name that summed up the wretchedness of my life. But I couldn't lie to God, so I said with a great sense of despair, "My name is Jacob", and I remember how I hung my head, and oh, how my hip hurt in that moment. I just looked at the dust and saw the marks in the sand of our wrestling. I knew God could not, and would not, bless Jacob. But then I felt warm hands cupping my face. He pulled my head right here – to his heart.' Jacob tapped his heart and his glassy eyes looked out across the river. 'So quietly did he speak. It was almost a whisper: "You will no longer be called Jacob, but you will be called Israel." In our language that means, "one who has fought with God." He went on, now stroking my face with such gentle fingers, "You have fought with God and with humans, and you have prevailed." And when he said, 'you have prevailed,' he pulled back from me a little and I saw the radiance of his smile. He just seemed so – well - happy.'

The old man started shaking. He continued to gaze out to the river, while a stream of emotion flowed from his contorted face. He was still leaning on his right arm, and with his left hand he stroked his cheek. Douglas felt embarrassed for him. Dorchadas sensed it and whispered, 'Let him be, Douglas.'

After a few moments, Jacob turned back to look at the others, and wiped his face with his sleeve. 'For the first time in my life I was being genuinely honoured,' he continued, 'not for what I was trying to be, but simply for who I was. This God whom I had patently so failed to serve, came to me in my dark night of lonely fear on the eve, so I believed, of a great fight with my twin brother that I could only lose, and in those dark hours of struggle he delved deep, deep into my soul. And do you know what, Douglas – he *liked* what he saw! He actually *liked* it! And in the liking, he *blessed* it.

'Well, I sat back in the sand on my right side, because my hip hurt so, and from somewhere within me I blurted out a question that took me by

57

surprise: "Tell me *your* name then!" But he would not tell me. Instead, he asked me to bow my head which I did, and coming over to me again, he laid his hands upon my head and blessed not the Jacob in me, but the Israel in me. My, that was some feeling. As he blessed me I felt power in my body and I knelt up as straight as my wounded body would allow. And then, as suddenly as he had come, he disappeared. Absolutely no trace of him, apart from all the scuff marks in the sand from our night-time battle. But, do you know, from that moment, I stopped running. He may have disappeared, but I knew he was with me, and he has continued with me.'

'And what about Esau and his four hundred men?' asked Douglas eagerly.

'Yes, yes, Esau and his men did turn up and actually all was well. I'd got it all wrong about him. As I said, it never pays to listen to judge life by your fears. We made amends and my life was from then onwards extraordinarily blessed. Not without its struggles and sorrows of course. But look at me now, Douglas,' he said, sweeping his arm over the grasses and river. 'My son, Joseph, is virtually running this country, and all my family are safe and well and God's work is being done.'

He yawned and looked up at the sun in the sky. 'Well, if you don't mind, it's time for my dinner. It's been good to meet you, Douglas – and you, Dorchadas you old rogue.' He clapped his hands for the serving girl.

'Thank you, Israel', said Douglas, careful to use the blessed name.

Jacob lifted his tired body out of the seat. 'Mm? Oh, yes, you called me "Israel". Hm, lots of people still call me Jacob, but inside I am always Israel now. I have enjoyed meeting you. I'm sorry, I never got a chance to ask you about yourself. Another time, I hope.'

The girl appeared again and took the old man's arm and slowly they started their walk back up to his home. Dorchadas and Douglas both watched him limp down the path. 'Now tell me, how's your mother doing?' he asked the girl, as they passed behind the swaying papyrus. Douglas never caught her answer for others seemed to now join in the conversation and the noise of chatter grew louder. The bright Egyptian sun dimmed and the lovely riverside scene was replaced by the everyday scene of a twenty first century Irish pub on a cold and damp October evening.

'You see, Douglas – the imagination is a mighty fine gift, don't you think?' said Dorchadas, draining the last of his Guinness.

Douglas could barely speak. He simply sat blinking awkwardly. He looked hard at Dorchadas, straining to understand what had just happened. Then, without saying a word, he drained the last of his Guinness, got up and made his way back to the St.Raphael Guest House. But it was the taste of honey cake, not Guinness that remained in his mouth as he walked swiftly through the cool Irish night.

God's invitation to the spiritual life
is a call to the high-risk venture of
being loved more fiercely
than we ever might have dreamed.

Belden C Lane
The Solace of Fierce Landscapes

CHAPTER 8

I want to write, but don't know what to write. So much has happened.
It's just gone 3am and I haven't slept much. Perhaps writing something
down will help clear my head. So went to the pub the first night and met
this guy called Dorchadas. Never heard of the name before - he says it
means 'dark'. Not sure what to make of that. But he's certainly an
intriguing guy. Quite liked him actually. Seems very popular here. But,
and how do I write this... Look, when I read this in years to come,
remember I came here in a pretty fragile state and my mind is not good.
I really do wonder about my mind actually. I can hear someone make
reference to 'mental health issue'. But I actually think my mind is more
lucid than it's ever been. Well here goes, I'll put it down in writing.

The first ridiculous thing is that the guy claimed to be an angel! He
clearly isn't, though I suppose I shouldn't be too quick to brand him as a
liar. But I have never read of an angel turning up in a pub with an Irish
accent and knocking back a couple of pints of Guinness. And what's
more, he said he was retired! Well I've not read that in the bible
anywhere! And I gave up believing in angels when she died. If angels
exist, then why weren't they there?

But there was another weird thing - and this is really weird. Last night
I went back to the pub and met him again. This next bit is hard to write.
The fact is, this guy got me to use my imagination and quite how he did
this, I don't know, but for a short while I was actually in ancient Egypt
meeting Jacob!! For heaven's sake, is that really likely? I think he must
have hypnotised me, which is a pretty unnerving thought. Just hope he
didn't use drugs. Well, however sinister the method, the experience was
actually rather wonderful. I've always liked old Jacob and I preached
about him in my last sermon at St.Philips (not my greatest by any
reckoning). Well, there Jacob was - right in front of me sipping wine and
dribbling it down his front. He turned up as an old man. He spoke
English which I suppose raises a few questions. But he did say a few
things that were wonderful. He told me about that wrestling match.

I can still hear old Jacob's husky voice: 'And do you know what,
Douglas – he liked what he saw! He actually liked it!' It took even that
old patriarch of faith by surprise – that God should look deep into the

murky shadows of his own clapped out soul, and actually like what he found there. I smile when I remember the look on the old man's face. But it's disturbing - I wonder about what God sees as he peers into my soul, assuming he exists? Apparently, nothing is hidden from his sight. Surely, he must disapprove? How could he condone my unholy thoughts - all the stuff that has gone through my mind these past two years. How could he possibly approve of my life in recent months where I have more or less abandoned all belief in him? How could he tolerate the terrible things I said to him when Saoirse died? How does an Almighty and holy God respond in any other way? Curiously my hip aches now as I remember Jacob's fight. How long would I have to wrestle with God until I believed in the very inner recesses of my shadowy soul, that God is far more keen to bless what he likes in me, than curse what is wrong? Longer than one night I think. Maybe a lifetime of nights, of dark nights like these.

*

4.15am

Still not sleeping. In the dark hours my fears and doubts speak so loudly. I find I want to see Dorchadas again. Every time I slip into a troubled sleep his voice rings in my ears. I see his sparkling eyes. As I lay in the dark, some lines of George Herbert came to mind:

O cheer and tune my heartless breast
Deferre no time
That so thy favours granting my request,
They and my mind may chime
And mend my ryme.

Will my ryme be mended here, I wonder? I fear my breast is too heartless now. Must try and get some sleep. Not sure what I'll do tomorrow. Don't think I'll go back to England just yet though.

*

The Americans were already ahead of him at breakfast in the morning, but Douglas' table by the window was waiting for him. He could hear Mrs O'Connell clattering away in the kitchen, and by the sound of the expletives emanating from the area of the cooker, the eggs were giving her trouble.

'How're you liking Dingle?' asked the American woman and before Douglas had a chance to answer, Mrs O'Connell breezed in and hailed Douglas with, 'Douglas, I'm getting your breakfast now, but for God's sakes those eggs are testing me this morning, they surely are. Do you mind if you do without your eggs this morning?'

'That will be fine,' answered Douglas and he observed that though the eggs may have declared war on Mrs O'Connell, it appeared that her hair was in a much more amiable mood this morning.

'We did the run around the peninsula yesterday,' said the American woman in a rather tired voice. Got to see all the sites. And today we head north up to Galway, then Shannon tomorrow and back home to Texas.'

'We've had a truly wonderful time,' said the man, shaking open his napkin before placing it on his lap. Douglas gained the impression that the man had enjoyed his holiday a good deal more than his wife who looked ready for home. 'They say Ireland is a good land for finding your healing,' he continued. 'Well, they're not wrong, they sure aren't.'

'No,' said Douglas rather formally. 'I'm sure.' He did not really want to engage in conversation.

'You been to the States?' asked the man as he spread a liberal supply of marmalade on his toast.

'No, no I've not,' replied Douglas. 'But I have a good friend who is a priest in California. I may visit him one day.'

'You would love it,' said the woman. 'A good deal warmer and drier than here. Don't know how the local people live with all this cloud and rain. It'd drive me mad.'

The man looked at Douglas and said, 'This is a land I love - I'm not sure my wife, Meg, quite shares my enthusiasm,' he nodded at his serious looking wife. 'But I believe what they say: there's healing here in this land, especially in these parts. It's done me a power of good, it sure has. We've had such a wonderful time. I hope you will be as blessed in your stay here.'

'Come on Ned, we need to get packed and on our way. We must leave this gentleman to get on with his breakfast' said the woman in her flat, tired voice.

'Sure, darling. On to new adventures!' the man said with a look of childish excitement on his face. He gathered his Stetson and they both left.

Douglas felt relieved, for he never felt very sociable at breakfast time. But he couldn't help notice the difference between the husband and wife. The one somehow so full of life and adventure, and the other so tired and withdrawn.

Soon after the Americans left, Mrs O'Connell returned and brought a welcome cafetiere of coffee over to Douglas, and as she poured the coffee she said, 'Dorchadas called in this morning, sure he did. All bright and breezy he was. Said to tell you that he'll be at Kathleen's Coffee House at ten this morning if you're interested.'

'Thank you,' said Douglas, not quite sure if he wanted to meet up with Dorchadas again. He was still reeling from the experience in the pub the previous night and he wasn't sure if this supposed angel had other tricks up his sleeve. When Mrs O'Connell came back with the full Irish breakfast she said, 'Kathleen's my sister. Been running that Coffee Shop for a hell of a long time now. God knows how she makes money on it. Apart from anything else, her coffee's crap. Her cakes are good, mind. It would be worth your having one of those. Anyway, that's where Dorch is if you want him. I hope the sausages are to your liking. Sorry again about the eggs.'

Douglas enjoyed the magnificent egg-less breakfast and as he did so he reflected again on the two Americans. The woman reminded him so much of himself in his present state. He too felt tired and withdrawn, just wanting to go home. And yet there was still an ember of life in his hearth that flared up a little when he heard the man speak. He may be depressed and still in deep grief, but at the same time he did not want to park his life forever in a siding of grief. As he cleared the final piece of sausage from his plate, he felt an energy rise - a kind of determination. Perhaps Ireland could be for him after all a place of healing. Maybe, just maybe, life could flare up in him again. And, despite the utter weirdness of the man, maybe Dorchadas could be someone who might help him find his life again. With this in mind, he resolved to seek out Kathleen's café and risk another meeting with Dorchadas.

*

Mrs O'Connell gave Douglas the directions for finding Kathleen's Coffee House. As he entered through a narrow front door, he discovered the café was no more than a small front room that just managed to accommodate four tables covered with plastic clothes. Each was decorated with a vase of faded plastic flowers. He also noticed a couple of chairs by a smouldering peat fire. The room smelt of stale cigarette smoke. As Douglas entered he heard the unmistakable, and for him unwelcome, sound of Dolly Parton coming from a back room. Other than that, there was no sign of life.

He settled himself at one of the tables, which rocked disconcertingly on the worn flagstones. He tried to stabilise it by folding up one of the many paper doilies that were everywhere, and stuffing it under the table leg. His table was next to a deep windowsill that was littered with more doilies and a variety of dusty ornamental ducks and a pile of stained ashtrays. There were thick, yellowing net curtains hanging either side of the window and the glass itself was decorated with an assortment of marks and stains that were highlighted by the sun. Douglas was just wishing Dorchadas could have found him a rather more attractive venue for their second meeting, when the very man breezed into the shop.

'Well, good morning to you, Douglas. How did you sleep now?' Dorchadas settled himself at the table. 'My, a table that doesn't rock! Has Kathleen been to take your order?' he asked.

'Good morning, Dorchadas,' said Douglas feeling surprising warmth towards his new friend. 'I slept OK, and no, Kathleen has not been in yet.'

'Just OK, eh? I thought you were going to have a good night, I must say. Now, Kathleen,' he called out. 'Are you there, love?'

'I'll be right with you,' came a voice from a room beyond a bead curtain. 'Just trying to get this infernal coffee machine working.' A hammering sound was accompanied by a rush of colourful swearing.

'Now you must be watching your language today, Kathleen. You have a priest in your café this morning.'

'Oh, God help us,' said the voice. 'Has he got time for my confession?'

'Not that much time,' said Dorchadas, and laughed, winking at Douglas. 'She's a great girl is Kathleen.'

'Were you all right about the meeting, Doug?' asked Dorchadas.

Douglas thought for a few moments and asked, 'Just how did you do it, Dorch? Is it hypnotism? Because if it is, I'm not really happy...'

He was not able to finish his sentence because he was interrupted by a flurry of activity as a large lady made her way through the beaded fly curtain, one string of which got caught in one of her expansive earrings. 'Och, the blessed thing,' she said as she disentangled herself. She eventually got herself free with the help of more swearing, and came and stood by the table clutching a notepad and a well-chewed pencil. 'Morning to you, Dorch.' She then looked at Douglas suspiciously and asked, 'You the priest?'

'Yes,' he admitted, 'but an Anglican one.'

'And an English one by the sound of it,' she said, somewhat fiercely. 'Always been Anglican, have you?'

Douglas thought it was a curious enquiry, and rather meekly answered 'Yes'.

'Very well, then. So, what will you be having?'

Douglas remembered Mrs O'Connell's warning, and said, 'Tea for me, please.'

'Aye, the same for me, please Kathleen, and bring some of those delicious cakes of yours if you will.' After she left the room, Dorchadas lowered his voice. 'Did Elsie warn you about the coffee?'

'She did,' replied Douglas.

'She's not wrong is Elsie. 'Only visitors to the town have the coffee. Seldom seen one finish a cup. But Kath has a heart of gold, that she does. Don't be put off by her gruffness. Been through a hell of a lot, she has.'

'I would have thought you wouldn't be allowed to use the word "hell",' Douglas said, teasingly. 'I'm far from convinced about this angel thing.'

'I'm retired, Douglas - remember? Retired. So, it's OK!' and he winked again and smiled his broad winsome grin. 'But I must remember you're a priest, so I'll try and be on my best behaviour.'

'I'll enjoy that thought, Dorchadas – you an angel trying to watch your language in front of a human!'

They both laughed as Kathleen came back with two mugs of steaming tea, this time weaving her way through the threatening bead curtain with great care. 'I'll be getting your cakes now,' she said as she plonked the steaming mugs on the table, spilling them a little.

Dorchadas poured some sugar into his mug and, as he stirred his tea, said, 'No, Douglas. To answer your question, it's not hypnotism I can assure you. Honest to God, I would not want to trick or deceive you.

Please believe that. I'll try and explain sometime. But did you like the old fella?'

'Yes, I did. It's not how I imagined him, you know. I guess I never really thought of him at the end of his life like that.'

'No, he was mighty different in his early life, I can tell you.'

'I've only got the Victoria sponge - will you be doing all right with that?' Kathleen had to raise her voice above the sound of her radio. A girl band had taken over from Dolly Parton.

'Grand for me, Kathleen,' said Dorchadas, and Douglas also agreed to a slice, even though the black pudding from breakfast was lying heavy in his stomach. She turned down the radio and returned with a cigarette dangling from her mouth. She placed two generous portions of cake on the table. 'Sorry about the ciggie, Douglas. It's not allowed you know in public places. But this is my home, so it's not public. At least that's what I tell the Garda if they're asking.' She took a big drag from the cigarette and then wheezed out a husky laugh in a cloud of smoke, waving her hands erratically in an attempt to disperse the smoke.

'Come and rest those legs of yours, Kathleen,' said Dorchadas.

'Aye, I don't mind if I do, Dorch,' she said. She disappeared for a moment and then came back clutching a mug of tea in one hand, and her pack of cigarettes and matches in the other.

'It's Douglas is it? We don't' get many Douglases in Dingle. So, what's this man been telling you about me, then?' she said, looking at Dorchadas cheekily and half closing her eyes as she drew hard on her cigarette.

'Nothing yet,' Douglas said, neatly forgetting the brief reference to her coffee-making skills.

'Well, I can't believe that,' she said. 'He knows a lot about my life, don't you Dorch. Has he told you he's an angel yet?' She laughed a wheezy laugh looking at Dorchadas who returned her look with a smile. Douglas noticed an extraordinary kindness in his smile. 'I don't believe a word of it,' she said after a deep inhalation. 'I've seen them angels in the church and he's not like any of them. Anyway, angels are supposed to be all holy and dressed in white with wings and that - and look at him!' She wheezed with laughter again. 'Mind you, he is a gentleman, Douglas, I will say that.' She reached out and grasped his hand, which was resting on the table. 'Come on you boys, eat up the cake, now. It's one of my best – made first thing this morning, would you know.'

They both cut into their cake. 'Delicious,' said Dorchadas. Douglas was also impressed by it.

'So you're a priest, Douglas? A Protestant one, then?' said Kathleen raising one eyebrow of her large, rather weathered face. He noticed her eyes were bloodshot – whether it was from the smoke or weariness, it was hard to tell.

'Yes,' he confessed. He felt disappointed. He was away from work and didn't want to be put into the role of professional Christian any more. But Kathleen put him at ease straight away.

'Makes no odds to me, Douglas. You being a priest and that. You could be the Archbishop of Shangri bloody La for all I care. I gave up on religion a long time ago.' She took another long draw from her cigarette, which took it down to the orange filter. She picked up one of the ashtrays from the windowsill and placed it on the table. Douglas watched her carefully as she stubbed out the cigarette. She seemed to do it with great feeling, as if to demonstrate the force with which she stubbed out her faith many years ago.

'Dorch knows all about it. Don't suppose I'd have told him if I had thought he really was an angel, mind. It's not the kind of thing I'd want reporting back to headquarters!' She wheezed with laughter again, and took a noisy gulp of her tea and leant back in her chair, which creaked alarmingly in protest. Dorchadas sipped his tea, keeping his eyes firmly fixed on her.

'You're all right, Kathleen,' said Dorchadas. He placed both hands around his cup and turned his gaze from Kathleen to the stained window behind her. Douglas noticed some emotion in him, but couldn't quite place it. It was something to do with melancholy.

'More cake, Douglas?' she asked. He had made his way swiftly through it, despite the lack of room in his stomach.

'No, no – I couldn't manage any more. It was delicious.'

'Doesn't shock you then - that I gave up on God?' She slurped again from her tea.

'No,' said Douglas 'We all have to make choices.' He hated how he sounded - he could hear the professional pastor in him, and his comment sounded like it had come straight from a training manual.

'Well that's it, you see. Some of us have made very bad choices.' Kathleen got another cigarette out of the box and tapped it on the table with her large and powerful hand. For a reason she could not understand, she felt she could trust Douglas with her life. And maybe it was that which caused her to continue. 'And I made one of the worst. I can't blame God for that, I suppose.' She lit up the cigarette and drew in the smoke, pulling her lips back as she did so, revealing her damaged, yellow teeth. As she exhaled she seemed to fill the whole room with smoke. Douglas was pleased they had left the door open.

'I was young, you see and loved my church. Such a sweet, pretty little place it was – beautiful windows full of saints. Beautiful one of Brigid. God, I loved that woman - used to chat to her in that window when I was little. I was sure she heard me. I wasn't living in Dingle in those days – we lived a few miles up the coast. I sang in the choir – loved the music I did.' She smiled and her large face lit up and Douglas saw a loveliness in her face. 'Father Gregory was an elderly priest – well, I was 17 and most men over 40 seemed elderly to me then! Anyway, he was a kindly old man and we all loved him. He also loved Brigid and he'd tell me stories about how she gave all her father's precious belongings to the poor. I was really sad when he retired. Then the new priest came.' She looked around her and lowered her voice. 'Father Peter was his name.' She drained the last of the tea from her mug and then wiped her mouth with her hand. Her rubbery mouth grimaced as she squeezed it. She took a deep breath. Her cigarette lay smouldering in the ashtray.

'Well, I was 17 when he arrived, Douglas – not far off 18 - and I was actually quite pretty in those days - don't disagree Dorch!' Dorchadas smiled and looked into his empty mug. 'Always a little overweight, mind. But Father Peter…' she sighed. She looked hard at the man next to her who was listening intently. 'Douglas, he was God Almighty beautiful and I fell head over heels in love with the man. I tried to hide it, but my sister Elsie spotted it, of course. You know Elsie - you're stopping with her at St.Raphael's. Well, she was three years older than me, and stepping out with Dan O'Connell at the time. They got married that same year as it happened. Well they both laid in to me – told me to stop ogling at the parish priest, and to find a man my own age, and not a priest for God's sake! Peter was twelve years my senior, he was. Hm – never felt an age gap, you know. We were – well, just – we just felt the same about so many things…'

She picked up her cigarette again and, knocked off the ash, then rotated it between her thumb and forefinger. A line of blue smoke went up and caught the sunlight that was straining to make its way through the window. She went quiet for a while as she fiddled with her cigarette. Douglas was longing to hear more, but didn't want to intrude so he kept quiet. Finally, she lifted the cigarette to her lips, but before she drew from it, she looked at Douglas. 'I think you can guess what happened next. He fell in love with me. Can you imagine it? A priest and a young girl head over heels in love. I knew it shouldn't happen, but I couldn't stop it, Douglas. He asked me to clean his house, and of course I said "yes". Mam and Da didn't suspect a thing.' She finally drew from the cigarette and then placed it carefully back on the ashtray.

'It was a Wednesday...' She smiled and looked up to the back of the café. Smoke swirled around her like incense and for a moment she closed her eyes as if in prayer. She kept her eyes closed as she said, 'Strange how it didn't feel at all wrong.' She opened her bloodshot eyes and looked down at her empty mug. 'He asked if I had done it before – he was so gentle, you know, especially when I told him it was my first time. He confessed it wasn't his first, but he said it was the first time with a girl he truly loved. Do you know, that touched me so much and made me feel so special, and I loved him even more, if that was possible. We lay under the sheet, and my, it was the most beautiful thing. I'd not had much happiness in my life up 'til then, but in those moments, I was the happiest girl in the whole of blessed Ireland.

'I hope to God I'm not shocking you, Douglas,' she said, emerging from her memories. 'I don't really know why I'm telling you all this. But you better get the whole story now I've started. We lay there afterwards and laughed so much. I managed to keep it very quiet. God knows how. But for four glorious months we loved each other – it was such bliss. If there is a heaven, then I do believe I tasted a little of it in those months. You won't accept this I know, but I truly believed that God loved our loving each other, and in those days my faith was as strong as the rock of Skellig.'

'So...What happened?' Douglas asked, his hands grasping tightly his empty mug.

'Well for a start, after a couple of months I started to suspect I was up the pole, and by the time I'd missed three months and feeling pretty sick, we both knew I was carrying our child. You'd think we'd be terrified, wouldn't you? But they say perfect loves casts out fear, and the love we had for each other and for the wee baby was so strong, we feared no one. How we thought we'd hide it, I don't know, but we figured that when the baby started to show, we'd come up with a plan. But all good things have to come to an end. It was, for sure, too good to last.' Kathleen sighed a long sigh, and her lip started to tremble.

'You take your time, Kathleen,' said Dorchadas with great tenderness and cupped his hand over hers.

'He had an aunt who lived in the next-door village,' she continued, as she pulled another cigarette out of its box, forgetting the first was still alight in the ashtray. 'A nasty piece of work if ever there was one. Well, it was a Friday – as cold as a confessional it was – November. November 18th at half past three. Peter never locked the front door to the Presbytery. We never heard her come in. We were lying in bed, cuddled together for warmth and having a smoke when the door suddenly banged open. She had been suspecting for a while, the nosey bitch. She looked so evil standing in that doorway, so full of hatred. I was that frightened I pissed myself – I so hate that, pissing in his poor bed.' Her eyes filled, as she thrust her jaw forward. 'God, if there's a hell, I hope she's rotting there right now. You'd think as family she'd protect her nephew. But, oh no! She was out to ruin him, she was. She was one of those purer than pure, goddy Christians who felt the whole town would be defiled by this – she said so! She said she would have to tell people 'cos if we kept it as secret sin, then the whole town would be cursed by God. I mean, where the hell does she get that from? God, poor Peter. I can still see him now, desperately trying to pull on his trousers, tears pouring down his beautiful face, and pleading with his aunt. I ran home, and locked myself in my room. Terrified I was, and desperately alone.

'Well it all came out. The village was shocked, of course, and the bars were full of the gossip for months. I had to tell me Mammy about the baby. Dear God, I can still see her face now. She made it clear it was the worst sin of all. She screamed at me, told me the family could never show its face in the village again. We'd have to emigrate. On and on she went. I don't know if she told my father – he was usually too drunk to notice anything. He never noticed me, for sure. I stayed for hours and hours on my own in my room, nursing my swollen belly.

'Mammy told no-one at first, and just as well I suppose, 'cos within three weeks of that horrible day my dear wee child passed away. I lost it one terrible, terrible night – dear God, there was so much blood. Mammy told me it was a cursed child anyway so it was better dead. Can you imagine anyone saying such a thing? I so wanted to care for the tiny remains, but she burnt it on the fire. She said dreadful things about God's punishment. It was then I knew if there was a God in heaven, he surely hated me. Well, the loss of the baby meant I could stay at home, so I had a roof over my head, even though I hated my mother. We never spoke of it again.'

She finally lit the cigarette that she had been fiddling with, and drew it slowly up to her mouth and breathed the smoke in deeply, letting it escape through her nose as she shook her head.

'And what happened to Peter,' Douglas asked.

'Peter was defrocked, of course, poor soul. We were never allowed to see each other again. Never seen him since. A truly horrible English priest from Tralee came to see me to tell me all about hell and that I was excommunicated. He accused me of seducing Peter and he even quoted the story of Jezebel in the bible, can you believe? He said if it weren't for God's mercy, I'd be like Jezebel – dead in the street with the dogs licking up the blood from my broken body. God, it was evil. God, God, God.... And would you believe it, that priest changed his religion - went Protestant so he could marry a girl in the town. And they had a kiddie soon after the wedding - very soon. The bloody hypocrisy of it all. Presume the evil sod's dead now.'

Douglas had listened intently to this eruption from Kathleen. He felt a disturbing mix of horror and guilt. The frequent references to the church and clergy thudded into his soul and he felt somehow responsible for Kath's misery. He also felt for Peter. He himself had not been far from surrendering to beautiful eyes when he was a curate. There but for the grace of God... The grace of God? What was that now? Douglas was shaken out of his depressed thoughts by Kath who was looking at him.

'So you see, Douglas, if there is a God, then he is a cruel bastard, and I want nothing to do with him.' Douglas felt nervous of the fierce anger he saw in her face. But it then rapidly changed to a kind expression. 'I'm sorry, darling, you really didn't need to hear all that. Dorchadas, you should have stopped me, for God's sake.' She took a final drag from the cigarette and inhaled the smoke so deeply that Douglas wondered if she hoped it would somehow reach the inner recesses of her pain and work as an anaesthetic. He reached out a nervous hand and placed it on her elbow 'I'm terribly sorry, Kathleen - I... I really don't know what to say.'

'Och, don't you worry yourself, Douglas. You go ahead with your faith if it does you good. But it has very nearly killed some of us. Always remember that, Douglas. Damn nearly killed us.' She stubbed out the half-smoked cigarette with such force that Douglas feared she would smash the ashtray.

'You open?' A voice in the café doorway startled them. A young couple were peering inside.

'Oh, for God's sake, yes, do come in,' said Kathleen brightly, recovering herself. She stood up and brushed down her pinafore as if brushing off the story she had just told. 'Sorry about the smoke in here – it's Douglas, from England - you know what they're like. Terrible smokers! And I did say it's not allowed. I'll fetch you a menu.' She laughed her wheezy laugh as she headed off to the kitchen, and the couple settled themselves at a table. Douglas wasn't sure whether to apologise for the smoke or not, when Dorchadas said, 'Time for a walk, Doug?'

'Yes, let's pay up and go,' said Douglas.

'No,' said Dorchadas. 'Kathleen won't want us to pay.' He then called to the kitchen, 'We'll be heading off now, Kathleen.'

'Good man yourself, Dorch', said a voice from behind the curtain. 'Be good now!' She turned up the radio to hide the sound of her smoker's cough.

'I should have the tea,' said Dorchadas confidentially to the young couple as he and Douglas made their way out of the café into the fresh air of the main street. Douglas noticed Dorchadas looking noticeably more hunched as he walked silently down the street. It would not be long before Douglas discovered why such a story as this disturbed his new friend so much.

CHAPTER 9

The calm, dark water lapped over the smooth stones. A part-submerged oak tree stretched out a blackened branch. Its brittle fingers had caught the remains of a fishing net which trailed in the current. In the tops of the tall ash trees, a crow's caw grated at Douglas' nerves. A tired wasp buzzed around an untidy mass of salty seaweed. The sunlight felt warm, but the light gusts of air that swept over the estuary were chilly, heralding the colder winds that would be on their way before too long. Dorchadas was lobbing stones into the water. He was aiming at nothing – just watching the splashes and the ripples on the incoming tide. There was stillness over the bay, but it felt a troubled stillness. Neither man had spoken for almost an hour, so when Dorchadas did speak it took Douglas by surprise.

'Not a nice story, Douglas.'

'No. No. Poor thing,' he answered. Even with the prompting, Douglas could find no words to talk about Kathleen's sad story. He had observed that the wound was still raw in Kath, even after all these years. And her pain was caused by the church and its teaching and he, whether he liked it or not, was therefore a representative of the perpetrator of her hurt. He felt sick in his heart. He looked up at Dorchadas – the first time he had looked at him since the café. He noticed such sadness is in his eyes. The furrowed lines on his face seemed deeper than ever. He looked gaunt.

'The darkness…,' said Dorchadas, looking out over the water, almost in a whisper. He threw another stone far out into the estuary water. 'That stone, Doug. It is sinking into the deep waters. How long will it stay there? Will it be washed back up into the light by a merciful tide? Or will it sink down and be locked in the dark for tens of thousands of years? And if it does, should it get used to the dark, or should it yearn for the light? Some darkness, you see, Doug, is a darkness of mystery, of searching. It is a luminous darkness, full of treasure, of possibility, of life.' He continued to gaze out over the water, and threw another stone far out into the estuary. 'But there are other darknesses, Douglas, that should never have been. Darknesses of wound and hurt, loss and guilt and all that stuff that steals away precious life. I hate that darkness. I do so hate it.'

He had taken Douglas completely off his guard. He was getting used to Dorchadas being the wise man who seemed to have answers. By comparison, Douglas was the novice, asking the questions. But here was this man, who claimed he was an angel, asking him the most profound and puzzling question, as if he felt Douglas could actually offer some sensible insight - which he couldn't. So there was another long silence.

'You never get the chance to choose, you see.' This time Dorchadas' voice was louder and he spoke with feeling as he threw a large stone far out and Douglas watched it fly out into the bay, somewhat taken aback by the strength of the man who had hurled it such a distance. As the stone landed in the water with a deep clunk, Dorchadas continued, 'Well, which of us would choose this? I mean, which of us would choose to dwell in the valley of the shadows? You see, we *can't* choose. No, *He* chooses – it has to be *His* choice. I understand that, but why did He choose *me* for this, Douglas?' He looked pleadingly at the Englishman as he offered another question that Douglas could not answer.

'I'm sorry, I'm really not with you, Dorch...' said Douglas and started to feel a tender compassion for his curious companion.

'If I had wings, Douglas, then every time I saw one of the dear children of God hurt, I would shield my eyes and ears. But he gave me no such defences. I *have* to hear. I *have* to see. I *have* to witness. I cannot turn my face away. You humans – I know it hurts you to witness these things, of course it does. I see how deeply it hurts you. But you see, for an angel of Paradise, whose eyes were made for the most wonderful scenes of light, when we witness the dark – well, we feel like the stone sinking deep into the mud. And you never know how long you're going to be there. It hurts, Doug... It hurts so much.'

Douglas was thrown into a conflict of feelings. He could see that something was painfully troubling Dorchadas. And yet, here he was again, making his ludicrous claim to be an angel. If only Saoirse was here. She had such a good way of managing people like this. Quite a few of her friends were distinctly loopy and yet she had a wonderful way of respecting them. Even her Cornish friend, Franny with her flowing dresses, wild make-up and love of fairies. Yes, Saoirse and Franny would not have batted an eyelid at this Irishman purporting to be an angel. In fact, it would have endeared him to them. He looked back at Dorch.

'You heard the story before, Dorch?' Douglas asked, turning the focus to the conversation with Kath.

'I was there, Douglas,' he said looking so mournful. He stared out into the dark blue water and pushed his heel into the pebbles. 'I was on duty that day, because darkness was in the air.'

Douglas felt an indignation arising - the indignation of one who many times questioned what heaven was doing while the one he loved so much suffered so greatly. In an angry tone he barely controlled, he spoke out over the water, 'Well, then, if you are such a great and powerful angel, couldn't you have done something – stopped that beastly aunt or something?'

Dorchadas turned and looked at Douglas, and leaning towards him said, 'You humans always want us to get you out of trouble, don't you? And sometimes we do. But I was never that sort of an angel. I had to dwell *in* it, you see. *He* had to dwell in it, and some of us have had to journey with Him.'

Douglas wasn't satisfied. 'Yes, but if I've read my bible right, He got a lot of people out of trouble – those sick people, and the hungry people on the hillside, the disciples on the stormy sea…Surely you could you have done something to help Kathleen?'

Dorchadas looked so pained. 'Please, Doug. Don't ask me that. You have no idea…' He pulled his knees up to his forehead and said nothing for a few moments. But then, he breathed in, looked up and said 'Mind you, they were being pretty naughty, don't you think?' He turned and smiled his mischievous smile, and his whole demeanour changed. 'Kathleen and that priest?'

'Well, yes, of course, a priest is not exactly allowed to carry on like that.'

Dorchadas laughed, 'You humans love that word, don't you – "allowed". Do you know, we have never used that word.'

'Come on, Dorch – lots of things are not allowed – think about the 10 commandments and all those "thou shalt not"s. There's quite a bit of "not allowed"s there!'

'Aren't they beautiful, those lovely commandments,' said Dorchadas and he lifted his head back and closed his eyes. 'That was some mountain, that was!' A glint of sunshine made its way through the thin clouds, and Dorchadas breathed in its warmth.

'Dorch, I'm getting a bit confused here,' said Douglas, shifting his body which was getting stiff and cold. 'You were the one who raised the issue of their naughty behaviour. Then you say we shouldn't talk about 'not being allowed', and now we're back to the 10 commandments.

What's your point?' He was feeling impatient, still raw from hearing Kathleen's story.

'The point is this, Douglas,' said Dorchadas, turning and looking hard at Douglas. 'I am not here to tell you what's wrong and what's right. That's for you to work out. But I notice one thing, my friend. You were more upset by the aunt's reaction and the priest's bullying, than you were by the fact that Kath and Peter were sleeping together. Now what does that tell you, Doug? Think about that. Are you going soft? Where are those fine evangelical principles of yours? I think principles are important to you. But the thing that you noticed was the darker story, the one that caused most damage in the long run.' As he said this he rose to his feet and said, 'I think we need some help.' He stretched himself. 'Come on, Doug. How's the Emily Brontë in you doing?'

'How's the what?'

'You'll need a drop of that old 'Benignant Power' just now,' he said as he stood up. 'Come with me a little way, I want you to meet a friend of mine called Svetlana.'

'That's a new name on me, Dorch,' said Douglas as he pulled himself up, grateful to be freed from the cold pebbles. Dorchadas walked ahead, purposefully and fast for a while. Douglas felt curious, but anxious.

'There she is!' said Dorch, pointing to a lady walking along the lane just ahead of them. 'She's got quite a story to tell us, Douglas. You listen to this. Hey, Svetlana, love. How's it going with you today?' Dorchadas' voice echoed off the nearby houses. 'That's the name she uses when she's travelling, by the way,' he said quietly to Douglas.

The woman stopped, and smiled when she saw the tall figure of Dorchadas. 'My goodness, it's you Dorchadas! I've not seen you for a long time!' Douglas looked carefully at the woman as she turned round and hastened towards them. He guessed she was a similar age to him. She was slim and had long, dark hair that was showing signs of greying. She was wearing jeans and a navy Arran knit jumper with a bright, cerise scarf wrapped around her neck. She sounded foreign, and Douglas guessed she was Russian or Eastern European. 'Where have you been, my old soldier?' she asked.

'Oh, here and there,' answered Dorchadas. Now, I want you to meet my friend, Douglas. You time for a wee chat?' As Svetlana reached them, Dorchadas threw his arms open and gave her a bear hug. She responded warmly and then came over to Douglas and offered her cheek, which he duly kissed. Dorchadas told them that he had just the place for them to go for a chat and he led them to a nearby playground. Svetlana gave a whoop of delight and leapt on to one of the swings. 'Come on, Douglas,' said Dorchadas and within moments the three had mounted the three swings that were beside each other in the playground. They swung back and forth enjoying the freedom and the rush of air.

As the swings slowed, Douglas started to suspect that he was in for another interesting and significant meeting. He was not wrong.

CHAPTER 10

'So how come you wanted to meet with me – I take it that it was you that called me, Dorchadas?' said Svetlana as she brought her swing to a halt, dragging her feet on the tarmac. Though she had a strong accent, her English was excellent.

'Yes, it was, Svetlana,' said Dorchadas. I thought my friend Douglas here should meet you. We've had a tough morning, you see, and I think he'd be helped by hearing your story.'

'How much does he want to hear?' asked Svetlana, releasing the swing's chains that she had been holding so tightly. Douglas looked at her more closely and could see she had a slight scar on her upper lip. He felt she had a genuine beauty about her, and a strong face, yet one that betrayed a life that had not been without considerable pain.

'Well not the full story,' replied Dorchadas. 'We've not got three weeks you know! Just tell us about your meeting with Him.'

'Now, does he know who I am, Dorchadas. You've had me speaking to your friends before now, and the poor creatures are confused. So you've not told him yet - correct?' she looked teasingly at Dorchadas.

'Correct' he said. 'But go gently on him. Douglas is only just getting used to these meetings. He had his first meeting last night.'

'Oh, really – who did he meet?'

'We went to meet the old man, Jacob, don't you know. Doug had been preaching on the man, so I thought it was time he met the old codger.'

Svetlana's face lit up. 'Oh my, how splendid! Why, it was by Jacob's well that I had my best meeting of all.'

'I know lass, that's what I want you to tell us about, so kindly get cracking.'

Douglas was witnessing this conversation in a whirlpool of inner confusion. He had twigged that Dorchadas was doing his thing again, of somehow hypnotising him, or releasing a powerful imagination, only this time they weren't travelling to another world to meet someone from the past; rather that someone had travelled to meet them in the here and now. The 'someone' in this instance was still very unclear. Douglas assumed it was a character from the bible, but to his knowledge, there was no Russian sounding woman called Svetlana in his bible. However, his

79

curiosity was stronger than his protest, so he said to her, 'Please, do tell me who you are – I would like to hear your story'.

Although Douglas found his swing to be not the most comfortable place to sit, nonetheless he settled as best he could, turning it a little so he could listen with full attention to Svetlana's story.

'Well, I'm not going to lie to you, Douglas, I was in a bit of a mess. I was – how do you say? Let's say, I had a first-class honours degree in broken relationships. My first marriage lasted only a few weeks. My second husband – well he dropped dead. My third was the cruellest man I have ever known.' Here she pointed to her lip and to various other parts of her body. 'Oh, you don't want to know all the details. Just say, on it went. I got through five husbands – hard to believe, I know, and in my part of the world, that does not make you a great favourite in the town. To be honest I gave up on men, until I met a man called Victor, and for the first time, at last I met a man I really loved. Well, I was such a sinner and failure by this time I didn't bother to marry. Truth be told, he was just as bad as me and had a few marriages behind him as well. So we lived together – shock and horror in the whole neighbourhood as you can imagine. So, I was sort of happy with my relationship with Victor – at last – but inside I knew I was still desperately unhappy.'

Dorchadas climbed off his swing and went over to a small roundabout that was nearby. 'Keep going, love' he said as he kicked the roundabout into motion. Svetlana took hold of the chains of her swing again and looked out towards the estuary.

'I would cry at nights, and Victor was so sweet. But I just felt I had failed so many people. My family disowned me and I had very few friends. But most of all I felt I had failed God. I mean, what must He have thought of me? The rabbis were very clear what they thought God's opinion of me was. But do you know… forgive me, what did Dorchadas say your name was?' She paused and looked now intently at Douglas, a look Douglas thought about quite a lot afterwards. It was a look that conveyed a sense that her motivation for the telling of her story was not simply to get it off her chest, but to give something of value to Douglas. And she needed to know his name, because it was a personal gift.

'Douglas,' he said with hesitation. 'A bit of an old-fashioned name, I always think. I was named after an uncle.'

'Ah yes – "Douglas" – it is a new name to me – but I like. So, back to the story, Douglas. I felt so terribly alone. Apart from Victor, the whole world really was against me – the rabbis and the scribes, the town of Sychar where I lived hated me, and I was assuming God hated me too. But you know, Douglas, despite all my many failings, I still loved my God. Even if he hated me, I still loved him. I felt him here'. She formed her left hand into a fist and patted her stomach with it. 'You know what I mean, Dorchadas, don't you,' she said, calling out to the roundabout.

'Aye, I do lass. And I do know how deeply you loved him, ever since you were a child. You never lost it.' Dorchadas was now kicking his feet on the ground to get the roundabout moving and for a few moments both Svetlana and Douglas smiled at the comic sight of this tall man sprawled across the slowly spinning roundabout and gazing up at the sky.

Svetlana turned back to Douglas. 'Dorchadas is right – I loved God so much as a child. You know, I often think that even as a child I yearned for the divine love. In my dreams I met God – it was so precious. But mine was not a happy home, you see Douglas. There was cruelty and I was unhappy. I just wanted to get out of the home, so when my parents arranged the marriage, though I didn't like the man, I was glad to get out of the home. That man never understood my love for God. He told me that religion was not for women – it was the men who worshipped God, who made the sacrifices. It was men that God blessed, not women. I tried to tell him of my dreams, but he would not hear of them.' As she said this, she sighed a weary sigh and looked out to the estuary again. Douglas noticed that the roundabout was now picking up some speed.

'And so it went on,' continued Svetlana. 'He divorced me after a year and I married again. Do you know Douglas,' she said turning back to me again, 'I really think that what I was searching for in my marriages was actually the love of God. I know it sounds crazy, but I also thought that through sex I would meet God. Does that shock you, Douglas?'

'Sure it does!' said the voice from the roundabout.

Douglas was taken aback at her frankness, but he didn't want her to think he was shocked, so he said rather feebly, 'No, of course not.' The spinning Dorchadas chuckled.

Svetlana now planted her feet on the tarmac so that her swing was quite still. 'You see, it is so hard to find the words for this – surely the sex act between a man and a woman is the highest expression of union, no? So, I thought, naïvely I suppose, that if I found a man I really loved and adored, then when we had sex – well, we would draw close to the great love of God. Well, that was not a view that my sisters or friends shared! Oh, no – they did not like that kind of language at all!' She chuckled and put her slender hand up to her mouth.

'The thing is, Douglas, I made those wrong decisions about the men. I never wanted to marry all those men. I was just longing to find a safe place of love, and a home where my love for God could spring up like a fountain for the whole home – and for the whole community!' Her face lit up and she smiled again. She got off the swing and stretched herself for a few moments turning her head from side to side and reaching up her arms to the sky. 'The swing is not so comfortable, no? Shall we go to sit on that bench?'

They moved across the playground to a bench. The roundabout was slowing as Dorchadas' heels dragged on the tarmac.

As they sat down, Douglas said, 'What about Victor?'

'Yes,' said Svetlana with a smile. She adjusted her scarf and crossed her legs, clasping her hands over her knees. 'Victor was wonderful. Victor is the name we use now. He knew exactly what I meant about the divine love. He went to the synagogue, though wasn't popular because of me. But he had such a good mind, and would remember the Scriptures used that day in the worship, and he would come back and we would chat about them. And we had long discussions about the Jews and Samaritans – all that was very important to people then. I won't bore you with all that now. The fact is that Victor and I found a deep and passionate love.'

'And what about the sex?' asked Dorchadas from the now stationary roundabout.

'You mind your own business!' shouted Svetlana, and then looked at Douglas smiling, 'Angels should not be interested in such things, should they?'

'I'm rapidly changing my view of them,' Douglas said, raising his eyebrows and looking in the direction of the figure slumped over the roundabout. The same figure was slowing stirring itself but looked decidedly unstable and was struggling to get itself upright.

'To be honest,' said Svetlana confidentially to me, 'the love-making was wonderful – Victor totally understood what it was I was searching for. We couldn't tell others. But there was, we discovered, a meaning in that act of love that was – well, there are no words, Douglas. I think maybe we discovered something of what it was meant to be. But few would understand that.'

Douglas felt uncomfortable with the discussion of sex. It had been a wonderful part of his life with Saoirse and yes, he couldn't deny there had been a spiritual dimension to it. But it was private and he certainly was not going to discuss it with strangers. And besides, it all brought back too much sadness.

'It is all right, Douglas,' said Svetlana, reading the anxiety in Douglas' face. 'This is a gift that has caused great joy and great sorrow. Few understand the true nature of his precious gift.'

'Dorchadas and I heard a very sad story this morning which involved sex and religion, and the two did not go well together,' said Douglas, partly as a diversion from his own story.

Dorchadas managed to get himself off the roundabout, and swerved over to the bench like a drunkard with very little control of his legs. He eventually landed on the tarmac near to Svetlana and Douglas, saying, 'Dear God, these human bodies can be mighty frail, can't they. Don't know how you cope with them, Douglas, that I don't. Sorry, lass, don't let me interrupt you now. Where were you?'

'One day,' said Svetlana, ignoring the voice from the tarmac, 'I was going up to the well – Jacob's well – I am so pleased you met that old Patriarch!' She patted Douglas' knee and smiled happily.

'I had to choose my time carefully to go to the well,' she continued. 'The other women didn't want me to go with them, so I had to go in the middle of the day, when it was really hot. So off I went to the well, and to my annoyance I saw a man sitting by it. Well, you probably know, Douglas, it was the culture of the time that a woman and a man could not be in public together. So as I got closer I hoped he would politely withdraw. I did not want to wait until he had finished using the well – it was too hot to hang around. So I got nearer, and coughed loudly so he could hear me coming and I expected him to hurry away. But no, he stayed sitting there and even watched me approaching. Well, I had been in enough trouble in my life, so breaking one more rule was not going to make much difference. I carried on expecting him to look disapproving and give some rebuke, but he took me completely by surprise.'

She turned in her seat and faced Douglas. 'Do you know what he did, Douglas? He asked me for a drink. I mean, it was the last thing I expected! A man not only speaking to a woman, but actually asking her to help him!' Her eyes were wide open in delighted surprise.

'Whatever next!' said a slurred voice from the tarmac.

'In our culture, you see Douglas, that is unheard of. And what's more he was a Jewish rabbi, and I was a Samaritan woman – you have an expression I think, something about chalk and butter?'

'Try "cheese"' advised the slurred voice.

83

'Yes, well, chalk and cheese – it should not have happened. So when I saw that this rabbi wanted to talk to me, I knew he had to be different. Here at last was a rabbi who would talk to me! Can you imagine how excited I was! I stood there in the hot sun, no longer minding the heat and asking him question after question. He invited me to sit with him – so shocking! I cannot tell you what this meant to me, Douglas. Here was a rabbi from Judea telling me the most wonderful things, helping me to understand things that had been mysteries to me since I was a young woman. And, what's more, it was the *way* he said them. There was...' Svetlana leaned forwards, and placed her elbows on her knees, and rested her chin on her hands for a few moments, her fingers patting her cheeks. 'There was something in his eyes, Douglas. I will never be able to describe those eyes to you – if only I could.'

Dorchadas was now starting to sit up and looked more like his normal self. 'Aye lass, it's what everyone noticed – them eyes. You would give your whole precious life just to spend a moment in their gaze. So many lives were changed by just one look of them dear eyes, so they were. So they were.' Dorchadas breathed in deeply and looked out toward the sea.

'And mine was one of them, Dorch,' said Svetlana reaching out and resting her hand on his shoulder. 'We spoke about living water, and that day I learned to drink from water of life. Sounds rather grand when I say that – but I know what I mean. But then just as I was so happy, I came crashing back down to the earth. He asked me the one question I dreaded. He said, "Go and call your husband." I froze when he asked me that. I can still see myself now, straightening up and clasping the leather water-carrier to me, somehow hoping it would defend me.' She enacted the scene as she spoke, clasping an imaginary water vessel to herself.

'For a second I thought of telling a lie. Surely he would reject me if I told the truth, but then I knew I could not lie to those eyes, so I sort of owned up. I said, "I have no husband."' She looked a little sheepish as she said this and drew in her bottom lip and looked shyly at Douglas. 'It was the truth, Douglas, but maybe not really the whole truth.

'As you can imagine, he was a prophet, so he told me that he knew all about the husbands I had had, and that Victor was not my husband. When he said that, I thought that would be the end of it. I was expecting him to say, "So, you like talking all about living water and worshipping God and loving God, but you are living a sinful life, so you will never taste that good water." So, I decided to distract him and start talking

84

about the proper place to worship – you see it was the hot argument of the day – should we worship God in Jerusalem or Samaria? And do you know what, he forgot about the husbands and he was happy to talk about worship. He said nothing about Victor!' She started laughing and looked at her intrigued listener. 'I mean, Douglas how could that be? He was a rabbi! He could not possibly approve of how I was living my life! And I don't think he did, it is just that there were more important things to get right first. For the first time I was with someone who did not judge me because of my story – he looked into my heart, with those eyes of his, and saw my longings and my dreams and my hope. He knew my lifestyle had been wrong, but he was moving beyond that to the very depths of my soul, like the deep waters of the well next to us, and he knew that if pure water started to flow from those depths, then the rest of my life would fall into place and become clean. It was extraordinary…'

All this she said with dramatic gestures, recounting so vividly the story that had meant so much to her. She leaned back in her seat and looked up to the sky and smiled. 'Quite extraordinary. Extraordinary! In those moments, I felt I was in one of my childhood dreams of God. But it was no dream – oh my, it was no dream, I can tell you. I was so happy at this point. I wanted it to last forever. But then I saw some men coming up the path towards the well, and I felt so sad that this special time would be ended by disapproving men. But just before they arrived I told him of the deepest yearning of my heart. I said, "I am longing for the day when the Messiah will come and this dark, dark world will finally be put right, and we will all be well" At that moment he leant across and grasped my hand.' She grasped Douglas' hand as she said this. 'I mean, so shocking for a rabbi to touch a woman! But he said so softly, yet clearly, "I am he – this man who is speaking to you. I am the Messiah." I looked at him, and knew then that if he really was the Messiah, then he was everything I was hoping for – I knew that if the world was ruled by one like him, we could all live in peace and there would be justice at last.'

Svetlana closed her eyes and inhaled a long breath before continuing. She let go of Douglas' hand and continued. 'By now the men had arrived and it turned out they were friends of his. I thought they would make comments – you could tell they did not approve, especially when they saw him holding my hand! But they said nothing, and I went back and decided to tell everyone I met. Victor first, of course, who was so excited. But I also told all those who hated me and, do you know, they could see something had happened to me. The rabbi had said, that living waters would flow from me, and incredibly that is what happened! In fact, he came and stayed with us for a couple of days and so many in my town found their freedom in those days. It was extraordinary, Douglas!' She threw her head back and laughed, and Dorchadas chuckled with her.

There was silence for a few moments. This was a story from the gospel of John that Douglas knew well. He had studied it, preached on it, and delivered many fine points on it. But he never imagined meeting a curious, modern Russian version of the leading lady of the story. It was all insane, and yet, and yet, this companion on the playground bench was touching something in him. That something was very tender. In these moments Douglas felt that whoever this person was, Svetlana was definitely someone he could trust.

All three sat quietly for a while, until the silence was broken by two small children who charged into the playground making a dash for the roundabout. A man and woman with a child in a buggy followed close behind and sat down at a nearby bench. Dorchadas was sitting on the sunlit tarmac with his legs outstretched, one crossed over the other, and his long arms reaching out behind him. With his eyes closed, and his face turned up to the autumn sun, he looked like a mystic in a trance.

Finally, Svetlana said, 'Well, I have to go now.' She looked warmly at Douglas. 'I have really enjoyed meeting you, Douglas.' She lowered her voice as if sharing a confidence, 'I know I touched something in your heart when I was talking. He was a prophet you know, and, truth be told, I am also one, in my own way. I look into your heart and I see a troubled sadness. I think you have lost someone who was once dear. I see violence, Douglas, a violence from the valley of destruction.' Tears appeared in the corner of her eyes as she moved closer to Douglas and studied his face, reading his wounds. 'Oh, Douglas. I am sorry.' She brushed the side of his face with her hand as if she were comforting a child. 'You have lost so much. But you will also find so much. Do not be without hope, Douglas. He will help you.' She reached forward and kissed him gently on his forehead and whispered, 'I promise you. He will.'

Douglas was so shaken by what she said to him, that he shut his eyes for quite a while. When he opened them, it was Dorchadas who was sitting next to him on the bench, not Svetlana who must have very swiftly left the playground.

The children were now on the roundabout and the man was pulling at the handles making it rotate at speed, much to the delight of the children.

'I shan't be going on them things again,' said Dorchadas. 'Don't know how the children can stand it. Well, it's been a long morning. Shall we meet for dinner again, Douglas? He smacked Douglas on the knee as they got up. 'Meet me at the pub at 7? The one at the harbour on the corner, all painted blue. You know the one? Unless you have other plans?'

Douglas didn't really want any more conversation that day, but didn't know how to decline Dorch's offer, so he meekly agreed. It would turn out to be another very significant evening.

CHAPTER 11

Douglas still felt rather full of black pudding and Victoria sponge, so he skipped lunch and strolled rather aimlessly around the town for a while. He walked away from the Marina to a higher part of the town and for a time enjoyed the view over Dingle Bay. There was still warmth in the sun despite the advance of autumn, and Douglas found a low wall and rested on it for a while.

He was about to close his eyes to enjoy the sun on his face, when a group of animated primary school children rushed past him on the way to some adventure. He checked his watch and noticed it had gone 3pm, and realised it was the end of the school day. His thoughts turned once more back to Saoirse who loved the school of which she was head for only two short years. Saoirse's style was not to everyone's taste. The South Yorkshire community was not always welcoming of some of her more radical ideas, but in the main her teaching staff respected her, and the children adored her.

Another group of children passed Douglas chattering away to each other in Gaelic. And then a lone child walked slowly past and something about him reminded Douglas of an autistic child called Ben that Saoirse especially loved. It seemed that Saoirse loved all her children, but it was clear to Douglas that Ben was one of her favourites and this was all the more surprising for the fact that most people in the school found Ben very difficult. Several times, in exasperation, his class teacher would march him to Saoirse's office and plonk him there, for she knew Saoirse was the only one who could calm him when he got distressed.

Douglas was in the school one day leading an assembly, and towards the end of it something rattled Ben. His class teacher made several attempts to pacify him but without success. Douglas, sensing an imminent disturbance, brought the assembly quickly to a close and in some desperation Ben's teacher hauled the restless child across the room to Saoirse. Douglas watched in admiration as Saoirse knelt down in front of Ben and smiled her winsome smile and whispered something in Ben's ear that had an immediate calming effect. As children swirled around them, Ben and Saoirse were a little oasis of calm. When she was sure he was ready, Saoirse stood up, and led Ben back to his class.

Douglas had no evening meeting that night and Saoirse's school prep was done, so after supper they slumped next to one another on the sofa, each clutching a glass of wine. For a time, they sat in silence, enjoying the closeness to one another. Then Douglas broke the silence by asking, 'When did you become a child whisperer, then?'

'A child whisperer?' asked Saoirse, sitting up and looking at Douglas with a half smile and an enquiring look on her face.

'Yes, this morning,' said Douglas, sipping his wine. 'With Ben. Everyone finds him wild, but the moment you come near him you whisper in his ear and he's an oasis of calm.'

'Mm... Yes, well not always...' replied Saoirse thoughtfully. 'I did quite a study of autism at Uni, and became fascinated by it. I think we're all on the scale, you know - especially you!' With that she prodded his arm and laughed a teasing laugh. Thankfully he had put down his wine glass.

'No, I'm not,' protested Douglas.

'Oh, don't be so sure, Reverend Romer. I've seen signs, sure I have,' she said with a beaming smile. 'And I love them!'

'Well, I'm not like poor Ben. It must be a nightmare for his parents.'

'That's where you're wrong. You've not met them. Yes, it can be embarrassing when they are in public sometimes, but they love him, you see, Dougie. And that's what all children need, isn't it.' She sipped thoughtfully at her wine.

Douglas sat up and leaned forward in the sofa. He was frowning. 'Yes, I'm sure they love him, but...'

'But what, Dougie? He's not loveable? Is that what you are trying to say? He doesn't like being hugged? He makes high-pitched screams? He is obsessional? I mean, is it only the sweet little kiddies who get loved in this world?'

Douglas looked hard at her. 'You really love him, don't you?'

'Yes, Dougie. I really do. Maybe I just see what you and others don't see. I see what his Mammy and Daddy see. I see how he does his way of loving, and it is beautiful. I see the way he tries so hard to learn and he works *so* hard, sure he does. I've seen him tie his shoelaces as if he is completing a work of art. I see him gazing at the window pane at a wee fly trying to escape, and I can see how much he admires the very fly that everyone else wants to swot. I see how he looks around after he has a hissy fit and it's so vulnerable, Dougie, it makes me want to weep buckets it does. I see all this, and if I believed in God, then I think I

89

would be seeing what he or she would see. I don't find it easy to see it, Dougie. It really hurts inside something awful sometimes. And I guess if there is a God, then a kind God would feel the same too. In fact, come to think of it, it would be an awful painful thing being God if he saw such things. Can you imagine?' She paused, and drained her glass.

Douglas felt somehow caught out. He had preached about love so many times, but it was always so correct and theoretical. Now, here was his atheist wife demonstrating a love that he did not think was possible in this world. He looked at her and stroked her cheek. 'And what do you see in me, my love? Or daren't I ask?'

She leaned up from the sofa, and grasped his arm with both her hands. 'All that I see, I love, my Dougie. That's enough.'

'Then there must be a whole lot you can't see,' said Douglas looking away.

Saoirse smiled. 'Don't be so sure! But what about you? What can you see in me?'

Douglas knew he would never be able to find the right words, but he made an attempt. 'My Saoirse I see a heart that I did not know could exist in this world. Until I met you, I only lived a half-life. I did not know humans could love like you love. I…', he sighed as he tried to find more words to articulate such deep feelings. They both looked into each other's eyes for several minutes without speaking and Douglas was surprised at feeling utterly comfortable in her gaze. In those moments he utterly believed that she really did love all that she saw within him, and he knew she saw much more than even he could see. And Saoirse also knew that at last she had found what she had been longing for all her days - a heart to rest in.

After a few moments, Saoirse looked down and took Douglas' hand. She looked up again and said, 'I'm afraid it came again this morning. No wee kiddie for us this month, Dougie. I'm so sorry…' Her watery eyes looked for reassurance to Douglas, who simply wiped them and said, 'One day we will be given a child, I know it. Until then, my sweet, we will just enjoy the time we are given on our own. We have our whole lives ahead of us…'

Douglas recalled every word of the conversation as more children passed him on the pavement. It was beautiful to remember this conversation, but it was also a torture to his soul, especially the fact that he was so wrong about their future. She never did conceive. And, as it turned out, her 'whole life' turned out to be only a few more months.

As more children from the local school passed him, his mind wandered back again to the dreadful day when he went into the school to tell the children. It was a terrible thing to have to do, but he felt Saoirse would have wanted him, more than anyone else, to communicate such news to her children. The staff had already been informed and were in a terrible state. It was clear that in her two years, Saoirse had won the affection of both staff and governors. So they agreed Douglas could tell the children. Douglas was full of apprehension as he walked down the drive to the school door and entered the assembly. The school was alive with the buzz of children's chatter. The Deputy head called for quiet and said the Vicar had a very serious announcement, and from somewhere Douglas found not only the strength but also the words to tell the children the fearful news. It seemed that every child in the school wept that day and none of them knew what to say to Douglas so they avoided him. Apart from one child, and that was Ben who, with his shining eyes and a wave of his hand, beckoned Douglas to listen to something he had to say.

Douglas knelt down and Ben whispered in his ear. 'I know, Vicar,' he said.

'You know what, Ben?' Douglas asked.

'I know she is all right. I have see her.'

'What do you mean, you have seen her?' asked Douglas, his frown betraying his anxiety.

'Last night, Vicar. She was in my room. She was glowing bright - like a firework - sparkling. She was beautiful. And she whispered to me, like she used to.'

Douglas felt a mix of panic and yearning as he asked, 'What did she whisper, Ben?'

'Just one word, Vicar.'

'What word, Ben?'

'"Peace", Vicar. She just said "Peace".' That's what she was, Vicar. She was sparkling peace. And she wanted you to know, Vicar. She wanted you to know. I've told you. I must go to my lesson now.' And with that, he sped off to his class.

The road was quiet now and all the children must have left school and were on their way home. The sun continued to shine warm on Douglas as he remembered Ben. He never knew quite how to understand this visit granted to this young child from his beloved. He certainly had his days of anguish wishing it was he who would be granted such a visit, but as the months went by no such visit was granted, and in the end he decided it was for the better, for if he had been given so much as a glimpse of his Saoirse he would have done whatever was needed to leap over the divide between this world and the next and join her. Indeed, there were very grey days when he even worked out how he would make such a journey, and more than once he was precariously close to taking such drastic action.

The sun went in and the air became distinctly chilly. Douglas got up from the low wall, and walked back towards St.Raphael's. He remembered he had agreed to meet Dorchadas again in the evening, and he found he was rather anxious about it. In the last twenty-four hours this so-called angel had somehow contrived to introduce Douglas to two figures from the bible. Just how many more such meetings were going to happen? Douglas wasn't convinced he could handle too many more of them.

As he approached the house that was becoming his Dingle home, Douglas realised he had felt warmed by the memories of Saoirse earlier in the afternoon, and he felt just maybe, he could tell this new strange friend of his how her precious life had come to such an untimely end. It was a story he had seldom told to anyone - he let most people find out through others. But there was something about Dorchadas that felt safe. And sure enough, he was to discover that his new friend most definitely was someone he could trust with this story.

CHAPTER 12

Douglas arrived at the pub promptly at 7pm and he spied Dorchadas propping up the bar, chatting to the young lady serving behind the bar. True to a form that was becoming familiar to Douglas, the two were both laughing.

'Och, there you are Doug,' cried Dorch, waving at Douglas. 'Ciara here has reserved us a nice table in the corner, that she has. But let's be getting a drink first. Will it be the Guinness as usual?

'Er, yes, yes, thanks Dorch, but it must be my turn by now,' said Douglas feeling for his wallet.

'Why not do the next round? Could you bring them over, love?' he called to Ciara, and led the way to their table. Shortly she brought over the welcome cream-headed drinks.

'You hooked on the dark stuff, now Doug?' said Dorchadas as he took the glass to his lips and smiled as he sipped.

'I thought you were the expert in the dark stuff, Dorch,' said Douglas, enjoying his first sip and, what he considered to be his rather subtle joke.

'Aye, that I am supposed to be,' said Dorch, but his smile quickly faded, and Douglas felt bad that he had joked about something that clearly was no laughing matter to Dorch. So, he quickly changed the subject.

'So that was the woman at the well in Samaria,' Douglas said with a barely concealed hint of scepticism. He was still struggling to work out whether Dorch had arranged an actress to come along and take her part, or if there really was some kind of weird alchemy around that could mysteriously lift biblical figures from the past and drop them into the modern day. It would take more than a couple of pints of Guinness to even begin to think this was possible. And yet, he really was moved by the encounter, so he didn't try to challenge it in any way.

'Yep,' said Dorch, pulling in his lips after drawing from his glass. 'You preached on her I expect?'

'I have – but I have never introduced her as an Eastern European woman in jeans, pullover and bright scarf.'

Dorchadas laughed an endearing laugh and put his glass carefully on the beermat. 'No, I thought that would surprise you! She's Russian actually,' he said as if that solved the puzzle.

'Why, though?' Douglas asked, 'I mean, why Russian?'

'They've loved her the most,' said Dorchadas cryptically.

'Sorry – who have?'

'The Russians of course. They called her Svetlana – or Photina. They have all sorts of stories about her. Some not far from the truth as it happens, though some others are pretty fanciful. They said she had two sons Victor and Josiah, and loads of sisters too. But the thing is Douglas, they saw into the heart of her. So many of your so-called bible scholars are all on about the "the significance of the theme of water in the fourth gospel" and stuff like that.' As Dorchadas said this he mockingly wobbled his head and put on a posh English accent. 'As ever, Douglas, it is good to study with the head, but most of the real learning is done with the heart, don't you think? Ours is a religion of the spirit, you see. Now them Russians loved her heart and they made something of her in their stories, and she liked that. So when she does a visit, that's how she often comes. Though I did see her come as an Inuit once when I was doing some work in the Arctic. Her furry hat was so big you struggled to see anything of her face, but she got her story across all right and it made a big difference to the poor lass she was meeting that day. Quite a difference, I'd say.' Dorchadas looked thoughtful, pausing in his recollection, and then took another sip from his drink.

The pub was more modern than the one Douglas ate in previously. Dorchadas assured Douglas that this was the best place for the local fish pie, which they duly ordered from the young waitress. There was a moment of quiet in the conversation after they ordered. Douglas was wanting to say something but couldn't quite find the words.

'Go on, Douglas – what you trying to tell me?' said Dorchadas in the way that Douglas found disturbingly knowing. Both his hands were clasped round his drink as he leaned forward and studied his English friend.

'Well, Dorch, I'm thinking about Kathleen and Svetlana. I suppose I just wish that Kathleen could meet Svetlana. Couldn't you arrange it?' It felt an awkward request, but it was at the front of his mind.

'Ah, there you go, Douglas. The Vicar trying to fix them pastoral problems again! It's not as easy as that, as you well know. You can lead a horse to water and all that. You see, you have had two visits, which is already more than many get in a lifetime. And why? Because despite what you say about yourself, you have a remarkably open heart, Doug. Kathleen, poor soul has a desperately sore heart, which is darkened by bitterness. I could lead her to meet Svetlana or the sweet Theresa of Lisieux, or even the Blessed Virgin Mary for that matter, but she wouldn't believe it. She would be protesting from the moment I made the first introduction and we'd be spending the whole time debating who's who. That kind of arguing does no good. No, Kathleen needs a different approach and we are working on it, son. In fact, I'd like to think that you were part of the plan.'

Ciara returned with the cutlery and a bottle of ketchup. 'You gentlemen visiting Dingle then?' she asked.

'Yes,' Douglas answered, slightly annoyed at having their conversation interrupted.

'Your man's from England,' said Dorchadas pointing at his friend, 'But don't hold it against him – he's nice enough!'

The girl laughed. 'And you – I've seen you around, haven't I?'

'Aye that you have, lass. I'm… I'm from these parts.'

'Ah well, enjoy your meal – it'll be ready soon.' And with that she went off.

'From these parts, eh, Dorchadas?' said Douglas teasingly.

'There are times when the full answer takes too long, Douglas!'

'Mm, I'd still like to hear that full answer sometime.' he said, reaching for his Guinness which was doing a good job of cheering him up.

'I dare say you'll get the main part of it before the week's out, Douglas.' And then, much to Douglas' surprise Dorch became very serious and said, 'You see, Doug, you are also here to help me, and God knows I need all the help I can get. But let's get back to the story of today.'

Douglas visibly flinched at this somewhat shocking confession. Not only did Dorchadas declare that he was in some kind of need, but he was also admitting that Douglas, of all people, might be able to help *him*. How could a clapped-out priest with a defunct faith possibly be of help to someone who purported to be as senior as an angel? However, he had no time to ponder this, for Dorchadas drew them back to the original conversation.

'I knew how cut up you were by Kathleen. I mean, it wasn't my plan that you should hear Kath's sorry story – it all came splurging out, didn't it? But you are a good listener, Doug, so I'm not surprised she coughed up all that stuff. But once we'd heard it, and I saw what was important to you in the story, I thought you should meet Svetlana. We learned a lot from her didn't we – especially about sex!'

'Yes,' Douglas admitted with some hesitation. He did not want to delve into the subject of sex again. As far as he was concerned it was a very private subject, and it alarmed him that this supposed angel should be so keen to chat about it. It was one of the things that made him seriously doubt if Dorchadas was an angel.

'I know what you are thinking, Doug. You are thinking that we angels shouldn't be thinking about sex. You see the thing is Douglas, it is a very sad thing for us angels to know that He gave such a beautiful gift of love to humans, which they have done their level best to destroy. Now take Kathleen – she found the gift. All right, it wasn't necessarily in the right place. Marriage is the chosen place. But the fact is, she discovered a purity in that act that many religious people have never come anywhere near finding in their marriage beds. Father Peter thought he would never taste of that gift, and when it came his way he couldn't resist it. He was such a lonely soul, you see, and so much wounding in his early years. But he did find love again, I'm pleased to say. Yes, of course it was "wrong" what happened with Kathleen and Peter.' Dorchadas made the inverted commas sign over the table as he spoke.

'It was not "allowed",' he said, repeating his actions. 'But you see where all this "not allowedness" gets you? It gets you into this tangled world of keeping the law and my, how religious people are obsessional about the law. You all know what is right and what is wrong, don't you just? You all have your rulebooks and know who's in and who's out. It drives us angels mad, it does, to see the way you suffocate love in your desperate attempts to work out what is allowed and what is not. For God's sake, Douglas, it is time for you religious people to think with your hearts. To think with *His* heart!' Dorchadas thumped the table with this, and the people on the table next to them stopped their conversation and glanced across.

'I'm sorry, Doug – I'm ranting, aren't I? It's just... I just hate to see religiosity. I have seen so many poor souls crushed by it, and it hurts me, it does.' Douglas could see Dorchadas' eyes shining as he quickly sipped from his Guinness and looked down at the table.

'I'm not sure I'm currently one of your "religious people" Dorch.' Douglas hadn't liked being included in a group that he had never found particularly endearing in the church.

Dorchadas looked at Douglas and leaned on the table, fiddling with a beer mat. 'I'm sorry, Douglas. It was wrong of me to say that about you. I think you know – I just have to have a blast-off every now and again. To see such a beautiful and precious gift being so - well…' Dorchadas was struggling for words. 'I mean you listened to Svetlana, didn't you? And you heard what He thought of her. Straight away she heard His heart, didn't she? But, just before we parted, she noticed something in you, didn't she Doug? Did you mind that?'

Douglas couldn't deny that he had felt very disturbed by what Svetlana was seeing in him. Did he really want Dorchadas now investigating his troubled past? He looked up at the rugged face that now felt to be such a familiar and comforting face. It was also a vulnerable face, and yet it looked to Douglas to be the kind of face he could trust more than any other he had ever seen. Apart, that is, from Saoirse's beautiful face. 'Yes, Dorchadas, I did mind that,' he said looking into the face that he trusted. 'But she was right,' he said, and sighed.

'Here's your fish pies, gentlemen,' said the cheery voice of Ciara. 'Enjoy.'

'Thanks, love. We will,' said Dorchadas as she placed the food in front of them. He picked up a fork and started poking at the potato covering. Douglas knew he was giving him some space to talk if he wanted to and so said nothing while Dorch took a couple of mouthfuls, sucking in the air to cool the hot food.

'Grand fish pie, don't you think?' he said, looking up at Douglas briefly, and wiping his mouth with the napkin.

'Saoirse, my wife, died two years ago, Dorch,' said Douglas as he squeezed the piece of lemon over his pie. 'Sometimes it seems like yesterday and at other times, like now, it seems a lifetime ago.' He took a mouthful of the fish. 'Certainly tasty, Dorch.'

'Aye, that it is - I said it's the best in Dingle and it is. Cracking pie as ever, Ciara,' he called to the waitress. 'Be sure to tell the chef.'

There was a pause for a while in the conversation. Dorchadas knew Douglas would continue when he was ready.

'She was more beautiful to me than I will ever have the words to convey, Dorch. All my friends couldn't believe it when someone as attractive as her fell for me. I was in my forties and unmarried and that's the way most people thought I'd stay. Quite a few assumed I was gay, including my mother. But when I saw Saoirse for the first time, it was love at first sight for both of us. She had the kindest smile. She was the head teacher of our local school. The children at the school adored her and they were delighted when we announced we were getting married.' Douglas paused and prodded his food with his fork.

'She was not a Christian, Dorch, and that shocked some of my friends and certainly most of the congregation. I even got one or two complaints about being 'unequally yoked'. And yet, there was something so genuine in Saoirse - she would have loved to have met Svetlana. She had a way of stripping away all the religious trappings that had somehow piled up in my life. In many ways it was really disturbing - and yet liberating too. It's not that she attacked my faith - no way. She was so sweetly respectful. But she wouldn't let me get away with any religious bullshit.'

Dorchadas, who was clearly enjoying his meal, smiled and said, 'I do love an honest human.'

Douglas piled some fish on to his fork and drew it to his mouth, but before consuming it he added, 'She was helping me to become fully *me*, Dorch. She really was. I was shedding so much rubbish. My faith was becoming more real by the day. And it really didn't matter that she didn't believe.' He didn't notice the taste of prawn as he chewed on it, because his mind was now occupied by a memory that absorbed all of his attention.

'She sounds wonderful, Doug,' said Dorch with great tenderness. 'I wish I had known her,' and in that moment Douglas wished more than anything that she was there now in that Dingle pub so that he could introduce them to each other. She would have loved this curious character next to him, chomping away at his food.

'So how did it happen - how did you lose her?' asked Dorch with great care. 'Only if you want to, son. I know it's tender.'

Douglas put down his fork and wiped the napkin across his mouth. He sat up straight and inhaled. 'She had a friend at Uni. Everyone called her Lolly. She was Egyptian and no one could pronounce her real name. I still don't actually know what it was. Well, Lolly got engaged to an English bloke and three months before the wedding - that is two years, two months and five days ago - Saoirse, Lolly and three other friends went off to Cairo for several days. It was going to be a sort of hen party with Lolly introducing her friends to her Egyptian family. Only it never happened.' Douglas pursed his lips and looked down. He paused for some time, then said, 'This is where it gets difficult, Dorch.' For a few moments both men ate their meal in silence.

'Once they landed at Cairo, they made their way out of the terminal and I imagine they were full of excited chatter as they looked forward to their adventure,' said Douglas, staring down at the table in front of him. 'Saoirse sent me a text telling me they had landed safely and that they were on their way to get their hire care. It was... It was the last text she sent me.' He sighed, then continued. 'Lolly was the driver as she'd been on the local roads often enough, and Saoirse was sitting beside her in the front. They set off from the airport to go to Lolly's home village where a big party awaited them.' He paused and looked up sharply. Dorchadas watched Douglas clenching his jaw for a while.

Dorchadas was taken aback by the coldness he saw in his friend's eyes. Douglas continued, speaking almost as if in a dream, 'They were not far from the airport when.... some loathsome bastard decided British people were not welcome in their land.... A car had followed them apparently from the airport...' Douglas was now gazing past Dorchadas into some distant place. He paused, breathed in and said, 'As it overtook their car, a man wearing a balaclava pulled out a gun and opened fire. I believe they call it a drive-by shooting.' Douglas turned and looked at Dorchadas. 'Lolly was shot in the shoulder, but Saoirse was hit in the head. The other girls were unharmed, even though the gunman clearly wanted to massacre the lot of them. Amazingly Lolly, though injured, managed to stop the car safely. The police and ambulance were there quickly, but by then the terrorists were miles away and have never been caught. Later a message was received to say a Jihadi group were responsible.' He took a couple of breaths and then stuffed some fish pie into his mouth and chewed it forcefully, and swallowed hard. Dorchadas remained still, watching his friend intently.

Douglas continued, 'I had taken Saoirse to the airport that morning, and I don't know if she sensed something but she really seemed so sad to say goodbye to me.' He winced as he remembered the final farewell at the airport, and took a sip of his drink before continuing. 'I felt sad, but also excited for her and knew she would love this little adventure with her friends, and she was only going to be away less than a week. So I drove back home and was glad to get the text from her to tell me they had landed safely in Cairo. I did start to worry a bit when there were no further texts for several hours, but I assumed the connection was poor where they were. Just as it was starting to get dark, the doorbell rang and two police officers were at the door. I remember little of the conversation with them, but I remember a feeling of utter helplessness and dread after they left. They said she had been in a serious accident and was critically injured. They didn't mention the shooting at that stage. I so desperately wanted to be with her, Dorch, but they told me not to go out to Cairo, and that preparations were being made to bring her home. I was in such shock, and realised how lonely I was - Saoirse was my best friend, but now in the greatest crisis ever to hit me, she wasn't there. I just sat in the dark on my own, longing for news - longing for good news. I didn't think she would die - she was far too strong for that. I assumed she would recover and be back with me soon.'

'Everything all right with your food gentleman?' Douglas was jolted out of his recollections by Ciara's question and he blinked hard as he looked at her. Dorchadas quickly said, 'Aye, lass, it's delicious, thank you.' Then, turning his attention back to Douglas, he said, 'Carry on, son.'

Douglas breathed in with his eyes closed, and returned to his story. 'That night was terrible. I had no sleep. I made a phone call to my parents who were not much use. Thankfully the police in Ireland told me they were going to see her parents, so I was spared having to call them. I couldn't sleep and I found it pretty difficult to pray. I was in such shock. But at dawn there was a phone call to tell me that she was being flown home, and my heart leaped. If she was coming home, there was hope.

'I drove to the hospital to await her arrival, but the medical staff there were very gloomy - you know, all the stuff about she may not come round, and if she did, she had a brain injury and they warned me about how that might affect her. I didn't really listen to them - I just felt someone as alive as my Saoirse could not die, and could not suffer brain injury. It was also while I was waiting that someone from the police came and spoke to me, explaining that it was not a road accident but a shooting. That, of course, was incredibly shocking to hear - that someone wanted to kill those girls who were doing nothing to hurt anyone. I mean...' Douglas shook his head.

Dorchadas said nothing and simply waited. Douglas continued, 'It was around lunchtime that the ambulance carrying her arrived, and I was taken to Intensive Care to see her, and there she was, Dorch. My beautiful Saoirse, lying so still, with a bandage wrapped around the top of her head. I sat by her hospital bed stroking her bandaged head and speaking to her for nearly two long days, but she never regained consciousness. Her face was quite untouched by the bullets and she looked so... so beautiful, Dorch.' He looked up, almost pleadingly at Dorchadas. 'I couldn't believe she would die, Dorch. Not her.

'It was quiet on the ward and I thought I'd recite to her one of her favourite Shakespeare passages - Caliban's beautiful speech in Shakespeare's *Tempest*. I was holding her hand and... I still know it, of course:

> Be not afeard. The isle is full of noises,
> sounds and sweet airs that give delight and hurt not.
> Sometimes a thousand twangling instruments
> Will hum about mine ears, and sometimes voices
> That if then had waked after long sleep,
> Will make me sleep again. And then in dreaming
> the clouds methought would open and show riches
> ready to drop upon me, that when I waked
> I cried to dream again.

Dorchadas had closed his eyes as Douglas recited the words, and when he opened them they were glazed with moisture. Douglas was now looking at a beer mat that he was turning over and over on the table in front of him. 'I remember the words so well - I wanted her to have such dreams in her sleep, but I wanted the riches from the clouds to include a wonderful healing and recovery. But she never woke from her long sleep and by the time I was reciting "I cried to dream again" she had left us.' He stopped turning the beer mat and looked at Dorchadas. 'And since that day, Dorch, I have cried and cried to fall into a sleep that will take me into a dream where I can be back with my beautiful Saoirse, but of course that sleep will never come - not in this life. And so, I am left here, crying for a dream that the clouds will never give.'

Both men were quiet for a while. Douglas then lifted up his sad eyes to his new friend and said, 'Even when she slipped away, she was still so lovely. Even with bandages covering much of her gorgeous hair. But... but she'd gone. All that life. All that love - just... gone.' He looked down at his meal and pushed it away from him. He was battling hard with the emotion and was determined not to cry. Dorchadas had also stopped eating. Deep anguish was etched on his face as he listened to his friend.

'The days that followed are something of a haze now,' Douglas continued. 'It was national news of course and there was much in the papers apparently, but I never read them. People tried to comfort me. Lots of people talked to me about her being in heaven, but to be honest that was little comfort - what use was she to me in heaven? One of my clergy friends, Frank, was a great comfort to me actually. He was an American priest from California who was Vicar of a nearby parish at the time. I didn't know him very well before this, but he was wonderfully kind and understanding - far more so than anyone in my church. I asked him to take her service, which he did beautifully - it was a real comfort to me. I wanted to give the eulogy and I took hours and hours preparing it. How do you summarise such a wonderful life in just a few words, Dorch? Well, in the end I was quite pleased with what I prepared.

'But it was a desperate day. It was cold and drizzling. I walked in behind the wicker coffin and was overwhelmed with a sense of wrongness about the whole thing - she should not have been in that basket being prepared for burial. But I was too weak to make any protest and I struggled in behind her and slumped to my seat and watched Frank as if I was in a dream - or nightmare. He then came over and told me it was time for the eulogy, and I got up and.... Well, I couldn't do it, Dorch. I couldn't get one word out. Frank gently eased my notes from my hand, and he read out what I had prepared and everyone said they like it. But as far as I was concerned, I failed her...'. Douglas looked down into his chest and chocked back the emotion as best he could.

Dorchadas reached over and gripped his arm firmly and said, 'You're all right, Doug. You don't need to tell me any more if you don't want to. Honest you don't.'

Douglas sniffed hard and then looked up opening and closing his eyes wide to clear them. 'Thanks, Dorch, that's about it really. That's my story.' He took a sip of his Guinness. 'And the fact is, I am not "over it" as my mother so aptly puts it, and I don't believe I ever will be "over it", and in church last Sunday I... I finally cracked and decided to have my breakdown in the full glare of the congregation that I was supposed to be leading.' He took another, longer sip. 'The whole thing has finally come tumbling down. In a nutshell, the whole God enterprise has not worked for me, so there's little point in my trying to sell it anymore.' He pursed his lips, opened his hands in a gesture of helplessness and then looked down and fastened his gaze on the uneaten food.

Dorchadas had also given up on his dinner. He was too distressed to eat. The force of compassion in him was so strong that for a while it prevented any words from breaking out. He looked at Douglas and said, 'My God, Douglas. You poor, poor soul. There are no words...'

'It's OK, Dorch. Nobody knows what to say, and to be honest I tell the story to very few people now. In fact, I'm thinking of inventing a different story to explain her death - no-one knows what to do with a story like this. But I'm sorry, Dorch. I know religion is everything to you. But you can see why I can't believe you are an angel. If God really does exist, then things are twice as bad as I thought they were. Not only have I lost the love of my life, but there is also a God in heaven who either doesn't care what happens to people, or he is utterly useless when it comes to protecting them. And please, please don't go doing what some of my friends have tried doing, which is telling me about my learning a precious lesson, and how I will be such a compassionate priest as a result and all that godforsaken rubbish. If this is God's classroom then I'm going to play truant for as long as I live, because no lesson could be worth that cost!'

For a while the two men sat in silence staring at the plates of half-eaten meals. Then Dorchadas leaned forward and grasping Douglas' hand said, 'Douglas, would I be right in thinking that we have reached the point where I should order us each a double whisky?'

Douglas was so dreading a lecture on the problem of human suffering and divine mystery, that the question from Dorch felt an immense relief. 'Dorchadas - you are inspired!' He watched his tall friend make his way to the bar. Whoever this man was, Douglas felt he was the first person to somehow hold his terrible story. He did not seem afraid of it, as so many others did. He didn't try and explain anything, or defend God, or quote Scripture. In fact, he said very little, but in that moment, Douglas had a strange feeling that of all the people he knew in his life, this was the one person who really understood how it was for Douglas. He sat back in his chair and was almost tempted to eat the remains of his food, but thought better of it when Dorch returned with the two whiskies.

Dorchadas was just about to say something, when there was a cry from the door. 'Dorchadas, you old rogue, fancy seeing you here now!' Both Douglas and Dorchadas looked towards the door, and coming towards them was Kathleen with a younger man beside her. 'Well fancy seeing the two of you here for God's sakes,' she said thumping both of them on the back when she arrived. 'And look who I have brought with me - none other than my rascal son, Kevin.'

Though Douglas felt a fondness for Kathleen after she shared her story in the café earlier, he was disappointed to have such an important conversation with Dorchadas interrupted. However, he realised there was nothing he could do about it so he tried to be as polite as possible. He stood up to greet Kath and her son. He glanced at Kevin and estimated him to be a man of a similar age to himself. He was of stocky build with receding hair and a short beard that covered a face scarred from acne. 'Pleased to meet you both,' he said quietly.

Dorchadas was also standing. He kissed Kathleen and shook Kevin's hand, and then said, 'Now I'm going to be frightful rude to you both, but we have both had an awful long day today we have, and we'll be going off very soon. Will you forgive us if we don't chat tonight, but how's about tomorrow night?' Douglas felt very relieved and so grateful to Dorchadas.

'Aye, that would be grand, Dorch,' said Kathleen. 'I may not be here as its the bingo tomorrow, but Kevin will be - it's your favourite group playing tomorrow, son, is it not?'

'That it is, mother. It is indeed. It will be good to chat to you both tomorrow night it will. Mam has spoken of you, Douglas. And it would be great to catch up with you, Dorch. And no worries at all about tonight. How's the fish pie? Looks like you've both left it - should we choose something else tonight? The fish pie's usually so good.'

'It is, Kev,' responded Dorchadas. 'But as you can see, our eyes were too big for our stomachs. The pie is as excellent as ever. You go ahead and order it now.'

'So, we will. Come on Mammy, let's find us a seat. The band will be starting up soon, so they will.' And with that the two departed.

'Thanks, Dorch - I'm really grateful,' said Douglas.

'Aye, I know lad - I would think you have had enough for one day. And to be frank, there is a bit of a story with Kevin, and, well, tonight would not have been the time for it.'

'Sounds like they are quite a family,' said Douglas

'Oh, yes, that they are, Doug. That they are.'

So, the two men drank their whisky and Dorchadas made no further mention of Douglas' story. But inwardly he was struggling greatly. And even he, the one who seldom knew fear, was distinctly anxious. Of all the people that Dorchadas would *not* want Douglas to meet during his time in Dingle, Kevin would be top of the list. If he should tell Douglas anything of how he lived as a young man, there's no telling how it might affect Douglas. Very badly, he suspected. He felt that if only he had the power to arrange things like this, then without question he would have ensured that Kevin was out of town this week.

CHAPTER 13

<u>Journal 10 October 11.15pm</u>

Another strange day with Dorchadas. Still claiming to be an angel, even when he's not drinking Guinness. Met Kath, a poor soul who had been terribly treated by the church. Awful story. Made me feel ashamed of being a Christian minister. Sometimes we do much more harm than good. Also met a Russian woman called Svetlana who claimed to be the woman at the well from John's Gospel!! Somehow magicked into the 21st century. I can't work out how Dorchadas is doing this. He assures me he is not hypnotising me, but one way or another he got me to believe that I visited ancient Egypt to meet an elderly Jacob, and that the woman from Samaria turned up in a children's playground here in Ireland. As if. But here's the thing - however he is doing this, the two people I met were really special, and even if they are not the actual characters from the bible, then they were still such fascinating people. Felt really moved by them. This Svetlana talked beautifully about her meeting with Jesus. Could have done with knowing her before I preached on that story - I learned so much. Felt sad actually that I had given up my faith. For all my anger and distress, there is still something about the Jesus of the Gospels that touches me. But I'm in no mood to try and trawl for my old faith now. I'm pretty sure it's sunk without trace.

Had supper with Dorch and I ended up telling him about Saoirse. I didn't intend to tell him. Can't bear the usual trite bible quotes and people's desperate attempts to hurry me out of my grief. But Dorch was really different. I told him the gist of the story - not all the details of course. For the first time I felt someone <u>really</u> listened to me. He said virtually nothing in response, and yet I knew he had heard me. Felt quite healing actually. I know he was curious about it, but I get the impression that unless I raise it again, he won't pester me about it. Kath turned up at the end of our conversation. Had her son with her who looked a bit of a bruiser. By then I was feeling really tired, and I was so glad Dorchadas told them we were soon leaving for the night. He wants us to meet up tonight. Should be OK I think.

I've decided to stay a few more days, and this Dorchadas is intriguing. I really don't get this pretending to be an angel thing, but I can live with it. He's actually a great bloke - never met anyone like him.

I can cope with the weirdness and I'm beginning to think he's just what I need actually. A bit disturbing when he said he felt I could help him. That won't happen - not me in my present state. And I told him I'd given up on God. Even that didn't seem to shock him. I mean, if he really was an angel, that should have been enough to ruffle a few of his feathers, surely? But no, it didn't seem to worry him at all. Still worries me a bit though. I have given up on God, but I still have that feeling that someone (Someone?) is watching me. As I walked back tonight, I thought of poor old Francis Thomson pursued by his heavenly hound...

> I fled him down the nights and down the days
> I fled him down the arches of the years
> I fled him down the labyrinthine ways
> Of my own mind; and in the mist of tears
> I hid from Him...

Am I fleeing him? Hiding from him? Certainly something very disturbing is going on in the labyrinths of my mind. Will I - could I - experience what Francis knew at the end of his poem?

> Halts by me that footfall;
> Is my gloom, after all
> Shade of his hand, outstretched caressingly?

What does that mean? Not sure that I know, but oddly can't get those words out of my mind. Too tired now - time for sleep. Just remembered how Saoirse used to curl up beside me when we went to bed and sometimes, if she knew I was unhappy, she would sing the Gaelic lullaby her mum sang to her. I never told her how those were some of the most precious moments of my life. There's so much I never told her. It's her outstretched, caressing hand that I need tonight. Does grief ever heal?

And in the night, when Douglas was in his deepest sleep, he heard that very voice singing the self-same song, only in English:

> Sleep now my love, sleep softly in the quiet
> let fears subside, let troubles fade into the dark
> This is a kindly night
> for tender angels watch,
> and Christ's own love will freshening daylight bring.

He never knew how this voice came to him, and by the break of day he had forgotten it, but when he awoke, he found his pillow damp with tears.

106

*

He was late for getting up, but just made it down in time for one of Mrs O'Connell's breakfasts. He felt he needed a break from the intensity of the previous day's meetings, so he decided to drive down to the little town of Inch. He enjoyed a very breezy walk along the sandy beach and stopped off at the pub for a diet coke and a bowl of soup which came with an ample supply of soda bread and butter. He decided to check the emails on his phone, something he had not done since arriving in Ireland. There was once a time when his mail box would have been packed full of parish business, but now it was virtually empty. However, there was one which caught his eye and it was from Mavis, the one person in the parish that he now counted as a true friend. He took a sip from his hot soup, and then read:

Hello there Douglas - your old friend Mavis here. Not sure where you hived off to, but hope you pick this up sometime. Felt so worried about you after your funny turn on Sunday and I must admit I have been worrying that you have gone and done something silly. Well, you know what a daft old worrier I am. But for the sake of my nerves, I'd be so grateful if you could drop me an email or text to let me know you are all right.

I'll be honest and say I'm relieved you've taken some time off work. You've looked so pale and drawn recently. But what's really upset me is the congregation - at first they were all over you with sympathy, but now they seem to do nothing but complain. They say you've turned your back on God, and so you can't expect to get better without his help and all that nonsense. Honest, Douglas, how cruel can people be? To be truthful, this is not really the Christianity that I like. It never was really - it was only because you were so kind to my Bert in his last days that I got coming to your church. And you helped me to see that God is a kind God.

Anyway, you don't need me wittering on. Do let me know how you are doing. I hope you don't mind me saying, but you've become a bit like a son to me, Douglas, and I do care about you so. I don't suppose my prayers are much good, but I do tell God about you in my prayers every night, I do. Not sure what he makes of them, but

107

you told me he didn't mind if I didn't use proper language and that. So maybe they will do some good. I do hope so.

You will get right in the end, and your poor heart will heal. Honest it will.

your friend, Mavis xx

Douglas read the email several times and then gulped back most of his coke. He imagined Mavis slowly typing out the email with her two arthritic fingers on her ancient computer, peering at the screen through her thick glasses and screwing up her nose as she checked the frequent corrections of the spellchecker. He saw the ashtray on the table, and the half-drunk tea next to her *Daily Express*.

Douglas recalled how Mavis had knocked on the door of the Vicarage one Saturday soon after he and Saoirse were married. It was Saoirse who answered the door and she invited her in for a cup of tea. When Douglas came in later from a meeting, he found the two of them sitting at the kitchen table. Saoirse's arm was wrapped around the shoulder of Mavis, in front of whom was a cup of tea and a pile of tissues. He learned that Mavis' husband, Bert, to whom she had been married over forty years, was in his last days after battling with cancer. Mavis had been a churchgoer as a child and the desperation of seeing her beloved Bert entering his last days, reawakened a spark of faith in her that led her to this Vicarage door in the hopes that the Vicar might be able to deliver the last rites.

Douglas did indeed visit her Bert that night in the hospital and anointed him with holy oil and prayed for him to know peace in his final hours, a prayer that Mavis felt was beautifully answered. Two days later Douglas was standing by the hospital bed making the sign of the cross on the pallid forehead of the recently departed, while Mavis knelt sobbing at the bedside gripping the cold hand of the man she had loved so deeply and for so long. Douglas took many funerals, and usually he lost touch with the bereaved family, but he and Saoirse felt an unusual affection for Mavis, and she soon became a very good friend and they did their best to help her as she struggled along on the thorny path of grief. She started coming to the Sunday services which gave her much comfort, but she was shy by nature and would usually slip away after the service and avoided having to make conversations with people she deemed far more confident and assured in their faith than she felt herself to be.

After a few months Saoirse discovered that Mavis was struggling financially, so they employed her to come to the Vicarage twice a week to clean and do some work in the garden. She was constantly grateful to Douglas and Saoirse for their friendship, but it was most certainly not all one way. She was the only church attender with whom Saoirse felt comfortable and there was many a time when Saoirse would come home from her teaching and the two of them would sit at the kitchen table talking over a cup of tea. Saoirse found Mavis to be a very compassionate and understanding listener as she shared with her the various strains and stresses of her teaching day. She also welcomed the fact that Mavis was quite unfazed by the fact that Saoirse was not a church-goer. In fact, she was the only member of the church to be unfazed by this. Mavis had the unusual gift of being entirely free of the need to judge others.

Saoirse's death had hit Mavis very hard, but despite her own personal grief, she had proved a strong support to Douglas and she was one of the very few people he allowed near those parts of his soul that were so terribly wounded. As Douglas read her email through a second time, he felt bad that he hadn't told her where he was going - he was in such a state when he left. So, he ordered a coffee to follow his soup, and replied immediately.

> My dear Mavis - I am so sorry I never told you where I was going. I'm afraid I wasn't really myself after Sunday's service, but I'm really quite all right now and you needn't worry. I've actually come to Dingle which is a little seaside town in the South of Ireland - Saoirse's homeland. I was hoping to meet Saoirse's aunt, but discovered she sadly died a while ago. But I've made a new friend here - a local man called Dorchadas— you'd love him. He's very eccentric, but he's showing me around the place and we have interesting conversations. So you don't need to worry at all. I shall stay for about a week and then come back and we can have a coffee and catch up. Do keep working at the house and garden, and I'll settle up with you when I get back. Take care Mavis - I really do appreciate your friendship. Any son would be so proud to have you as his mother. With love, Douglas

When he finished his coffee, Douglas drove back to Dingle. Once back in town, there wasn't much else to do, so he went off walking again as it was a pleasant sunny afternoon and he found himself walking near the playground where he had experienced the curious meeting with Svetlana the day before. He walked into the playground, partly just to reassure himself that the playground actually existed and he was pleased to discover that it did and looked just the same as it did when he and Dorchadas had visited it. So, he wasn't being transported this time to some other place. He sat on the very same bench where he had sat with Svetlana. He looked around half expecting to see her, and even found himself rather hoping that she would turn up. His mind was still struggling greatly to work out quite what had taken place at this meeting, and who this Russian lady really was. He had to admit that she was extraordinarily convincing as the biblical woman at the well in Samaria.

A girl in school uniform came into the playground. Douglas guessed her to be in her early teens and he watched her slump on to one of the swings. He had seen many such girls in England and this girl's body language looked familiar, and he decided that she was a stroppy nearly teenager who was best to be avoided. However, he could not quite avoid her, for she called across to him, 'Not seen you here before.'

'No, I'm visiting. From England'

'Oh. You a tourist, then?'

'No, seeing friends.' Douglas was battling with various issues. For a start, he did not want anyone to think he was chatting up a young girl, and all his safeguarding training flashed warning buzzers in his nervous mind. But also, he was racking his brain to think of any teenagers in the bible who might be leaping out of their pages to present themselves to him in modern day guises.

So, he decided to move, when she said, 'You look sad.' It took him aback.

'So, do you,' he replied.

'Aye, I am,' she sighed. 'Complicated home life, shall we say. Think I might head off somewhere new soon.'

The safeguarding buzzer was still sounding in Douglas' head, but nonetheless he asked, 'Where would you go?'

'To England, of course. Get away from this dump.' She looked down and made imaginary circles with her toes on the tarmac.

'I came here, away from England which had become a dump for me,' he said and smiled.

'Is the whole world a dump then?' she asked not expecting a reply.

Douglas realised he was actually now of the view that yes, the whole world was a dump. It was a dump because he had been dumped in a story of violence and death and it was a dump from which he was unlikely to ever escape. And yet, he hated the thought of this young life that was sitting on the swing opposite him believing such a thing to be true, so he replied, 'No. No I really don't think it is.' He looked harder at the girl and saw past the stroppy teenager, and felt he spied something really strong. 'I suspect you could make anywhere a wonderful place.'

She looked surprised and cocked her head to one side and asked, 'What's your name, then Englishman?'

'Douglas.'

'Hm. Don't know any Douglases. I'm Grace.'

Douglas got up from his bench and walked towards her. He said, 'Well, good to meet you, Grace.' He was about to leave the playground when he paused for a moment, and asked, 'By the way, have you ever come across a guy in town called Dorchadas?'

'I've heard of him - is he that tall guy that's a bit weird?'

'Yes, that's the guy.'

'You a friend of his?' she asked, looking up at Douglas and shielding her eyes from the bright sky behind him.

'Yes, I am,' said Douglas, surprised at himself at owning to being his friend after so short a period of time.

'Well, then,' said the girl, 'he's probably all right then. I'll look out for him.'

'Please do. Been nice chatting to you, Grace' said Douglas. Then he added, 'Can I just check one thing. You're not... not a bible character, are you?'

'You what?' said the girl, looking at Douglas with a horrified look on her face.

'No, I didn't think you were. I was just checking. Don't worry. But if you do meet Dorchadas, you'll probably find out why I asked the question.'

The girl laughed, 'Well, I don't think anyone would expect to find someone in that holy bible that was like me.'

'You'd be surprised,' said Douglas. 'You would truly be surprised.'

The girl laughed and then turned to her phone and her fingers danced at speed across the keyboard as she responded to a text. Douglas walked out of the playground. Once again, he had been faced with another story of human failing and hurt and it troubled him. In days gone by he would have probably given the girl some advice and maybe some Bible verses, or even offered to say a prayer with her. But not now. However, he noticed that he had no hesitation in recommending the services of Dorchadas. He surprised himself by discovering how much confidence he put into this curious character who, surely, was only half sane, if that.

CHAPTER 14

Douglas and Dorchadas had arranged to meet back at the same pub in the evening and they settled themselves on a couple of stools at a corner table, reserving a third for Kevin. Kath had sent a message to let them know that the call of the bingo was too strong to resist and that Kevin would be along later. Douglas and Dorchadas had a meal together while they waited. Douglas noticed that Dorchadas seemed nervous, and the chatter they had together was fairly mundane compared to the weightier discussions of previous days. Douglas told Dorchadas about his visit to the playground and the meeting with Grace and they spent some time discussing present day teenager culture. Douglas was impressed by just how in touch Dorchadas was with the world of young people. Just as they were finishing their meal, Kevin arrived coiling his fingers carefully around three glasses of Guinness.

'Well, I expect you gentlemen will be needing these, to wash down those steaks now,' he said as he skilfully placed the drinks on the table without spilling any. Douglas had already had a couple and was feeling a little light-headed, but he didn't want to refuse the kindness of this new friend.

'I assume Dorch has converted you to this fine Irish water, has he?' said Kevin, lifting his glass proudly.

'Oh, I didn't need converting - I've always been fond of a Guinness', and Douglas knew that it was something about the way he said this that made him sound unbearably English in contrast to these two very authentic Irishmen.

'Well, we all need a little converting, isn't that so, you old angel rascal,' said Kevin, punching Dorch on the shoulder, causing him to spill some of the drink. As Kevin smiled his broad smile, Douglas noticed that he had quite a few teeth missing. Douglas found that he felt somehow apprehensive in his presence.

'How long have you known each other?' Douglas asked, taking a sip of his Guinness. Kevin was already half way down his glass.

'Too long!' said Kevin and laughed loudly again - a little too loud for Douglas.

'Actually,' he went on, now much quieter and leaning across confidentially to Douglas, 'I owe my life to this man. No word of a lie.'

His pale, rugged face took on such a look of sincerity as he said it, that Douglas' initial view of him shifted - just a little.

'How come?' asked Douglas, now sounding a bit more like his normal self.

'It's a long story, Douglas…' He placed his glass with care down on the mat before him. 'It's a shame we can't smoke in here,' he added as it was now his turn to act a little uncomfortable.

'You know we enjoyed some good craic with your Ma yesterday, we did,' said Dorchadas. Douglas was surprised to see Dorchadas a little nervous.

'She's a very impressive lady,' said Douglas, sounding rather Vicarish again, he thought.

'Oh my, she is that. She certainly is,' said Kevin. He then rather took Douglas aback as he said, 'But tell me about yourself. Ma says you're a priest, are you not?'

'Ur - sort of,' said Douglas, faltering a little, and taken aback that Kevin should refer to his profession right at the beginning of their conversation. But what sort of a priest could he own to? Yes, he was, but he wasn't Catholic. Yes, he was, but he was a pretty miserable specimen of one. Yes, he was, but he would probably soon be defrocked. Yes, he was, but not like the sort that had been so brutal to Kevin's mother. From his inner confusion he asked, 'Do I look like a priest, then?'

'Well now, from experience, yes, I would say that you do,' said Kevin, and looked strangely sad. 'I learned to read people in my old trade. I never trusted a soul and was suspicious of everyone. That's how it was, so I found myself looking hard at everyone and, by looking hard, I often guessed their trade. You'd be surprised by how many priests were involved in the troubles.'

'I'm not Catholic,' said Douglas.

'No, I know - you're a British Protestant. True Church of England if I'm not mistaken. It shows, but don't let it worry you, Douglas. It's of no concern to me now. It would have done, mind you, had it not been for this gentleman here, eh Dorch?'

Dorchadas looked uncomfortable and said, 'You see, Douglas - you need to know, because it will come out sooner or later.' Here Dorchadas lowered his voice, 'Kevin was a captain in the IRA. Long time ago now. Water under the bridge.' He took several small sips from his beer. 'You had a good day, Kev?'

'There's no need to lower your voice, Dorch. The whole of the Dingle knows what I was. It's no longer important. It's what I am now that counts.'

Douglas was sitting upright in his chair with has hand clasped around his glass. He felt the coldness of it. Mention of the IRA drew his mind straight to the horrors of terrorism, and to the particular personal horror that terrorism had inflicted on him.

'D... d... did you arrange this Dorch?' he said, addressing Dorchadas but staring hard at his glass. He was dismayed to discover his stammer was returning, a sure sign that the disturbance within him was serious.

'Oh God, Douglas, I'm sorry if I've offended you,' said Kevin.

'Did you, Dorch? said Douglas, ignoring Kevin's apology and turning to look at Dorchadas. He was the one now raising his voice, and one or two people nearby stopped their conversations and looked over at the tense group of three.

'No, no, Doug, you must trust me, I swear to God I didn't. Kevin and Kath are good friends and I didn't know they would drop in on us last night. But, Doug, listen. It might just help to hear his story, that it might, son.' Douglas found it disturbing to see Dorchadas so unsure of himself. 'Please believe me, my friend,' he said and he placed a warm hand on the cold arm of the English priest.

With reluctance Douglas believed him. He did not want a scene, but his stiff body language betrayed his discomfort. Was he now drinking Guinness with a man who was once as ruthless as the man who stole the precious life of his beloved Saoirse? He was indignant that such a criminal should behave in such a friendly manner, as if his crimes were no longer significant.

'Douglas,' said Dorchadas with surprising authority in his voice. 'Doug, listen to me. I know Kevin well. He's a changed man. Honest to God he is. People can change - and do, believe me. Surely you must know this?'

Kevin was not unaccustomed to this reaction that he was observing in his new acquaintance. He had once been a man of violence, and he had come to understand why any who had suffered from that violence would look on him with mistrust and hatred. In fact, he had become very skilled in interpreting people's reactions. Even from these few moments of conversation, he guessed Douglas had somewhere in his life suffered because of violence. Kevin knew well the signs. He could see the judgements forming quickly in the minds of those who learned of his

115

past. But he knew himself to be a profoundly changed man, and he was determined that Douglas should know this and not judge him by his former life. He had changed so much. And it was down to this tall stranger called Dorchadas who, by some curious alchemy, had transported him to a meeting, the remembrance of which always filled him with powerful emotion. But even that extraordinary meeting had not healed all his guilt.

He still struggled greatly with the fact that he was responsible for stealing the lives of innocent people through the fiery idealism that drove him when he was a young man. And there was something in this English priest that was activating the old guilt again. He sat silently at the table looking down and rubbing his finger over a patch of spilt beer. His knee was up to its old tricks, frantically bouncing up and down.

Douglas sat back on his stool and breathed deeply a couple of times to calm himself, as Dorchadas took a long sip from his drink and looked up at the ceiling.

'You were a Captain, then?' said Douglas. Douglas felt that conversation was better than this prickly silence, and there was part of him that actually was curious about Kevin's story.

'Yes, that I was, Douglas,' said Kevin, relieved that Douglas wanted some conversation. 'Truth be told, I rose quickly in the ranks because I was... well, I was passionate. In those days I believed in the cause, and I would go to any lengths to achieve it. Young men can be like that - young Irish men, especially.'

Douglas took his gaze away from his glass and looked more carefully at the man now and could see the signs of passion still in him. He was slim - quite gaunt in some ways, yet handsome, and when he did smile, despite the missing teeth, it was a wide and generous smile. The eyes were dark brown, intense, yet with kindness. But those same eyes had also at one time expressed such venomous hatred. There had been times when, for some poor victim, those eyes were the last they saw on this earth before violent bullets robbed them of their lives. Such a thought caused Douglas to look away from him.

Kevin then leaned forward and asked, 'Have you ever had cause to hate, Douglas?

'Yes' said Douglas, somewhat ashamed of the speed and strength of his answer. But yes, he did. He hated the loathsome assassin who stole his precious beloved from him. Yes, he did hate him, enough to murder him if ever he laid eyes on him. 'Yes, I have, Kevin. Some people

116

deserve to be hated. And if you want the honest truth I hate all t…t…terrorists, because they are the ones who have robbed this world of some of the sweetest and k... kindest lives that ever lived. So yes, I…'

He stopped himself. The stammer was a bad sign. He knew he had to step back from the rush of emotion that this former terrorist was arousing in him. And he did not want to get into his own grief and anger here in public. He breathed in again, and looked stubbornly at the glasses on the table avoiding Kevin's gaze.

Kevin was quiet for a moment and then said, 'You see, Douglas, and I don't expect you to understand this, but when your parents, your grandparents and your great grandparents going back centuries have been bullied and butchered and humiliated with every kind of humiliation, it does something even to the most holy of us. I can't excuse any of us, Douglas, but the fact is that I drank hatred with my mother's milk. We loathed the English for what they had done to us. My Granda was part of the Rising. He was the son of a sweet Irish girl who after he was born was raped by an English soldier and her mind never recovered. You can see where his hatred came from, Douglas. And my grandma told us again and again the stories of her forebears who starved to death, did most of them, in the Great Hunger. Many of them here, in these parts of Ireland. I could go on, Douglas, but it is not a pretty story. As I say, I'm not trying to make excuses, I'm just trying to explain why some of us became as we did. The hatred was just shovelled down from one generation to the next. It was terrible, it truly was.'

None of this was new to Douglas. He remembered Saoirse talking about her family and the violence and horrors experienced by previous generations of her family. When she told him, he was astonished that she could ever contemplate marrying an Englishman, but she was adamant that she would live up to her name, as a free person, and not be driven by her history. It was clear to Douglas that Kevin was, early in his life, shackled to the cruel history of suffering in his family, and in that cycle of violence he added further to the wretched tales of suffering in his land. And yet something had clearly happened to him to cause him to step away from it all. But then Douglas felt the darkness again - this man had killed people, and killed people like his Saoirse. He could not just excuse him as being a victim of his history.

No-one spoke for a few moments. Douglas was very aware of the powerful feelings churning within him, and yet here was an opportunity to actually speak to someone who, at one time in his life, lived with

117

similar values and drives to the one who had murdered his wife. He could learn something that might help him at least gain some understanding of the motive for the atrocity.

Dorchadas was terribly aware of the tension and in a poor attempt to defuse it asked, 'Would either of you gentlemen like another drink?'

Douglas ignored the offer and asked, 'Tell me, Kevin. What do you think about the modern day J... J... Jihadists, and the suicide bombers, and t... terrorists and d... drive-by assassins in the Middle East who randomly shoot innocent B... British tourists for no other reason than they are from a Western nation?' He hated the way his stammer had returned and felt angry with himself.

At this Kevin looked up at Douglas and said, 'Oh, God, Douglas. I'm so sorry. I can see now - you've lost someone haven't you? It was a terrorist, wasn't it? Oh God, I'm truly sorry. I don't want to add to your suffering.' He rose to leave, but Dorchadas put a firm hand on his arm.

Douglas wasn't totally surprised that he had guessed, but he was not going to give an inch to this former murderer, and would certainly not tell him anything about his personal story. He would leave it in generalities for the moment. He was surprised to see that he was near the end of the Guinness - nervousness had caused him to keep slurping. He was feeling decidedly unsteady now, but there was something he wanted to say.

'Mm. Yes, I did... I um, yes, I d... did know someone. A member of the family actually, and it was... well. Yes, it was sad, b... b... but we move on. You know, we have to move on, don't we?' He knew the alcohol was affecting him now, but he also felt a need for a further supply so he looked at Dorchadas and said, 'Yes, please Dorch, to answer your earlier question. Perhaps a Jameson's now please. Perhaps a double. Just one ice.'

'And for me please, Dorch,' added Kevin in a low, flat voice. 'No ice.'

Dorchadas dutifully rose from the table to collect the drinks.

A table nearby erupted in raucous laughter and it took a while for it to subside, while one rather inebriated man added comment after comment, each one apparently more hilarious than the other. As he bellowed out, 'And it was only Monday!' it seemed that the whole pub erupted in laughter, apart from a little island of tense seriousness in the corner. Kevin smiled an unconvincing smile.

When it was finally quiet enough, Douglas breathed in and leaned towards Kevin, 'I really don't want to make any enemies, Kevin. I - I... well, I mean I know there are reasons. And I realise we Brits have been appalling to you. I'm no historian, but I know enough to know our violence over the years has been terrible.' Douglas could hear himself slurring, which he felt was preferable at the moment to stammering so he continued. 'But what makes one of these Jihadis do this? I mean, a group of friends were just arriving and driving away from the airport to go and have a few days holiday and a hen party. So, tell me, what's so evil about that? What hideous stain of Western Christendom are they supposed to smear on that country by doing that, eh? How can five young women, travelling in a car possibly be a threat to anyone? What conceivable crime have they committed to warrant someone to drive up and just shoot randomly at them? Mm? What, Kevin? said Douglas, almost as if he was putting Kevin on trial. The alcohol had loosened his reserve and some of his raw questions were escaping.

Kevin felt genuine and terrible sympathy for his new English friend. He was still haunted by the fact that there were people now, even twenty-five years on from those fateful bombings and shootings, who still tenderly stroked photographs and treasured toys, letters and trinkets, and their grief and suffering was due to his terrible actions. He looked at Douglas and said, 'You see Douglas, no-one can excuse those Jihadi guys, of course not. But they also have a terrible history of hatred, and I'm sorry to say the British have their part in that story too.'

'Oh b... blame the British again,' stammered Douglas sourly, and then regretted butting in. 'I'm sorry - carry on'. He clutched at his now empty glass so hard that Kevin feared it would shatter in his hands.

'No, it was not right of me to say that,' said Kevin. 'I apologise. But the thing is I know what it is to be bottle-fed hatred from birth. It's a terrible, terrible thing Douglas, and only those who have experienced it know what it is like. If you have been loved from birth and have not known hatred, then count yourself blessed indeed.'

'Indeed, you should,' said Dorchadas, having squeezed his way through a now very crowded bar and placed three double Jamesons on the table. 'Sláinte, my friends.'

'Yes, I suppose I have been blessed,' said Douglas calming a little. 'And I have only known hatred these last couple of years, and to be honest I don't like it being in my heart, but it's there whether I like it or not. Well done you, Kevin if you, through some of Dorch's magic, have

119

got rid of yours. But mine doesn't look like budging. I thought my faith would help, but I'm sorry to say, it's proved utterly useless. So it looks like this hatred in me is here for life. There's an encouraging thought. So, cheers to hatred and all who sail in her.' He looked very weary as he raised his glass and swigged back most of its contents, wincing as it burned its way down his throat. 'That should help' he said in a rasping voice, trying to make a joke of it, and another roar erupted at the table next to them which drowned the sound of his indiscreet burp.

'But,' said Dorchadas when they could hear themselves think again, 'you've not met the person who helped Kevin. I'm not saying it would cure you, Douglas, but it might help. I could introduce you.'

'Oh, not one of your b... b... biblical fantasies again Dorch, surely? Who is it this time? The W... Witch of Endor? Let's raise her up from the dead, shall we? Or Judas Iscariot - he'd have qu... quite a tale to tell. Let's see how he's getting on these days. Or how about one of those f... fanatical prophets who seemed to love going around slaughtering people. Come to think of it, there was a fair bit of m... mayhem and murder in the name of God in the Old Testament, don't you think, Dorch? Some of those so-called heroes of faith in the book of Judges could give the Jihadists a run for their money, don't you think?' It was clear to all now that the alcohol was affecting Douglas as he swigged back the remains of his whisky, and slurred out louder than he realised, 'Anyone for another? Come on C... Captain, I'm starting to get into the mood. The night is still young...'

'Time to get him home, I think,' said Kevin.

'Aye - time to get us both home, I think, as I'm none too steady myself,' said Dorchadas as he helped Douglas to his feet.

'I'll remain here for while I will, Dorch,' said Kevin pushing his undrunk whisky away from him. 'It's great to see you again - not seen you for too long in these parts. Go well, friend.'

Without any further conversation, Dorchadas and Douglas, both looking as if they were on board a ship on a rolling sea, made their way out of the pub. A young couple who had been standing for a while quickly grabbed their chance and sat on the two recently vacated stools, next to a man who seemed to be in prayer as he pressed the palms of his hands to his eyes. He was no longer aware of the noisy pub as he drew into his soul once again the extraordinary scenes of Paradise that he glimpsed on that day he first met this curious and beguiling man who claimed to be an angel. Never did he imagine Paradise would look like it did. Never did he imagine he would meet who he did. Never did he guess that his life would be so dramatically changed by that meeting. And yet even such a meeting as that could not heal the sorrow he still harboured in his soul. He said nothing as he got up, and the couple assumed the moisture around his eyes was caused by the drink. Once he had left, the young man at the table took the glass and swigged back the contents. 'A wee gift from the angels of heaven,' he said laughingly to his girlfriend.

CHAPTER 15

Soon after they left the pub, Douglas made it clear that he wanted to walk back on his own. Dorchadas stood for a while and watched his English friend career along the lamplit pavement. Things had not gone to plan. He had done so well recently helping several humans who had got themselves into fixes, but this one was difficult. The hurt and the hatred had delved so very deep into his soul. Had he been hurt just too much? No, no-one was beyond the healing. Dorchadas made his way back to his lodgings, and battled with the inner doubts that were seriously questioning whether he had done more harm than good. The last thing he wanted, was to hurt this human that he had come to greatly love, despite only knowing him such a short time. Oh, life had been so much easier when he was an angel. At least until the terrible moment...

As Douglas made his unsteady way back, he felt the need to wretch and was horrified to find himself turning into an unlit alley and emptying the contents of his stomach. He felt appalled - how often he had been critical, even in his sermons, about drunkenness, and here he was being revolting because of alcohol. But he also knew it was not just the alcohol. Meeting Kevin had churned his stomach. He wanted to understand the mind of the terrorist, and yet when Kevin started to tell his story, he couldn't take it. There could be no excuses, no reasons, no rational explanation for acts of such hideous villainy. He did not want to meet any redeemed terrorists. Such people would want to be forgiven, even have reason to be forgiven, and this was something that Douglas could never do. He could never let them off the hook.

Elsie O'Connell heard her front door shut loudly, and turned over in her cosy bed. She recognised the sounds of an inebriated guest, but at least he was back, and on his own, which comforted her religious sensibilities. All her guests were in now, so she could go off to sleep, and she speedily slipped into a world of welcome repose. For Douglas however, his world of sleep was far from peaceful. He still felt sick and woke a couple of times and wretched his way to the bathroom each time feeling disgusted with himself.

It was just before daybreak that he awoke with a start from a nightmare. The dream had started well, in bright, warm sunshine. He was in a busy place where cars and busses were dropping off and collecting passengers. He made his way to an entrance of an airport. The place was bustling with people and he made his way to the arrivals gate. He was going to collect Saoirse and he felt such excitement. He elbowed his way to the barrier where many were waiting to welcome friends and relatives. There was a large glass door, and there, on the other side of the door, appeared his Saoirse. He leaped like a child and waved frantically. Saoirse however looked lost and disturbed. She saw Douglas and then banged her fist against the glass door which did not open. She was shouting at him. Her distraught face was so clear, and he could see she was shouting out 'help me!' Douglas tried to get over the barrier, but soldiers prevented him. He fought with all his might, but he couldn't get through. He watched helplessly as Saoirse frantically pounded the glass, and he watched in horror as she seemed to be sucked away from the glass door into a shady chasm that lay behind her.

Waking from the nightmare provided no comfort for Douglas. He sat up in his bed, straining to catch his breath. It was as if he was right back in the first days of his grief again. This trip to Ireland had been a terrible mistake. He could take no more.

Though hungover, he moved fast. He grabbed his case from under his bed and stuffed his belongings in it. He showered and dressed. Though it was early, he could hear the sounds of Mrs O'Connell downstairs. He went down and chatted briefly with her and paid his bill. He gave her a note and asked if she could get it to Dorchadas. She said it would be no trouble, and after she watched through her kitchen window his hire car leave the parking bay, she glanced at the note. It simply read, 'Dorch - thanks. you've been kind. But I need to get home. Douglas'. For reasons that quite surprised her, Elsie O'Connell found herself feeling unusual concern for this guest. She quickly told herself off, and bustled into the kitchen to prepare the breakfast for the other guests.

*

Douglas was relieved to discover there was a seat available on the midday flight and it was not long before he was back on English soil. His home, however, felt distinctly unwelcoming. Mavis had not known he was coming back, so she had not put on the heating and the house felt cold and damp. He made a black coffee and sat in his front lounge in front of a gas fire that hissed out some welcome warmth at him. A beam of autumn sunlight was making its way through the glass, casting a narrow rectangle of light across the floor. He sipped at his coffee and studied the bright shape that was silently inching towards him.

Ireland now seemed so far away. Did he really go drinking in the pubs with a half-mad Irishman? He chuckled to himself as he thought of Dorchadas' spinning on the roundabout. Mrs O'Connell had probably got Douglas' note to him by now. He wondered what he made of it. For a few moments he found himself missing him. But it had all become too complicated - too many memories were erupting and disturbing him. His journal lay on his lap - he wanted to write, but how to write about such things? After a few moments he attempted to gather his thoughts.

Journal 12 October.   England
I'm back. Don't really want to write about it. Felt rather ambushed by Dorch. Not sure he meant it, but he introduced me to Kath's son Kevin, who turned out to be an ex IRA captain. Of all things! The last person I wanted to meet was a terrorist who had merrily gunned down innocent people in his youth. Actually I don't think Dorch planned this - was just bad luck. But chatting to Kevin brought back far too many memories. My stammer returned which was embarrassing. And I got pissed. Had terrible dream - can't bring myself to write about it. Another dream in which I failed to help my Saoirse. Awful guilt. And such hatred for the assassin. Funny how it no longer bothers me that I don't pray. Bit of a relief in a way. But also makes me feel lonely. Anyway, here I am back home. Not sure what I'll do now.

*

Douglas put the journal and pen down on his lap and breathed in deeply. He settled back in the armchair. There was nothing much to say, really. No profound thoughts, just a sense of nothingness. He closed his eyes and, in contrast to the previous night, he fell into a tranquil sleep. He was awoken by his journal falling to the floor and he found himself bathed in sunlight. He blinked and picked up his journal, and taking a sip of cold coffee, he read through the past couple of days. After reading it, he put it down on a side table, and sighed a very deep sigh. Everything felt stationary. His life seemed to have come to a standstill. He wasn't sure if he was comforted or disturbed by the thought that if he just stayed here for days, probably no-one would know or care where or how he was.

124

But he was wrong, because he was startled out of his rumination by a loud knocking at the front door. 'Is that you, Douglas?' came a muffled voice through the letter box, followed by another burst of knocking. 'Looks like you're back. Just checking you're alright.' Douglas recognised the voice and got up from his chair. The voice belonged to faithful old Mavis.

He opened the door and Mavis shuffled in, her arms full of bread, milk and other bits of groceries. 'I'm so pleased to see you, Douglas. I thought you were still in Ireland, but then I noticed your car in the drive, so I've been out to the shops. Thought you might need these. Oh my, you do look thin, son.'

'Thanks Mavis,' said Douglas, taking the various bits of groceries off her and putting them on the kitchen table. He made two cups of tea and they sat at the table. Douglas filled her in on some of his experiences in Ireland, being careful not to sound too weird, thus sparing her the stories of encounters with biblical characters. He was very keen that she should not start doubting his mental state of mind.

'And how are things here, Mavis?' he asked, nibbling at one of the rich tea biscuits she had brought.

'Oh, you know, much the same, much the same,' she said, slurping her tea. 'Have you been into your study yet, Douglas?'

Douglas had not been in, so Mavis continued, 'Well, I left you a note there. The bishop has been trying to contact you, you see. She wants to meet with you. I was here when her secretary phoned wanting to book a meeting with you. I mean, it's not really my business as the wardens are in charge of things, but it's just that she phoned while I was here, so I took the message and said I'd leave a note on your desk.

'I see,' said Douglas, 'When is it that she wants to see me?'

'Well, the first time she offered is Monday at 8.10am,' said Mavis, 'but I don't suppose...'

'Typical,' said Douglas with a smile. "Not 8am or 8.15, but 8.10. I'm surprised it wasn't 8.07.'

'Well I've never met the dear lady, but they say she does seem a bit stern like. But a nice lady, Douglas, a nice lady, I'm sure.'

'Yes, Ok Mavis. I'll go and see her on Monday then.' It was not a meeting he would look forward to. The wardens had probably already been on to her, and almost certainly Gerald had - he was Chair of the Diocesan Board of Finance and on the Bishop's Council and was always saying how well he knew her. By now she probably held a very dim view of the Vicar of St.Philip's. He had no energy to change any of those views and it was more with a sense of resolution rather than anxiety that he phoned the bishop's office and left a message confirming the meeting.

After Mavis left, Douglas ordered a Thai takeaway, watched some TV with a few beers, and went to bed early. Even now, two years on, he found it difficult to clamber into the bed which should have been welcoming two of them, not one. However, he soon drifted off to sleep and awoke the next morning somewhat refreshed. He decided that after breakfast he would drive out to the Peak District - he did not want to spend too long in the Vicarage in case some well-meaning or not-so-well-meaning people decided to call on him. As it turned out, he should have made his escape sooner.

CHAPTER 16

As Douglas was brushing his teeth after breakfast and looking forward to a day of peace and quiet, he heard the doorbell. He assumed it was Mavis on her way to church, so he went down stairs and breezily opened the door, only to discover, to his dismay, the two wardens and Gerald Bentley.

'Excuse us, Douglas,' said Glenda, who was wearing her Sunday best, 'but we noticed you were back and we thought we would pop in for a few minutes before we go to church.' She smiled an unconvincing smile.

Her co-warden, Brian stood behind her with his hands in his pockets looking at the dead heads of the rose bush that was climbing up the wall next to the front door. 'These could do with a prune, Doug,' he said. 'Let me know if you want to borrow my secateurs - they're brilliant. Got them off eBay last month. They've done a great job on my roses.' His face supported the grin that seemed to be an almost permanent fixture.

Before Douglas had a chance to say anything, Gerald pushed in front of Glenda, saying 'We've not come to discuss roses, have we Brian? Now we won't take much of your time, Douglas, but we do need a conversation. May we come in?' Before Douglas could answer, Gerald was in the hallway, with Glenda and Brian following. As they entered the lounge, he said to Glenda in a hushed tone, yet one that Douglas could hear, 'Let me do the talking.'

Douglas invited the three of them to sit and offered them a coffee which they declined. He made an attempt at clearing the beer bottles and wrappings from his takeaway. He was very aware what a poor impression such refuse would make on his visitors. The three sat on the sofa, with Gerald in the middle. Brian started fiddling industriously with the corner of a cushion. 'It's good to see you back, Douglas,' said Gerald, sitting forward as the sofa was a little too tight for three people. 'We understand you have been away. Been far?'

'To Ireland,' said Douglas wearily.

'Oh, *In Dublin's fair city, where the girls are so pretty...,*' chimed up Brian rather tunelessly, leaving go of his work on the cushion and smiling broadly at no-one in particular.

'I hardly think we need a full rendition of Molly Malone, Brian,' said Gerald. 'And you're on churchwarden duty in five minutes, so we have not got long.'

Still smiling, Brian returned his attention to the cushion, which he now placed on his lap. 'Ireland's lovely, though, isn't it? I'm so glad you managed a little holiday,' said Glenda, offering some kindness into the conversation.

'Thank you, Glenda. But can we please move on to discussing important matters?' said Gerald, his impatience growing by the minute. 'Now Douglas, clearly you had a bad turn last Sunday and I regret having to speak up as I did during your sermon.'

'I doubt you regretted it at all,' said Douglas, surprising himself at being so direct to a man who normally overawed him. If nothing else, his few days in Ireland seemed to have made him more assertive. There was very little to lose now.

'Er, indeed,' said Gerald, a little taken aback, yet determined not to be deterred from his path. 'As I say, it was a difficult Sunday for all of us. Indeed, many Sundays have been very difficult in recent weeks. But, let's move on.' He coughed and wriggled further forward so that he was now sitting on the very edge of the sofa. 'It won't surprise you to hear that the Standing Committee had an emergency meeting during the week.'

'No, it doesn't surprise me at all,' said Douglas. He leaned far back in his chair and folded his hands on his stomach and sighed. 'Go on,' he said.

'Well,' continued Gerald, somewhat disturbed by Douglas' nonchalance, yet determined to make his carefully prepared comments. 'At the meeting we had to discuss contingency plans. We obviously are very concerned for you and wish you God's speed as you recover. But clearly, with your... er... how shall we put it? Your current crisis of faith, the Standing Committee felt it was not in the best interests of the church to be led by someone so... shall we say... unsure of their faith. St.Philip's is a strong church and has always prided itself on upholding good orthodox Christian beliefs. Isn't that so?' He looked behind him to left and right to the two wardens appealing for their support.

'Er, yes,' said Glenda.

'Bang on,' said Brian, and then continued, 'Is that carriage clock genuinely antique, Douglas? I was looking at it when we had the bible study here a few months ago. It's a really special one, isn't it?'

He was just about to stand up to go to the mantlepiece, when Gerald seized his arm, pulling him back and saying, 'If we could just leave the appreciation of the Vicar's belongings until after this conversation. May I continue?' Douglas could not help smiling at Brian. He had appointed Brian as warden last year. No-one else was willing to stand, but for some reason Brian's name had been put forward, perhaps because he was always so relentlessly cheerful which provided a happy balance to the mood generally held by the Vicar. Though he was pretty useless as a warden, he did brighten up the meetings with his relentless cheerfulness and in recent months, Douglas had grown to appreciate him. He provided a pleasant contrast to Gerald, whose dominating presence in the church had always felt oppressive to Douglas.

'So,' continued Gerald, '- and forgive me for being so direct, Douglas - we are faced with a crisis in our church. We cannot afford to lose ground. We've lost a lot of people this past year which, apart from anything else, has seriously depleted our finances, as you know. To be blunt about it, there is a general consensus that this decline is not unrelated to your state of mind. We need strong leadership to enable us to recover. And, what's more, we have the Bishop's Five Priorities that we have signed up to, not to mention the expensive tower renovation to manage. So, you see, it is clear to all of us that, in your current state of mind, you are not able to provide the kind of leadership that this church now urgently requires.'

Gerald breathed in deeply, before continuing. 'So, the Standing Committee asked me to speak to the bishop. As it happened there was a Board of Finance meeting on Wednesday evening and so I took the opportunity to speak to the bishop after the meeting and I appraised her of our difficult situation. In the brief conversation that the time afforded us, I was given to understand that she is of the same opinion as myself - er, as the Standing Committee, I should say - that you be encouraged now to formally stand down from being the Vicar. That is - and forgive my bluntness again, but it is important we are clear - we are expecting your resignation, Douglas.'

As Gerald said this, Glenda looked down hard at her fidgeting hands. Brian frowned and looked at Douglas and said, 'Sounds a bit final, Doug, doesn't it? Shall I call for the firing squad, eh?' He laughed a high and rather nervous laugh. Gerald pursed his lips and looked hard at his Vicar, whose ministry at the church, in his opinion, had declined the moment the Irish girl had come on the scene. In his opinion she had been most definitely a bad influence on the man who, up until he met her, had been a reasonably good Vicar.

Douglas felt deeply weary and it would have been so easy to have given in there and then. But he felt a strong determination not to be bullied by Gerald, so he said, 'Thank you, Gerald. You have put your views across with your usual candour. I will give careful consideration to your request, but it would be irresponsible of me to decide such things speedily…'

'Yes, yes,' said Gerald, edging so far forward on the sofa that he was in danger of slipping off it. 'But, with respect, you do need to appreciate that it takes a very long time to get a new Vicar, and we need to be moving on this. You have made clear your faith position and there is no doubt it is no longer compatible with St.Philip's. I would encourage you to put the church first on this occasion and think about what we need now. You don't want to see all the work you put in during your good years go to waste, do you? I can't see…'

'Oh, stop it, Gerald,' said Brian, now patting the cushion that he had placed on his lap. 'Give the poor man a break. I think he's got the message. Let him have some time to have a think about it. We've not all got pots of money like you have, Gerald. The man's got to make a living. We can't just chuck him out on the street, poor bloke, can we? Now, perhaps we could have that coffee, Doug?'

'We are not stopping for coffee,' said Gerald, getting redder in the face by the minute. He always resented it when people referred to his hard-earned wealth.

'Gerald, you need not worry too much,' said Douglas. 'I have an appointment to see the bishop tomorrow. We shall discuss all this then. And yes, be assured I am concerned for the church and I am not quite as selfish as you imagine. Now, you mustn't be late for the service.' He stood up and the other three stood with him. Gerald was quite taken aback by the confidence that had taken hold of the Vicar. With his bearing this kind of attitude, the job of removing him would be harder than he had imagined. 'I hope the service goes well this morning,' said Douglas as they made their way to the front door. 'Do send them my greetings and tell them I am all right.'

Gerald said nothing as he passed through the front door. Glenda put her shaky hand on Douglas' arm and said, 'Thank you, Douglas, for being so understanding,' and followed Gerald.

Brian smiled broadly and nodded at Douglas and then sang, '*She was a fishmonger, and sure was no wonder, so were her father and mother before...*'. Douglas chuckled as he heard Brian singing his way out of the house, and heard Gerald's irritated rebuke that brought it to an abrupt halt. After they had departed he decided he needed to get out of the Vicarage quickly before anyone else came knocking at the door, and he was soon on his way driving out into the Dark Peak.

He spent the rest of the day walking along Stanage Edge and returned to his Vicarage as the autumn night was drawing in. Thankfully there were no other visitors to the Vicarage around the time of Evensong, and he spent the evening in peace in front of the TV and then went to bed early, in preparation for his visit to the bishop in the morning.

*

Douglas drove up the tree-lined drive to the elegant home of the bishop. The scholarly-looking chaplain welcomed Douglas at the door and told him to wait in a small room, next to the bishop's study. At 8.10 precisely Bishop Pauline appeared in the doorway, and said, 'Thanks for coming, Douglas. This way.' She led him into her front room, where two antique and upright chairs were strategically placed either side of the fireplace, which housed a couple of smouldering logs. The intention was to convey an impression of comfort and informality, but somehow it all looked to Douglas' eye rather artificial, and he was feeling far from comfortable.

The bishop sat her smart and slim figure on the chair opposite Douglas and studied her iPad. She tapped on it a few times and read something on it saying 'Mm' as she read it. She then brushed her greying hair behind her ear, took her glasses off her nose and looked briefly at Douglas and then returned her glasses and looked back to her iPad saying 'It may not surprise you to learn, Douglas, that I have had an email from your wardens and one or two others.' She looked back up at Douglas, removing her glasses once again. Douglas could see she was also a little nervous.

'Er, no, it doesn't surprise me, Bishop.'

The bishop shuffled in her seat and then put on what some clergy called her 'sweet face', and said, 'I do realise Douglas that this has been a difficult time for you, and I do hope you appreciate our concern for you. But I think in this meeting we need to get down to some practicalities.'

'Yes, Bishop.' Douglas braced himself for the worst.

Her sweet face was soon replaced by her business face, which was rather less sweet. 'This email is questioning your competency and they are talking about a pastoral breakdown.' She put the iPad on the table beside her, crossed her legs and said, 'It very much sounds to me Douglas that they want to get rid of you.'

'Yes, I think they probably do,' said Douglas. He had no energy to fight this one, and he decided to come clean with his bishop. 'Bishop Pauline, I'm so sorry about this, but I'm going to be honest with you. As you know, the loss of Saoirse has hit me very, very hard. So hard in fact, that I'm afraid I have now lost my faith, and therefore there is obviously no use in my carrying on. You can't have an unbelieving priest serving in your diocese. So, to make life easier for you and everyone, I offer my resignation.' He felt a great sense of relief as he said this, and he leaned back in his chair, letting his arms fall to his side, and he took a deep breath, enjoying the heady scent of lilies that stood tall and radiant in the window.

Bishop Pauline uncrossed her legs, and to Douglas' great surprise, she leaned forward and took Douglas' hand. He looked up and was astonished to see moisture in her eyes. 'I'm so sorry Douglas. I…. I too lost my way once, and it wasn't easy finding my way back.' She released his hand but continued to look most kindly at him. 'May I… Can I suggest you don't offer your resignation just yet? I think it is always good to have time to think. What I would like you to do is to take a three-month break, and then, towards the end of that time, come back and see me. It will be like a sabbatical - you are probably due one anyway. I'll sort out your wardens and Gerald. He won't be pleased of course, but I'm learning how to manage him.' She smiled and leaned back in her chair, once again marshalling a stray lock of hair and securing it behind her ear.

Douglas was silent for a few moments. He was feeling bad about all the times he had judged this bishop and spoken about her behind her back. It would not be the last time that he would see that behind the rather stiff, formal business-like exterior, there resided a fellow human who knew something of the trials and tribulations of parish life. Indeed, of what it was to be human.

'Thank you, Pauline,' he said, rather surprising himself that he had used her Christian name. 'I'm really happy to take your advice. It's so kind of you to do this. I really am sorry to be one of your problems.'

The bishop smiled warmly and said, 'Douglas, I have never seen you as one of my problems, and I never will.' She then replaced her spectacles, stood up and was back into her formal self again as she straightened her suit jacket.

'I'll ask Janet to get on to HR and your leave will be sorted in the next couple of days. Do contact me at any time if you need to.' They shook hands and as Douglas drove away from the bishop's house, he chuckled as he thought of how angry Gerald would be to get this news. He was always pleased when Gerald did not get his own way, as he so often did. And as he drove through the Sheffield streets, Douglas felt a welcome sense of contentment. Three months felt good and they felt spacious. Quite what he would do with the time was hard to say. He certainly could not stay in the Vicarage. So, should he - could he - return to Ireland? He was far from sure.

*

On returning home Douglas was still wondering how to use his time, when he decided to check out his emails. He was somewhat surprised to see one entitled 'Missing you' from an email address which was *dorchadas@cherubim.com*. It read:

> Hello there, Douglas. I do hope your trip home went OK and you are settling back into life in England. Not sure how you'll manage without the Guinness or Jameson's mind!
>
> Seriously Doug, I feel I blew it the other night and I just want to offer you my apologies. I should have known it would be tough for you to meet Kevin, and I should have made sure you didn't have to meet the fella. God knows, I can be an idiot at times. You wouldn't think it, would you? Angels are supposed to be pretty perfect, but I can assure you that once we step into human skin, we pick up all kinds of frailties. Not blaming humans, mind you - it's just a bit confusing for us. And I know, you don't think I'm an angel, so you can disregard this last bit. Just put it down to me being a foolish old man, then.

133

The point is, I really enjoyed meeting you and learned so much from you. I do hope we can meet up again. I'll be in these parts for a few weeks, so maybe you might be back again. You'll know where to find me if you do.

I do hope you come back, Douglas. I hope you can forgive me. And never lose track of the benignant power. Remember another of that sweet girl's poem, Doug. The last she wrote:

No coward soul is mine,
No trembler in the world's storm-troubled sphere:
I see Heaven's glories shine,
And faith shines equal, arming me from fear.

I know, lad. You're telling me your faith's shot to pieces, so there's nothing too shiny about it. But Emily Brontë had her doubts too, you know. I think your turn will come, Doug, to see a touch of heaven-shining glory. And yours is no coward soul - no way. I love your courage - I can see it, even if you can't.

Now I won't witter on like I usually do. I shan't write again - not unless you want me to. I don't want to be a bother to you.

Take care and much love - and thanks again.

your friend, Dorchadas

Douglas stared at the computer screen for quite a while. He had felt angry with Dorchadas for introducing him to Kevin but this email touched him as he read it several times. He chuckled at the humour of it. He also felt stirred by the Brontë poem. Did Dorch know it was one of his favourites? He felt he had been such a coward in recent months, and yet here was Dorchadas saying that he saw courage in Douglas? Was he just flattering? No, that was not Dorchadas' way. It would take courage to return to Dingle. Did he have enough? He read the words again and smiled. It really seemed that Dorch was missing him. No-one missed him these days, and so the experience was one to be treasured. And Dorchadas had said that Douglas might be able to help him. Could that honestly be possible?

So, there it was. He now had to choose: should he return to Ireland and see Dorchadas again who had a curious knack of being both disturbing and comforting? He slowly pushed back his chair, left the computer and went to his drinks shelf in the kitchen, that turned out to be disappointingly empty. However, there was a quarter bottle of *Highland Park*, so he carefully poured himself a good measure, popped in his cube of ice, and returned to his computer. For the best part of an hour he sat almost immobile, save for the occasional sips from his glass. As he finally drained the last drops, he knew what he must do, and he started typing his emails.

As Gregory of Nyssa observed
in his reflections on the Song of Songs,
the bride is most joyously met by the bridegroom
in the darkest part of the night -
at that very point of uncanny, shuddering feeling,
when she does not know who or what is there,
when she expects terror,
but suddenly breaks into the joy of recognition and love.

Belden C Lane
The Solace of Fierce Landscapes

CHAPTER 17

After only a few days home, Douglas was on his way back to Ireland. He had booked a flight easily, and he had phoned Elsie O'Connor who was pleased to report that his room had not been let out to anyone else. Despite a few nagging doubts and fears, he instinctively felt there was more for him in this land than back in the UK. He increasingly disliked the thought of a sudden breaking of the friendship with Dorchadas, and Dorch was clearly sorry for the Kevin meeting, so Douglas felt he could trust him again. Further, the meeting with bishop Pauline had been surprisingly healing for Douglas. Despite his confession to her of his loss of faith, she still respected him, and showed a genuine understanding of how he was. It felt like he was now not so much running away, but was being obedient to his bishop by taking some time off work. Despite the wardens, Gerald and most of the church viewing this as an annoying delay to their getting on and finding another Vicar, the bishop was in the end the one in charge, and Douglas was happy to rest in her wisdom and authority.

So it was a rather more confident Douglas that made his way out of the arrival hall at Cork Airport. He had intended to go straight to the hire car park, but he was arrested by a shout of 'Douglas, lad! Over here with you, now!' He looked across the road, and there was Kath waving from the window of an old pick-up truck that was parked directly under a sign that read "Strictly No Parking". 'Put your case in the back Doug, it's not going to rain,' she called, and Doug dutifully did as commanded and climbed into the passenger seat.

He left his window open as the cab was full of smoke. 'Look, I hope you don't mind me collecting you, son, but Elsie told me you were on your way back, and I thought it was the least I could do,' she said above the roar of the revving diesel engine.

'Thanks so much Kath - that's very kind of you.'

'Oh, no - think nothing of it, Doug. It's smashing to have you back again,' she said, and turned and smacked Douglas on the knee and said something in Gaelic. 'Now the thing is, Doug, I'm going to ask for your help with something. You can say "no", but before you do, can we call in at the Starbucks and I can just fill you in on something. The coffee's shocking at Starbucks - they don't know how to make proper coffee, they don't. But you can always have the tea.'

Douglas felt slightly apprehensive and wondered if he was being dragooned into another one of Dorchadas' ventures, until Kath said, 'Dorch doesn't know you're coming yet. We've not seen him for a day or two, but someone said he was going to be at *The Angels Rest* tonight. He'll be mighty pleased to see you, he will. He's missed you a hell of a lot. Strange, really as he only knew you a couple of days. But, he's like that is Dorch.' Kath carried on filling Doug in on local news as she navigated her way somewhat erratically away from the airport until they came to a roadside Starbucks, and they drew in.

'Let me get this Douglas. Don't suppose you'll want the coffee?'

'Actually, I'd really like a cappuccino please, Kath.'

'Oh, well, please yourself,' she said, and proceeded to order a cappuccino and a tea, and a couple of brownies.

'I know, I know,' she said as she squeezed her ample form on to the bench chair, tossing the brownies on the table, 'but I need the energy if I'm to drive you back safely. If I can't have me smokes, I'll take the brownies.'

'Thanks,' said Douglas, who was grateful for a bit of sustenance as he had missed breakfast.

'Well, now Douglas, I really appreciated the way you listened to my horror story in my caf the other day. You're a grand listener, you are. I'd not told that story for a long time. It really helped to get it off my chest. But that night as I had my last smoke of the day in bed, I thought about them two priests - Peter and the English nightmare of a priest. I don't know what became of Peter, poor soul. But Dorch told me he was happy, and I was so glad to hear that.'

'Well, horrible though it all was, it looks like your life recovered, Kath,' said Douglas sipping at the frothy cup in front of him.

'Aye, that it did. Not too long after it all happened, I met Kevin, a lad from up the coast, and we were soon married. He's passed away now, God rest his soul, but he was a good man was my Kevin. He was a fisherman and worked bloody hard on the boats he did. He was out in all weathers. That's what wore him down - the rough weather. And with a little help from the booze, the truth be told. But he was kindly - never laid a hand on me and a good pa to our lad, Kevin. It was the tradition in his family - the men are called Kevin going back centuries. But it's not that I need your help with.'

Here Kath lowered her voice and leaned towards Douglas in a confidential way. 'The English priest, Douglas, is the Venerable Cecil Oakenham. Don't suppose you have heard of him, have you?'

'No, I haven't,' said Douglas as he sipped his welcome cappuccino.

'Well, I have discovered he's still alive. Must be pushing 90 now I should think. And I'm told he's poorly. The point is, Doug, by curious coincidence, Elsie heard someone talk of him yesterday and to cut the long story short, I now know where he is.'

'Is he still in Ireland?' asked Douglas

'Oh, aye. He never left. Became an Archdeacon of somewhere or other. But he's now here - just down the road. In a little place called Ballincollig. Now Doug, I know this is asking a hell of a lot of you, but because you are an Anglican priest and English and that, you could be the one to help me.' Here Kath started to look awkward and started to shuffle in her seat. She was clutching tight her half-consumed brownie. Her large face reddened. 'God, I wish we could smoke in here. Still I've got this instead.' She bit into her brownie and continued with her mouth half full. 'The thing is Douglas, I believe I must meet with him before he dies. I think it would help me get this bitterness out of my guts. I've hated him all my life, sure I have. It's been a poison in me. I need to see him to help rid me of it. I want him to apologise to me, Douglas. I want him to know how badly he hurt me.' Kath breathed deeply and added, 'I just don't want to be the bloody victim in this - I need to... to just tell him. That's all. Doesn't actually matter what he says. He can't hurt me any more.' She stuffed the last part of her brownie in her mouth and chomped at it, looking at Douglas, waiting for his answer.

Douglas felt very taken aback by this request. He was feeling very fragile as it was, and to be the broker of this delicate conversation felt to be way beyond his mood or abilities. However, as he looked at Kath covered in Brownie crumbs, he felt a powerful compassion for her and, despite the riskiness of it, he found himself saying, 'No time like the present, Kath. Let's be on our way.'

Kath slurped down the remains of her tea, thumped her mug on the table and said, 'Oh God, Douglas you're a saint. I can't thank you enough.'

*

The St.Bride's Senior Care Home was a relatively modern building, set back from the road with a small pleasant orchard at the front. Kath drove her truck up the gravel drive and parked in the visitor's car park. 'Doug, would you do the talking please? Just at the start?' Kath asked. Douglas nervously agreed as they entered the vestibule and were met by a young nurse.

'Hello,' said Douglas with surprising authority, 'My name is Revd Douglas Romer and we have come to visit the Venerable Cecil Oakenham.'

'Oh, aye. You've come to see Cecil, have you?' said the nurse, looking a little surprised. 'Well you have chosen a good day as he's not had a bad morning. I think he is still in his room. Is he expecting you?'

'No - we are actually old friends,' lied Douglas, 'and it would be rather lovely to give him a little surprise.' Kath, who was standing behind Douglas, wheezed loudly.

'Oh, of course. He gets very few visitors actually.' The nurse lowered her voice, 'Which is not surprising as, to be honest with you, he's not the most friendly of gentlemen, if you get my meaning. Do come this way.'

The three walked down a long corridor and came to a door. The nurse knocked loudly and a gruff voice from within cried 'Come'. She opened the door, ushered in Kath and Douglas and said, 'Visitors Cecil - be nice to them please.' And with that she smiled at them and left.

'Who are you?' said the thin, elderly man who was sitting in his dressing gown at a chair by his bed, holding a newspaper in one hand and a magnifying glass in the other. He peered at the two visitors. 'I don't recognise either of you. Where are you from?'

'My name is Revd Douglas Romer...'

'No clerical collar - why not?'

Douglas ignored the rebuke and said, 'And this is Mrs Kathleen Griffin. I have brought her here, because you met many years ago and she has something she wishes to talk to you about.'

The former Archdeacon looked concerned and frowned a deep frown at Kath, leaning forward as if to get a closer view of her. He placed his newspaper and magnifying glass carefully on a table beside him and sat back in his chair. There was only one chair for a visitor and Douglas offered it to Kath who sat down. Douglas was about to sit on the bed, when the Venerable Oakenham abruptly commanded, 'Not on the bed. You'll have to stand.' Douglas dutifully stood, staying near to Kath.

'So, who are you? And what have you to say to me?' enquired the elderly gentleman, peering hard at Kath. 'I don't recognise you at all.'

Kath took a deep breath and started, 'I don't expect you to remember me, but I remember you. You were once a Catholic priest…'

'Oh, a very long time ago. I'm nearly 90 now and don't remember much about that time in my life. It's no good going back to those days.'

'Well I do remember them, sir,' said Kath. 'I was a young girl at the time and I had an affair with a young priest whose Christian name was Peter.'

The elderly man pushed his chin forward and clasped his brittle hands in front of him. 'Mm… I vaguely remember. He was a wayward priest, as I recall…. In the Dingle area, wasn't he?'

'No,' said Kath now with surprising confidence, 'No, he was not wayward, sir. He was a wonderful priest. We loved each other and we slept together. It was wrong, but both of us were young people who had been terribly treated in our lives and desperately needed love. We both needed help badly, but instead what we got, sir, was brutal punishment from the family, the community and from the church.'

'Well, well,' said the Archdeacon, pulling himself up in his chair. 'You will appreciate, madam, there are procedures if you are about to make a complaint.'

'With respect, Mr Oakenham, stuff your bloody procedures. What have procedures got to do with the love of God which you are supposed to proclaim through your life and witness?'

'Procedures are extremely important and I strongly suggest…' but Kath, who was getting redder in the face by the moment, would not let him continue.

'If you will let me finish,' she continued with a stern voice and steely stare. 'You were the priest they called from Tralee to "pastorally assist" with our problem. Can you remember this now, sir?'

Oakenham was frowning hard. 'Madam, you are talking about events such a long time ago. I… have a vague recollection of something like that…'

'My recollection is not vague, sir,' said Kath. 'Oh, not vague at all. Let me remind you exactly what happened when you came to our parish.' As Kath stared at the elderly and frail man now sitting upright in his chair, she was remembering him more and more. She remembered very clearly the tall, thin man with an angular jaw, and black hair, greased and brushed back leaving a high, shiny forehead. He had a small mouth and thin lips. It was disorientating to see this ancient version of the man who had caused her such terror all those years ago. But there was no terror now. A power was alive in her as she was finally able to have her say to a man who had forbidden her to talk when he first met her as a terrified teenager.

'You came to my house,' she continued calmly, but very clearly. 'You sat me in the chair and stood over me - you and my ma, standing there and pointing at me.' She thrust forth her finger as she continued. 'You forbad me to see Peter. And do you know what, Reverend Oakenham, without allowing me to offer one word in my defence, you told me I was excommunicated. You told me I had brought the church into disrepute. Worst of all, Father Cecil, as they called you in them days, without a shred of evidence, you claimed I had seduced Peter that I therefore was worse than a harlot. Yes, you did, sir and I'll tell you what you said next...'

'If I may sincerely object, this is utter...'

'Let her finish,' called out Douglas, surprising himself with the anger he felt on Kath's behalf. Oakenham looked furiously at Douglas as Kath continued.

'Yes, I will finish,' she said. She lifted herself out of the chair and stood in front of the frail old man who leaned back in his chair. 'Because you then said something else. And bear in mind this was you coming to "pastorally assist". Well tell me this sir, what was so bloody pastoral about you then telling me that I was no better than Jezebel of the bible and for seducing one of your best priests I should be dead in the street with the dogs licking up my blood. Oh, yes, sir, I remember it all right. I remember it word for bloody word I do. I remember every word of yours shuddering into my poor soul. And you made out you were all official and holy and that. But, Mr Oakenham, and I remember this very clearly, I do, it was not long after that terrible day that you, all of a sudden, changed to a Protestant. Gave up the Catholic faith so you did. Oh yes, I read about it in the papers I surely did, how you said it was God's call on your life. And then, lo and behold, not long after that what did I read? I read that you had got yourself married.'

'Madam, it was all completely proper. I converted due to my conscience...' cried Oakenham, visibly shaken now by the clarity of Kath's recollections.

'Oh, proper was it now? Proper? And tell me Mr Oakenham, was it proper to get married to the very woman who the whole of Tralee knew to be the lass with whom you were affairing with in the days when you were the priest there. Oh, yes, I know all about that, sir. Yes, I certainly do. And if I remember rightly she had a little baby who came a little soon after that hurried wedding, did he not?'

'I must protest in the strongest possible terms...' The elderly man, crimson with desperation and anger now gripped the arms of his chair and attempted to stand without success.

'No, you mustn't protest,' said Kath, now with her hands planted firmly on her hips. 'Yes, this is what I have wanted all my life - to be here, to be standing over you, to see you cowering, you being humiliated. How does it feel, eh? Well, let me tell you something else, Archdeacon bloody Oakenham, I was *not* guilty, but you are as guilty as hell. You are guilty of ruining a young girl's life, and guilty of defrocking one of the best priests in Ireland.'

Douglas was now getting worried, and he came near to Kath and pulled at her sleeve, saying 'Kath, Kath...'

'It's all right Douglas, I'm not going to harm him.' And she stepped back and said, 'I just want to know, Mr Oakenham sir, do you have any regrets about how you handled that pastoral case?'

'Absolutely not!', said the old man, leaning forward in his chair. 'As I told you, I followed the correct procedures and did exactly what was right. And, if I may say so, the way you are behaving now confirms I did the right thing to speak so severely to you. You were out of control then, and you are out of control now. Young women are prone to be flirtatious, especially with God's servants. They.... they wear dresses that reveal everything!' His elderly, creased face reddened alarmingly. 'They might as well walk around naked - look at them these days. And you were no better - you seduced a priest, madam! You dressed and behaved like a harlot. You are the one who should be apologising.'

Kath breathed in deeply and said, 'No sir, I am not.' She turned as if to leave the room, but then checked herself and said, 'Tell me this, sir. Do you believe in purgatory? Because if you do, then I should fear it if I were you, with all your goddamn might, because when you get there and you tell God and his angels you were a shepherd of the sheep of God, they will tell you that the shattered and broken lives of the girls you so cruelly humiliated and cast out as 'harlots' were perhaps the very sheep you should have been tending. I don't think them holy angels will be too impressed with that, Mr Oakenham. No, I don't! Come on Douglas, I've had enough.' She grabbed hold of Douglas' arm and marched him out of the room, slamming the door behind her. As they left, they heard the old man calling out, 'You spiteful little bitch - I'll be making a complaint about this, you wait and see...'

'Complaint, my arse!' said Kath as she marched up the corridor, lighting a cigarette as she did so, and brushing off several flustered nurses who in vain tried to stop her. She opened the exit doors with a crash that shook the building and strode out into the car park. She turned and looked at the astonished Douglas and called out, 'My God, that felt good Douglas! That felt bloody good!' and shrieked with laughter, before throwing her cigarette on the tarmac and falling on Douglas' shoulder, dissolving into shuddering sobs. Douglas gently stroked her head and when she was ready, he led her to her truck and they drove off to Dingle in a very full and thoughtful silence.

As they drove up over the Connor pass in evening sunshine, Kath was ready to talk. 'Douglas, I want to thank you for that - it meant the world to me, but I hope to God it wasn't awful for you, son. It must have been a terrible thing to witness. I mean, I was hardly lady-like, was I now? Don't suppose you have that kind of behaviour in England, do you?' She wheezed a little laugh.

'No, no. It wasn't awful or terrible. Kath, it was stunning!' and he smiled at the driver of the truck, because he knew he had witnessed a very courageous woman who had finally let go of a poison that had been in her system close on 50 years.

'I'm sad, though Doug,' she said as she navigated her way around the tricky twists and turns on the road to the summit unusually slowly by her standards. 'I suppose I had hoped that he might have changed, didn't you? But I could see from the moment we entered the room that he hadn't changed a bit. I was hoping to see him different - in his heart, I mean. But no. He was as cruel and bitter as when I first encountered him. I guess some people just want to keep hold of their bitterness. That makes me grieve, Doug, that sure makes me grieve. I didn't want to live with mine any longer. I'd had my fill of it. I had to find a way to rid me of it, and I did. Today I got shot of it, the saints be praised. I couldn't have done it without you, Douglas. I shall always be grateful, son. Always.'

They reached the summit of the Connor pass just as the sun broke through the clouds, bathing the peninsula in gentle autumn sunshine. Kath pulled into the parking area and they both climbed out of the truck to admire the scene. They gazed down on the bay of Dingle.

'Douglas, love,' said Kath, 'I don't rightly know what happened there in that room, and God knows I didn't exactly behave myself and I certainly wasn't holy! But I can tell you one thing: after I left and I stood in that carpark sobbing like a babe on your shoulder, I knew exactly why I was sobbing. Do you know why I was sobbing? It was because for the first time in many, many years, I felt a sense of peace, Doug. *Real* peace. And, I don't know how this can be, but the fact is that I felt, at long last, at peace with God. It's like... well, I don't know, Doug. I'm probably imagining it all, but it felt like God was pleased with what I said. Doesn't make sense, does it? Cussing and swearing at that old man. I mean the old man was a priest for God's sakes. How could God be impressed by all that stuff? But I actually think he was.'

She paused for a moment, then continued, 'But listen to me, Douglas. A sworn atheist talking like this! Whatever next! Now don't go telling Dorch about this for God's sake. He'll try taking the credit for it!' She wheezed her infectious laughter again. She pulled out her packet of cigarettes and then thought better of it. 'No... It's fresh air I need now,' she said and closed her eyes and breathed the cool Atlantic breeze deep into her lungs, and into her soul.

Douglas stood in the welcome sunlight listening to Kath with both delight and amazement. Kath was right, it all made little sense. But standing there in that afternoon light, Douglas felt he had witnessed a most surprising and remarkable redemption. His eye turned from Kath and followed the contours of the hills, down to the bay, over the waters, on to the hills and fields of Kerry and up to the soft clouds gliding gently in the blue Irish sky. For the first time in quite a while he felt it could be possible that he too one day might find a place of peace. It was a precious calm he experienced on that mountain that afternoon. But it would turn out to be the calm before the storm.

CHAPTER 18

'I can't tell you how good it is to see you again!', said Dorchadas and hugged Douglas so hard that Douglas feared for his ribs.

'Yes, and I have missed you, you old sod,' said Douglas laughing.

'Och, you trying to rouse an angel's anger by your bad language, are you? Well, as penance you can buy the drinks, that you can,' said Dorchadas smiling broadly, as he slipped his tall frame into a former church pew that served as one of the many forms of seating in *The Angel's Rest*.

'So how was England?' he asked, as Douglas returned with two full glasses that had taken an age to fill at the busy bar.

'Lonely. Sláinte,' said Douglas clinking his glass with Dorchadas'. 'But I actually had a very good meeting with my bishop, and she has given me three month's paid leave, so the world's my oyster, Dorch.'

'Well, it always is your oyster, son! It is good to have you back, and once again I'm sorry...'

'No,' interrupted Douglas holding up his hand, 'there really is no need, Dorch. I know you did not plot that meeting with Kevin, and to be honest, I think some good may come of it all. To be fair, I behaved pretty badly and I have been a bit worried about what Kevin made of it all, but Kath has put my mind at rest.'

'Oh, you met with Kath already have you?' asked Dorchadas.

'Yes, she picked me up from the Airport. You not heard?'

'What in that battle bus of hers? My heaven, Douglas, I'm glad to see you alive!' and Dorchadas chuckled and clinked his glass to Douglas' again. 'She didn't bring you over the Connor Pass in that thing, did she?'

'Oh yes, she did. But she not only picked me up, Dorch, but she took me to meet someone. But she told me not to tell you, else you'd take credit for it!'

Dorchadas laughed and said, 'Oh, that's Kath. She won't mind you telling me. She tells me everything. And I promise not to take the credit, sure I won't!'

So, Douglas recounted the story of the meeting with the former Archdeacon. Dorchadas listened intently, his face contorting in sorrow at the bitterness of the old man, but then lighting up at the news of Kath's new freedom. Both men were then quiet for a time, and then Dorchadas said, 'Douglas, perhaps we are starting to get closer to the heart of the problem here. Take a look at the world he has placed you in. Around every corner there are shafts of dazzling light if only you open your eyes to see them: the carefree smile of a wee kiddie; the luminous beauty of a dragonfly wing; the slender arc of the moon in a midnight sky; the matchless gift of a new day. But how many see such things? I mean, *really* see them?'

Before Douglas could comment, Dorchadas continued, 'Your man the Archdeacon, now. I mean, at some point he chose a lifeless path, did he not? And look where it has led him. it's a dark path - not the beautiful dark of mystery, but the wretched darkness of lostness and bitterness, and that's a cruel darkness, sure it is.' He paused for a moment as a group of young people shuffled past them, all laughing hysterically.

Douglas watched them with amusement, then Dorchadas grasped his arm and continued, 'The real pain is knowing how He saw His world when He walked this earth with us in those beautiful days. Course, I knew a little of what He saw, but He saw it all with even brighter eyes than those of us angels. I mean, He *really* saw this world, Doug. Can you imagine what it was like for Him? Think of Him in Galilee in the springtime - He loved that land, He did. But when He wandered through an olive grove with his friends, He didn't just see just a few old gnarly olive trees. When He saw an olive tree, He saw the radiance of Paradise shining through it, and you could see the delight on His teary face as He stroked the gnarled wood with his fingers. As far as He was concerned the very earth beneath His feet blazed with glory and appeared to Him as sparkling gold dust.

'Each morning he saw the world as if he were Adam taking his first steps in the Garden of Eden. And not just seeing, but the way He listened to the birds and smelt the fragrance of the flowers. Even in the dark, when He could not see, He *felt,* and such feeling caused him to see things that no daylight eye could behold. His world was full of wonder. So, imagine how terrible to be in this world, seeing all that there is to see, all the light and glory, but to be among people, some of whom only wanted to live in the dark. He has provided so much light, Doug. And yet some of his beloved humans would rather hanker after the dark.' Dorch took a sip from his glass. 'This is what puzzles me, it sure does.'

Douglas was entranced with this view of a Jesus who daily experienced this world in a way he had only glimpsed occasionally. 'But why, Dorch?' he asked, looking hard at his friend. 'Why do you

147

think that people hanker after the dark, when the light is plainly so much more attractive?'

'It very much depends on how you understand "light",' said an English voice nearby. A stranger had arrived and was standing at the other side of the table from the two men. He was of small stature, clean shaven with greying, close cropped hair and he appeared to be in his mid-sixties. He was wearing a black suit over a black polo neck sweater. He was holding a small glass of lager which he lifted delicately to his thin lips. 'Mind if I join you?' he said as he settled himself into a vacant chair, and placed his lager with great care on the beermat in front of him.

'Oh, I wondered when I would see you again,' said Dorchadas, leaning back in his seat and sighing.

Douglas was completely puzzled. 'Excuse me?' he asked, hoping someone would explain.

'Let me introduce myself,' said the stranger. 'My name is Annas. I believe you have read of me in your so-called gospels, no? How do you do.' He held out a limp, cold hand to Douglas, which Douglas shook with little conviction. So far, the day had gone well, but now Douglas felt very disturbed. It was happening again - he was being hypnotised, or drugged, or something, but one way or another he was being introduced to another character from the Scriptures. And this character was one of the high priests who conspired to hand over Christ for crucifixion. Though at this present moment, Douglas was hard pushed to remember precisely what his role had been.

'Dorchadas - we last met in rather different circumstances, however, it is a pleasure to see you again', said Annas with a very insincere tone. He offered his thin hand to Dorchadas who shook it briefly.

'May I enquire the name of your guest?' he said, looking from Dorchadas to Douglas.

Douglas instinctively began to dislike the man, and answered, 'Reverend Douglas Romer,' for some reason revealing his profession.

'Ah, indeed,' said Annas, again taking a tiny sip from his half pint of lager. 'And I suppose you have also believed the false reports about myself and my son-in-law, the honourable Caiaphas, both of us, of course, highly respected High Priests, yet treated abysmally by historians. Perhaps I can take a little of your time to put matters right. People so easily assume we were the dark and wicked ones, but you do need to know, Revd Romer, that there was much more light in us than the written reports suggest.' Douglas noticed that the eyelid of his left eye closed disconcertingly slowly.

'You see, we were called by God to keep order in Jerusalem at a very delicate time. Most of the local people were uneducated and they could be swayed by any wayward teacher, rabbi or rebel who happened to excite them. Now Pontius Pilate was a very generous Procurator of the people and allowed us to practice our divine worship and religious practices with a great deal of freedom, as long as we kept order. Our God, after all, is a God of order, and is justly angered not just by sin, but by rebellion, by false teaching, and by disrespect of those whom he has called to rule with authority.' Douglas felt he was speaking in a tone of a barrister setting out his case. He was feeling very wary of him, yet was also aware of the sinister power of his logic.

'So, you see, Reverend Romer - or may I call you Douglas?' he asked with a smile expressed only by his lips, not by his eyes. Douglas ignored the question. 'So, you see,' Annas continued, 'when we were presented with a rather scruffy looking Galilean from Nazareth, who had succeeded in starting a riot in the temple - using violence, don't you know - and who had been constantly challenging the accepted teaching of our law, we were going to need a great deal of convincing that the man was really worthy of our respect. Well, the last straw, of course, was that this man made the preposterous claim that he was - I can hardly bring myself to say it - the Son of God. Well, there is no question that this is the ultimate blasphemy.'

Douglas breathed in and was about to protest when Annas continued sharply, 'Now don't go telling me we should have recognised him as such, and we had blatant lack of faith, and we had failed to understand our Scriptures correctly. Let me tell you straight, young man, this supposed rabbi looked an absolute shambles, he talked in riddles no-one could understand, he flouted the well-known and accepted religious laws, and he was consistently disrespectful to those whom God had appointed in positions of authority. And the half-demented, uneducated drop-outs he hung out with were not much better. He had zealots and tax-collectors. And he even had some very disreputable women with him - yes, a rabbi with women in his troupe!'

'But...' attempted Douglas

'Let me finish, young man,' ordered Annas, holding up his hand like a policeman controlling traffic. 'I am simply asking you to recognise that we, the high priests, were the ones called by God to establish peace and order in the city and the land, and God had made it clear to us that if we kept order and the proper acknowledging of the law in the city, and protected the people from idolatrous worship, then he would bless us.' As he said this he started stabbing his finger hard on the table. 'This Jesus was clearly a heretic. He claimed he was divine, and he was someone who blatantly disobeyed our laws. He was also stirring up trouble, and civil unrest did not go down well with Pilate. It was essential that we kept on good terms with Pilate - he could easily have turned on us, and that would have been appalling for the people. Appalling.' He pursed his lips and breathed in loudly through his nose.

'So, this Jesus of Nazareth had to be stopped,' he continued. 'He was challenging the very fabric and foundation of our civilised society which, up until he came along, was working very nicely, thank you. Before we handed him over to the Romans we gave him a perfectly fair trial, where incidentally he was deeply disrespectful to us - especially to the Lord Caiaphas. He was a trouble-maker and definitely inciting the people against us high priests. So we had no choice, especially once our Sanhedrin had tried him and found him guilty. We handed him over to the Romans. It was clearly the only thing we could do.

'I have to say,' and here he put on an expression of compassion which looked most inauthentic to Douglas, 'I was sorry that he had to die a rather unpleasant death, and I would have preferred him to die in a more civilised way - but the Romans were like that, you know, and we had no control over their methods of execution. But I won't have you and all those like you, saying we were evil and dark, because we were not. We were simply doing our duty. We were the ones keeping the real light alive in very testing times.' He was now red-faced, and sipped from his glass, with his lazy eye staying closed for a few moments. 'And kindly remember, I was there. Oh yes, I know you have documents recording it all, but they are from a very biased point of view. Those writers were brain-washed by him, and they were out to get us right from the start, and twisted everything we said and did. They were jealous of our power and authority and they were trying to usurp us. No, what you have a is a very one-sided point of view. It is a pity a much more balanced view was not recorded.

'And now, if you will excuse me, I have another appointment.' He started to rise from his seat.

'But wait,' said Douglas, 'you have not given us a chance to reply to all the assertions you are making.'

'I did not come here to have a discussion with you, young man, but to give you the full facts and to redress the balance. You claim you know what is light and what is dark. Well, I am making clear that the stories you have been told are distorted and have made light look dark, and dark light.' He lowered himself down in his seat again and looked more closely at Douglas. 'It seems to me, Reverend Romer, that there is a deep confusion in you. Think very hard about what is right and what is wrong, what is light and what is dark.' Then, moving his face close to Douglas, he said in a confidential voice, 'And if you think this man here is an angel, then I suggest you reconsider. In fact, I should be very wary indeed of him, if I were you. In my estimation, he is most certainly not an angel. But he could very well be quite the opposite.' He then stood, and, leaving most of his glass undrunk, said, 'Good evening, Gentlemen,' and walked out of the pub.

'You might want to shut your mouth,' said Dorchadas after a few moments.

Douglas had not realised he had been sitting there gaping for a few minutes. He turned and looked at Dorchadas and said, 'Did that just happen, Dorch? Was that... Annas?'

'Aye, son. But not a meeting of my arranging. They happen sometimes when you are in the season for them.

'What season?'

'It's really not easy to explain. But you are in a season. It could be weeks, could be years. But in the season, you'll have some meetings. Better accept it. And no point trying to work it out. Benignant power is about as near as you'll get. But in my mind you are better off without those kinds of meeting. Ready for another?' He held up his empty glass.

Douglas did not notice the question and asked, 'But why him - why Annas?'

'That's not for me to answer, Doug. You have to work it out.' And with that, Dorchadas rose from the table and headed for the bar.

*

Journal 16 October. Ireland

It's been another crazy few days. Went to see the bishop. Well, despite what I've sometimes said about her, I actually found her very understanding. Told her about my loss of faith, but that didn't seem to shock her at all. Even called her Pauline by the end! Anyway, she's given me three months paid leave - amazing! Says it can be a sabbatical. And I got an email from Dorchadas while I was in England. So the long and short of it is - I am back in Dingle - feeling tired tonight and too much to write about. But suffice to say Kath picked me up and we ended up meeting her old nemesis, the very priest who was so awful to her. Retired Anglican Archdeacon and he's an old bloke now, but that didn't stop Kath giving him a piece of her mind! Seems to have done her a power of good. Power - I think that is what part of it is about. The man had terrible power over her at the time of that sad event, and in a way that power has hung about her all the years since. But today it shifted, and after the meeting there was no doubt about where the power lay. What misery is wrought by the wrong use of power.

Talking of which, there was another "meeting" tonight back at The Angel's Rest. It was great to see Dorch again, and we were having such a nice conversation - 'craic' Dorch calls it. Well, then someone else arrived. Dorch said he had nothing to do with it, but this guy sat down opposite us and he claimed he was Annas, the high priest. I know, the Annas of the Gospels turning up in Dingle… Well, whoever he was, what a horrible man. Obvious connection with that arrogant Archdeacon. Made of the same stuff. So many religious leaders have been like this and caused such misery. Religion and power is such a toxic mix. No wonder so many people are put off God and religion. I wonder how many I have turned off in my time?

It was my third 'meeting' with a bible person. Though I'm still puzzled by how this works, I'm sort of getting it. Dorch says it is to do with the power of imagination. Saoirse always said I had a good imagination, though it was never as alive as hers. Dorch says I'm in a 'season' of these meetings, so I suppose there could be others. Well, whatever they are, I can't deny they are doing me some good. Even the one with Annas. He helped me to see that I want nothing to do with that sinister use of religious, institutional power. I wonder what Gerald would have made of Annas! It's a worrying thought that they would probably have become the best of friends!

Today's meetings with the bitter Archdeacon and sinister Annas makes me more certain than ever that the further I can get away from the church now the better. And I'm feeling a bit better about giving up on my faith. I can actually write this down now, and not flinch. Don't actually feel that guilty about giving up on it all. Starting to feel my real self at last. But then I do have moments of wistfulness. Dorch said some beautiful things about Jesus that touched me.

Dorch carries on saying he's an angel - he's clearly convinced about it. To be honest, I'm really beginning to wonder now. What he says really sounds so convincing, and he's such a brilliant guy. I certainly don't buy Annas' suggestion that he is demonic. But if he is an angel, then what about God? And what about my abandoned faith? It's all a bit confusing. And I'm tired, and it's time for bed.

CHAPTER 19

Douglas slept more peacefully than he had done for many weeks, the result of which was that he overslept and was awoken by Mrs O'Connell knocking at his door.

'Are you still alive in there, Douglas, or do I go fetch the undertaker?'

Douglas was startled into wakefulness and made some sounds to reassure her that the undertaker was not needed.

'Well it's past the breakfast hour, but for you I'll make an exception, if you'll be down in ten minutes. And there's another note for you at your table.'

Douglas felt hungry, so he obediently made his way downstairs in time for one of Mrs O'Connell's specials. And sure enough, there was a note on the table which read:

> Morning Douglas. I hope you don't mind me disturbing you, but I'd love it if you were willing to have another wee talk with me. I felt bad after our conversation a few nights ago and would love to put things right. Would it be all right with you if we met at the church at 11am - I like to go to the mass at 12. If you don't turn up I'll quite understand and wish you God's speed. Kevin.

As Douglas launched into a large piece of black pudding, he considered the note carefully and decided that he would meet up again with Kevin. He was feeling a bit stronger.

'There's a storm coming in later, Douglas,' said Mrs O'Connell as she refilled his coffee cup.' Looks like it's a nasty one.'

Sure enough, when Douglas stepped out of the building a little later, he was met by a strong wind. He enjoyed the freshness of it on his face and he made his way briskly to the church where he arrived early. It was the same church that he had visited a few days back and, as before, he felt more comfortable in the building than he expected. He enjoyed the heady fragrance of incense. The sun was shining brightly through the east end windows causing the well-polished pews to gleam in its light. There was no one else in the building which pleased him and he wandered around the building looking at the various signs and symbols of Catholic worship.

He was particularly taken with a range of ceramics on the walls, and as he inspected them more closely he discovered they were the stations of the cross. Each picture depicted a scene from the final hours of Christ's life. There he was, with scars on his back, being mocked by the soldiers; then falling under the weight of the cross; there was Veronica mopping his face, and other women weeping; Douglas made his way towards the end of the display and studied the contorted figure pinned to the wooden beam with Mary and John standing beside him, bent with grief. This was the emblem of the religion he had tried to serve as a minister for fourteen years, a service which had now come to an end through his own failings.

He was just beginning to wonder whether this man hanging limply on the cross also had his moments of thinking he had also failed, when a voice at the back of the church roused him from his thoughts. It said, 'I'll be in the vestibule and ready when you are - no hurry.' Douglas turned from the painting and spotted that the voice belonged to Kevin who was standing by the glass screen that separated the worship area from the vestibule. He was clutching a couple of Costa coffee cups.

Douglas followed him through into the spacious vestibule, where Kevin had found a couple of comfortable chairs near a window. 'Do you take the milk, Douglas?' he asked.

'No, actually I take it black, but...'

'Then this one is yours,' said Kevin, handing him the cup. 'Should be quiet here for a while. People don't arrive early in these parts, so we will have a while to talk if that's all right with you.'

'Yes, sure Kevin,' said Douglas taking a welcome sip of his coffee.

'It's turning a bit wild out there, isn't it?' said Kevin taking a cautious sip of the hot drink. 'I thought,' he then said rather tentatively, 'I might just tell you a bit about my story, just so you understand where I'm coming from, but if that doesn't appeal, please say now, won't you?' Douglas noticed how Kevin looked genuinely anxious, and at this moment in this sacred and peaceful building it was very hard to believe that at one time this man harboured such grim hatred in his heart.

'Yes, Kevin. I'd like that. I'm afraid the other night I'd had a bit to drink and...'

'No, no. Let's not go there, Douglas!' said Kevin with welcome light humour. He took another sip of his coffee and then placed the cup carefully on the floor beside him. He leaned back and, for a moment, clasped his knee with his hands, revealing his awkwardness on embarking on a story, the first part of which always caused him distress. He sat back up again and said, 'I come here every day when I'm in Dingle. I go to the midday mass and every time I say prayers for my victims. Every time I come I am faced with my past and every time I leave I am comforted by my future. That's the grace of God for you.' He reached down for his cup and took another nervous sip from his coffee.

'I recognise the look in you, Douglas. I have been allowed to meet with a couple of families whose lives I have torn apart by my actions. I've seen something of the hurt.'

'I'm all right, Kevin. It's two years on...'

'Aye, but I know the pain and regret takes a whole lot more than two years to shift. So, I'm not coming to excuse myself, Douglas, nor to try and make things better. But I want to tell you about what can happen to even the darkest life. And my life was dark, I can tell you. I told you how much I hated the British and for a while I carried out my duties well and became a skilled sniper.

'Well, eventually I was caught and there began the next stage of my life. I always knew this was a possibility, but the horror of being banged up in jail and losing your freedom was much worse than I had bargained for. And when you are locked up inside, you mix with other souls whose lives are also filled with hatred and bitterness. It's not a grand place to be, I can tell you. So, I just got sicker. My mammy and sisters would travel north and visit me, all telling me what an arse I'd been, and yet they were also full of kindness, they were. They were a great comfort, a truly great comfort, God bless them.

'So, I was stuck there, and one thing I did not want to think about was God. I'd given up on him a long time ago - even though I liked to go the masses and that. Inside the prison there were the usual God-botherers who tried to pump bible verses down me, mostly to tell me what a pile of refuse I was, and I needed no-one to convince me of that.

'Then a guy called Kenny arrived. Small guy with bright blue eyes and a little goatee beard. He was the kind of guy that the moment you looked at him you wanted to laugh.' Kevin smiled broadly as he remembered him. 'And he did a lot of laughing, even though, like the rest of us, he hated the loss of liberty and the humiliation meted out by the guards.' Kevin paused thoughtfully for a moment. Douglas was fascinated. He had never visited a prison and was intrigued to hear about life inside.

Both of them sat in silence for a few moments, sipping at their coffee. A fly hummed in a nearby window, tapping against the glass in its bid for freedom. 'As I said, Kenny was different,' continued Kevin, breathing in deeply. 'He claimed he was innocent, which of course all the men claimed, but in his case, I was inclined to believe him. The thought of being inside and having done nothing to deserve it doesn't bear thinking of. And you would think he would be more bitter than the rest of us. But he wasn't, Doug. Amazing, isn't it?' asked Kevin, genuinely still surprised after all these years. He drained his coffee, crumpled the cup and threw it accurately into a nearby bin. 'Learned a few skills when I was inside,' he smiled, and Douglas smiled with him.

He continued, 'So I said to your man Kenny, "what's the secret?" Well it turned out the man was one of your actual Franciscans - third order he said, though I still don't know what that means. But he told me a lot about St. Francis who lived a long time ago in Italy, but who certainly left his mark on the whole world. Left it on Kenny, for sure. He said that this Francis had also been a prisoner in his time, and that he had a special love for prisoners. I remember one day we were outside, doing our walk in the yard, and he said, quite casually really, "So you see Kev, I now know God has called me into this prison, to serve him here, and to share his love, just as Francis would have done." Well, to be fair, Doug, that's not the kind of language you use inside the Maze. The guy could have lost a fair few teeth for that if he had been overheard, but I think he trusted me. And the thing is, Doug, something about the way he said it - well, it was like the love of God leaked out of the man there and then. I could sort of feel it, there in that prison yard. Well you don't let that kind of thing get to you when you are in the company of the other prisoners, I can tell you, so I controlled the wash of feelings inside of me as best I could.

'But that night when I got into bed, them feelings returned, and I bawled my eyes out. I think I cried all night like a new-born. And in many respects, I woke up a new-born. Not that born again malarkey that the God-botherers went on about. But it was as though hatred had drained out of me with my tears and, I have to admit it, love started to take its place. For a year after that Kenny and I would meet together for more chats and we'd go to the chapel services which, to be sure, had all the life of a morgue about them. But what we did do, was we met and

157

had silence together for 10 minutes a day. And my, they were special, Doug. They were special.' Kevin leaned back in his chair and closed his eyes and inhaled, as if he were drawing something of the strength of those meetings into his soul now.

'So how long were you inside, Kevin?' asked Douglas. He was fascinated by the story, the religion of which sounded a good deal more attractive than the one he had been peddling these last few years.

'Well, it was the time of the Good Friday agreement, you see. And, it felt like a fair miracle, it did, because it wasn't long before we blokes found ourselves walking out on the streets free men far sooner than we expected. It was truly incredible.'

'So, did you start going to church, then?'

'No, no. I came back down here where the family is and Kenny went back to his family in Donegal, so we didn't see each other after that. Those ten-minute meetings with Kenny were my church, and nothing else really appealed. Besides, whilst the hatred was cured in my soul, my guilt wasn't. The guilt was just terrible. Once I had come to my senses, so to speak, I realised just what terrible things I had done. Oh aye, I could give the line about why the war was just and the killing was necessary and so on. But it no longer worked for me. I could no longer justify my actions and I hated what I had done. To take someone's life, Doug. That's not something you forgive yourself for easily. And in all I took five lives. All soldiers. One of them female. For some reason, that's the one that haunts me the most.' He looked anxiously at Douglas. He knew he had to confess it. It was his lifelong penance to live with the shame of what he had done, and to behold the look on the faces of those to whom he chose to confess the specifics of his crime, and they were only a few. But the look on Douglas' face dug into his shame more than any response he had known.

Douglas knew he was on very delicate emotional territory now. He could cope with Kevin finding God in the way that he had, but hearing of these specific murders, especially the murder of an innocent woman, triggered a toxic mix of powerful feelings in Douglas. Hoping further conversation might lead them away from this topic and from the feelings within him, he said without conviction, 'That's OK, Kevin. Go on with your story.' A gust of wind buffeted the building, startling both men.

'I hear there's a storm, coming, and it sounds like it could be underway,' said Kevin. 'Let me finish the story quickly, then you can go. So, this guilt problem. Well, this is where that Dorchadas comes in. I was there, in *The Angel's Rest*, and this tall gentleman offers to buy me a pint and we sit down for a natter. Claimed he was an angel, which of course I didn't believe for a moment, but I liked the guy, and he'd bought me a jar, so the least I could do was listen to him. Well, then this really weird thing happened. He may have done the same to you, I guess. But we were kind of transported. I don't know how else to describe it, but I found myself with old Dorch, standing in the most beautiful place. God knows, Douglas, someone like me should never be found in a place of such beauty. I was in tears the moment I opened my eyes. I should never be able to describe such things to you, Douglas, not for as long as I live. Sure, I can't.' Even as he referred to this memory, tears were welling up in Kevin's eyes.

'Look, as you can see, I have to be brief about this, because the emotion of it all is inclined to get the better of me. So, I'm in this place, and walking across the grass to me was a man who - all I can say was that he looked at one level perfectly normal, but at another he was full of a kind of radiance. He went up to Dorchadas and they hugged each other like long lost pals. Well, he introduced himself to me as none other than that guy who hung on the cross next to Jesus - you know, the one that Jesus spoke to as he was dying. Now, I don't in the least expect you to believe any of this, Doug, and I've done my fair bit of speculating about it, I can assure you. But the upshot was that this lad told me he had also been in my line of business, and if his story is to be believed, well he took many more lives than I did - men and women. And he told me that he had been caught by the Romans and handed the death sentence, so he was, and was taken up to them fearful crosses on which the Romans pinned their victims. And he found himself on the cross next to...' at this Kevin started to cough, and pinched the bridge of his nose, squeezing his eyes shut. Opening them he said, 'I'm sorry, Doug, I'm not sure I'm going to be able to tell it all to you. Just to say... they hung on them crosses together on that fateful afternoon in fearful agony, so they did... One guilty and the other completely innocent...' Kevin kept trying to control the emotion that was so powerful. He failed to speak for a few moments, then muttered, 'He told me every word of their conversation... You'd never believe, Doug...'

Douglas felt a little embarrassed as Kevin took out a grubby looking hanky and mopped his face. 'Don't go on if it is difficult, Kevin,' said Douglas, feeling a mix of fascination and discomfort.

'You're all right, son,' said Kevin, breathing in hard. He checked his watch, then steadied himself. 'You see, after that kind of meeting, things are bound to change, are they not? This man spoke to me in that beautiful place and by the end of hearing his story I knew I was... well...forgiven. There's no other word for it. I was guilty of the worst crimes, but I was forgiven by God.' As he said this he looked uncertainly at Douglas, who grasped his coffee, drained it without saying anything and then crumpled the empty mug in his hand. Douglas had listened intently to Kevin's story but he became aware of an almost overwhelming sense of anger and indignation when Kevin spoke of being forgiven. Kevin was a brutal murderer, and here was God merrily forgiving him. The thought of a murderer being so quickly and so easily let off the hook did not sit comfortably with Douglas.

Douglas could not face pursuing a conversation on forgiveness, so stifling his feelings as best he could, he asked, 'How does he do it? How does D... Dorch do this thing of taking us to different places, or conjuring b... bible characters up from nowhere?'

Kevin paused. His face was red. He was squeezing one hand with the other. He looked up at Douglas and said in a voice so quiet that Douglas struggled to hear him, 'I think he really is... you know... the real thing...an angel...Or at least was once an angel. And it looks like this is just something that angels and ex-angels do. Simple as that.'

The two men sat in silence as another gust of wind shook the building. An early worshipper was blown into the porch trying her best to keep hold of an umbrella that seemed hell bent on taking to the skies.

'Kevin, thank you so much. I'm really grateful,' said Douglas, reverting to his polite English self, and rising from his seat. 'Really grateful. I think I'll go up to your mum's cafe and get something to eat.'

'Oh no, there's no point in going there, Doug. She's away today. She decided to go off and see that Peter - you know, the priest from all those years back. She's been wanting to go and see him for donkey's years, but yesterday gave her the courage she needed. She made enquiries and discovered that he lives in Adare - not too far off.'

'Oh... oh really? said Douglas, a little vaguely. There was such emotion whirling around in him, he hadn't much space to think of this highly significant meeting for Kath.

'Thanks so much for listening, Douglas,' said Kevin as he watched Douglas making his way out of the church past another windswept parishioner. He felt uneasy as he could see that Douglas had struggled with aspects of his story. He had been so sure that it had been the right thing to tell Douglas, and yet now he had his doubts.

Kevin made his way slowly to his usual pew. Today was his day for praying for the soul of the young lass from Lancaster whose life he had stolen when she was on her first week of duty in the army, and he prayed for the family who had firmly refused to meet with him and had sent vitriolic letters to him. He also prayed for Douglas, for he feared that in telling his story to him, he may have done more harm than good.

CHAPTER 20

Douglas was nearly knocked down by the force of the gale as he left the church, and he struggled his way to a nearby café where he ordered a toasted sandwich, but when it arrived he had little appetite for it. Kevin's story had disturbed him. In fact, he felt more depressed than he had for a long time. He liked Kevin, yet here was a man who had deliberately shot dead five people in cold blood, and one of them was female. One of them could have been his Saoirse. And then God comes along, whips Kevin off to Paradise so he can meet a penitent terrorist, and then says all is forgiven and you can get on with your life now. Well, wonderful for him. But clearly God didn't care much for that poor female soldier who was shot to pieces just as her life was getting going. Douglas prodded at the toast that was going cold and felt a mix of anger, resentment and grief building up within him.

He was startled awake from his thoughts by the door blowing open and in blew Mrs. O'Connell.

'Mary, Joseph and sweet baby Jesus, that's a fierce gale if ever there was one,' she cried as she fell into the café. She came over to where Douglas was sitting, desperately trying to arrange her hair which was a sure testimony to the strength of the wind. 'So there you are, Douglas. I've been looking high and low for you, sure I have. It's done my bad knee no good, it has.'

'Why, is something wrong?' asked Douglas in some alarm.

'No, not really. It's just that eejit Dorchadas - he's been wanting to meet with you and for some reason I said I'd goes to try and find you for him, as he was tied up with something this morning. Well, here you are now, thank God.' She continued working at her hair as she settled into a chair at Douglas' table. 'Well, he wants to meet you down by the beach for God's sakes. I mean, of all places - in this weather! God knows why he should choose the beach with a storm like this blowing up, but you know what he's like. Here - he's done a wee map for you, so you can see where he wants you to get to.' She handed him a piece of paper with a sketched map on it.

'Well, all right,' said Douglas compliantly, 'When does he want to see me?'

'Well now, it's just coming up to twelve, and he said it would suit him if you could be there for two. So, you best be there, Douglas. You'll want to get back and pick up your coat, you will. The storm's rough, sure it is. And do take care. It's a sheltered beach, but when there's a storm it's wild there, it sure is. Now I best be going because I want to nip in to the mass, just to keep on the right side of the Almighty, God bless him, and then I've got some new guests arriving after lunch. More from Texas, would you believe it. I swear to God, I've had half of bleeding Texas coming through my house this year, sure I have. Well, let's hope they've got some anchors on their toes, else they'll be blown to the other side of Kerry before nightfall. See you later, Douglas.' She got up from her seat and then scurried back out into the wind, where almost immediately her hair fell once again into disarray.

Douglas smiled for a moment at this character that he had come to love, and somehow her brief company had given him a little appetite for his lunch, most of which he managed to finish. Faithful to her command, he then returned to his room to collect his coat which seemed robust enough for the wind, a wind that certainly seemed pretty lively and the dark clouds it was bringing with it suggested that there was some heavy rain coming before too long.

He set off for the beach following the map's instructions, but as he did so the discontent returned and deepened. He felt he could see it more clearly now and the clarity of it was profoundly disturbing him. He kept thinking about the forgiven Kevin. Forgiven - it seemed so easy. Forgive and forget. Douglas knew he could never forgive the evil killer of Saoirse even if that killer was given a hundred visitations from heaven and became a haloed saint. Too much damage had been done in Douglas' heart. He paused for a moment by a gate and looked out to the sea which appeared to be growing wilder by the minute. He felt himself shaking - he was not at all sure he wanted to meet Dorchadas now. All his grief seemed to have opened up again. The telling of it all to Dorchadas, and then the meeting with Kevin who was a murderer, apparently let off by heaven, was causing an inner storm in him as fierce as the outer one he witnessed coming in from the sea. He also thought of the meeting with Gerald and the wardens and their clear intention to get rid of him. Not only his personal life, but his professional life was falling to pieces. And, worst of all, the crisis of the last few days brought back such clear and painful memories of the woman he had so deeply loved, yet was only allowed to know for such a short period of time. Familiar tears flowed as

163

he heard her voice. Was she calling out to him through this storm? Was she alive in a different form somewhere? Was there any way of making contact with her? She was the only person he wanted to meet now - every other life felt like it only caused trouble.

He nearly turned back to St.Raphael's, but something prompted him to head for the seashore and meet with this strange man, Dorchadas, who, though so likeable, seemed to be causing such huge disturbance in Douglas' life. He would make sure this was his last visit with him, and then he would have to get out of Dingle, out of Ireland and find some way of getting free of the pain. There was no harm in meeting with him, albeit in the midst of the wind and rain, just to say farewell. He owed him that. He would like to leave on good terms. He was walking fast and enjoyed the buffeting wind - something to battle with as he wrestled with the storm within him.

He arrived at the beach which was a riot of wind and spray, and down near to the water's edge he spied the tall figure of Dorchadas who was standing bolt upright like a century at his post. He was gazing out to sea, and despite Douglas hollering at him, he didn't notice him until Douglas went up close to him and smacked him on the back.

'Och, there you are Doug,' he roared over the sound of the wind and breaking waves. 'Thanks a million for coming. I just wanted you to be here with me. There's a bit of a storm coming in, and there's no better place to see it than right here, where you can see the surf and the spray and the sheer wildness of it all. And look at them gulls, will you? Don't they love it. What do you think, Doug? Isn't it stupendous? Doesn't it do your spirit good?' He turned his face away from the stormy sea and looked at Doug and yelled, 'It's just what your spirit needs today, Doug. That's why I wanted you here.'

'You got me here just to have a look at this?' asked Douglas, annoyed at being dragged out in foul weather to have a look at a stormy sea. He could taste the sea salt strong in his mouth.

'Well, why not?' asked Dorchadas, genuinely puzzled.

'Because Dorchadas, call me a wimp if you like, but I actually don't like being torn to shreds by a howling gale, and getting drenched to the skin by sea and rain when I'm already freezing to death! That's why. No, I don't think this will do my spirit any good at all, thanks very much.'

Dorchadas looked at Douglas carefully, and he could see a new fragility in him, and he regretted his decision to invite him to the

164

seashore. It's just that Douglas seemed to be getting stronger and he felt this experience would do him a power of good - a kind of flushing out of the old stale air, and a powerful inhalation of a new bright breeze. The forces of nature so often healed wounded spirits. He had seen it time and time again. But he could now see that Douglas was nowhere near ready for this. He felt an awful sense that he had got it wrong again - so much was not going to plan this week. 'What's happened, Doug?' he asked, steadying himself in the force of the gale.

'I met with Kevin just now,' shouted Douglas as a huge wave crashed into the sea beyond them. 'He told me all about his past and the shootings, and then he told me about the nice little visit you arranged for him in Paradise with another former murderer, and how he got over his hatred and his guilt. He told me God was very pleased to forgive him. All happily ever after for him, Dorch. Very nice. But not so good if you happened to be the husband or parents of the young woman he shot in cold blood, is it? Have you tried taking any of them on a little trip to heaven so God can explain himself to them?' Douglas kept having to steady himself in the force of the wind, but it was an inner force that was driving him now.

The rain that had been threatening for a while now arrived, and Dorchadas' normally wavy hair quickly became drenched and fell about his face. 'Oh, my, Doug. I'm sorry, lad. I don't think it's like that at all, I really don't.'

'No clearly you don't, Dorch. You're a blasted angel after all. You have to toe the party line, don't you? Keep the divine end up and do your best to make sure that God doesn't look bad. Well, I can tell you Dorch, from where I stand, he looks pretty bad to me these days. In fact, I would say just at the present time he looks cruel and nasty. I mean, what had those soldiers done so wrong that he comes down with his divine decree and snatches them away with one of Kevin's bullets, eh? What exactly was their great crime?'

The rain was becoming heavier, and the spray from the crashing waves was stinging their faces with salty water causing them both to screw up their eyes. But though buffeted by the storm, both men stood their ground facing each other, as if in mortal combat.

'But, Doug, dear friend...' tried Dorchadas.

'No, no, no! It's no use "dear friending" me now, Dorch,' interrupted Douglas. 'I've honestly had enough of all this stuff.' Douglas was slicing the air in front of him, cutting himself off from all the excuses

165

and explanations he had received that had failed to satisfy him. He knew now he had finally tapped the true feelings that had been locked deep in him since the day his Saoirse was taken from him. This, for him, was his moment of truth. The storm had blown off all his nice, English, Anglican defences, and now this so-called ex-angel could have it straight.

'Yes, it's been very nice meeting all these holy people through your hypnotism, or however it is you do it, but I'm finished with it all, and I don't need you trying to haul me back into a religion that is cold and cruel.'

Dorchadas was astonished at this sudden outpouring from Douglas. He honestly thought he had got the measure of this man, as he had with so many others he had helped over the years. He thought he was just about there - in a place where Douglas would finally be at peace with himself. This was his job now to do just this: meet the humans who were sent his way, and help them find peace. But now he was manifestly failing at this simple task - alongside his other appalling failure that he could never mention to anyone. He felt desperation rise in him. 'Douglas, for heaven's sake, let's go somewhere warm and talk this out. You're clearly not yourself, son.'

'Oh, that's where you are wrong, Dorchadas. I am *exactly* myself. This *is* who I am,' Douglas cried desperately thumping his chest. He no longer noticed the force of the rain and sea spray sharp against his face. His coat was sodden now and the rain was penetrating through to his skin, but he felt no cold. In the past such emotion would have engaged his old stammer, but the force of feeling was so strong in him now, that even that old, awkward restraint was thrust aside.

He took a few steps away, but then turned and came back and pointing up at Dorchadas he shouted, 'You see, Dorchadas, you may have been an angel in your time - so you say - but the fact is that I have been a Vicar, and yes, a pretty poor specimen of one at that, I know. But you see, you've not stood as I have by the gaping hole in the ground on a wet November day and watched while sombre men lower the coffin of a young child into the unforgiving earth. You've not held the quivering arm of the wretched mother as she wails at the thought of her kid lying in the cold clay, never to laugh and play again, never to grow up into all that he was born to be. You haven't sat by a ringing phone unable to answer it for dread of it being the voice of the undertaker with news of yet another cruel and untimely death. You don't know what it is like to be so battered and busted by human sorrow that you have nothing left to give.'

He turned away, plunging his hands into his soaked coat pockets. He stood looking out to the fuming sea for a few moments and then returned to Dorchadas, pointing accusingly at him again. 'And it's not just death. You haven't sat in a lounge lit only by the flickering light of an EastEnders bust-up raging on the telly, holding the slumped figure of a once strong man, who is sobbing with fear and grief at the news of his sudden redundancy and wondering what the hell he is going to do with his terrifying heap of debt. Well I have, Dorchadas, I have, and I can tell you, these are all hellish places to be, and if there is any heaven about, then why, oh why, can it not touch our earth when it desperately needs it?'

All the while Dorchadas stood there feeling wretched and helpless and eventually shouted out, 'Yes, yes, yes, for God's sake, yes, I know, Douglas. At least, I don't know what you've known, but yes, believe me, I have seen the horrors of this world. But, but... it's not the *only* thing I've seen. You humans are incredible! I've seen men and women torn to shreds by grief who look to the skies through their tear-drenched eyes, and, often to their surprise, they find something of heaven, and are mended, Douglas. I've seen children, horribly hurt, as children should never be, but lying on their damp pillows and feeling a touch on their cheek of a power greater and gentler than any human power, and they are given the strength they need. I've stood at the back of your great cathedrals and watched the distant figure of a priest lifting bread and wine to heaven, and seen tears on the cheeks of the browbeaten and broken who leave that building with peace and hope in their broken hearts.'

Douglas was far from convinced, and swayed towards Dorchadas grabbing him by the lapels of his drenched jacket, and looked up at him with such a hardness that even Dorchadas felt a stab of fear. 'Yes, that may be true for a privileged few. But for most of us, that's not how it is. And don't you see, you mighty angel from heaven, that pain and suffering has resulted in millions giving up on the idea of God, including this mortal standing here on this storm-tossed, godforsaken beach. If you don't mind me giving your God a piece of advice. If he wants to stop the flood of people exiting his church in these days, then I suggest that when people come hammering on his great door of Paradise for help when they are battling the hellish pains of this life, he does a bit more than offering such platitudes as "all things work together for good...", because manifestly, Dorch, they do not!' As he exclaimed this, he let go of Dorchadas' lapels and punched his shoulders. A huge gust of wind nearly threw him to the ground, but he steadied himself and glared at Dorchadas.

'Oh, Douglas... Doug, my sweet friend,' said Dorchadas, steadying himself and then leaning forward to Douglas so their drenched faces almost touched, 'It's just that I *see* other things as well, and I wish to God you could see them.' Now plentiful tears were mixed with the rain and sea on Dorchadas' face.

All the while the tide had been coming in, and some seawater flowed over Douglas' shoes. But the feelings of anger and grief were so fierce within him now that he did not notice it. He shouted back at Dorchadas above the roar of another crashing wave, 'Well, clearly I can't Dorch, and no doubt that's because I am a rotten, faithless, heathen waste of a sinner, and the world will be well rid of me. We have reached the end Dorch. We really have.'

At that he pushed Dorchadas away from him with such force that Dorchadas was nearly felled. Douglas then ran towards the raging ocean. For a moment Dorchadas stood still, looking in horror as he saw Douglas rip off his coat, throwing it to one side, and then plunge into the sea, and above the roar of the wind and the heaving waves he heard the voice of his friend, almost childlike, screaming, 'Saoirse, Saoirse my love, my darling, I am coming...' As he watched his friend disappear under the waves, Dorchadas took several huge strides and in moments he was alongside Douglas, grabbing him and pulling him up. Douglas tried his best to fight him off, but Dorchadas held him tight as a colossal wave crashed over them, dragging them down to the grinding shingle of the restless seabed.

*

Douglas could never explain what happened next, but in an instant, they were both standing on dry land and far away from sea and storm. Their clothes were mysteriously dry and the air was warm. They were still panting from the exertions of the struggle in the sea. The sound of their breathing was all the more conspicuous for the stillness and silence around them. Douglas was shaking with emotion and full of intention to fight Dorchadas, and yet, somehow in this place, the fight seemed

168

pointless. His fists were clenched around the lapels of Dorchadas' coat, and with slight reluctance he let them go.

They were standing on some rough, dry ground with grassy tufts around. As their breathing quietened they could hear the gentle sound of cicadas, and somewhere in the distance a dog was barking. It was dark, but there were a few burning torches scattered here and there which revealed they were in a small wooded area. They were standing under a small and ancient looking tree and a light breeze was causing the leaves to tremble. For a few moments neither of them uttered a word. For Douglas, there was only one explanation - they had both drowned in the sea. It had finally happened. His life had come to its end. And there was a world beyond life that they had now entered. The question was, were they in Heaven or Hell? Or could they even be in some in between world?

Somewhat to his surprise, Douglas heard the sound of a gentle snore, and just a short distance away he saw the shady outline of several men who were sound asleep. It all made no sense to him, so he looked to Dorchadas and asked in a reverential whisper, 'Where are we Dorchadas?' But Dorchadas said nothing. Douglas looked hard at him, and though the light was poor from the nearby torch, there was enough for him to see something in Dorchadas' face that he had not seen before: it was the unmistakable look of fear. 'What is it Dorch?' he asked, feeling concern for the friend that he had been berating so severely only moments earlier.

'Oh, Doug. Oh, dear God, please, no...' Dorchadas took a few steps backwards. 'Oh please no... not here...'

'Not where, Dorch? Tell me, where are we? Are we in heaven or... or the other place?'

'Look...' said Dorchadas and slowly held up his shaking hand and pointed to the distance. As he said this, a bright full moon slid out from behind the clouds and Douglas could see the clear outline of some more sleeping bodies, and in the distance, he saw a man on his own, sprawled on the ground, now being spotlit by the brilliant moon. It was difficult to make out quite what he was doing there, but from the jerky movements of his body, it looked like he was in pain.

'Who... who is that, Dorch? Does he need help?' whispered Douglas.

'It's Him, Douglas. It's Him,' said Dorchadas almost as if he were dreaming. 'And this, my dear friend, is where...' He paused, then continued, '.. is where I fell.' Dorchadas kept his eyes fixed on the moonlit figure in the distance, but pulled Douglas back several yards, as if he was pulling him out of danger. He pulled him to a grassy knoll and said, 'Sit here, Doug, but let's look the other way for a while.' They sat together and looked out over a valley beyond which they could see the flickering lights of a town and, as well as the sounds of cicadas they could hear the distant sounds of chatter and laughter.

'So, Douglas,' said Dorchadas who was shaking like a cobweb in a breeze, 'I'll do my best to explain - that's if there's time.' There was indeed just enough time for Dorchadas to tell Douglas why this was the one place in space and time that he dreaded visiting more than any other.

CHAPTER 21

Dorchadas breathed in hard through his nostrils and gazed out at the town across the valley. The moon returned behind a cloud. The comical sound of a donkey nearby was in marked contrast to the seriousness that was so evidently in the soul of Dorchadas. 'I know you find all this impossible to believe, Doug, but I'm simply going to tell it to you as it is, and you'll have to make up your own mind about it. But one thing I ask Doug, is that you respect the fact that for me, this is real. Oh, if only it *was* make-believe.' Douglas had never seen Dorchadas so nervous.

'Of course, Dorch. I'm with you,' said Douglas, and placed an arm on the tall man's stooped shoulder. He felt genuine concern and compassion for him.

Dorchadas looked back over the valley and started, 'I was in Paradise, waiting for my orders as per usual when I was told "You have been chosen to help Him." "Help Him to do what?" I asked. "You must go and give Him courage." There was something about the tone that disturbed me, but then the opportunity to be working directly with the Son during his time on Earth - well, who wouldn't leap at the chance? Well...' Dorchadas drew in his breath again and closed his eyes. 'This was where I was sent.' He threw his thumb over his shoulder, referring to the scene behind him. 'This is Gethsemane, Douglas - the day before... before He died.'

Dorchadas paused for a few moments, and then continued, 'As you can see, it was dark when the moon was behind the clouds, but of course that's not a problem for us. At first, I saw His friends and they were all asleep which seemed strange, because I assumed that if I was coming to help there would be a whole lot of trouble and commotion. But it was really quiet. But then I heard a whimpering sound from over there,' he nodded back over his shoulder. 'He looked all dishevelled, like - His hair all over the place - and He was kneeling on the ground with His poor hand thumping at the earth. I had longed to have this direct encounter with Him in this world - I mean, who wouldn't? But I never expected to find Him in this terrible state. Up until then, I had never personally experienced fear, but as I crept nearer to Him, I could feel this sense of terror tighten within me - I had never known such a thing before.

'As I got closer to Him, I realised He was talking to Father - well, not talking exactly, but begging, like a wee child in desperate distress. "Oh please, please - is there another way?" I heard Him say. "O God, let this cup pass from me. I'm not strong enough to drink from it." I couldn't believe what I was hearing. He was always so strong. I edged closer and I saw blood on His forehead - the vessels on His dear head were bursting with the strain of it! Can you imagine, Doug, how bad it must be for that to happen? He fell to the ground and then He saw me. He stretched out an arm to me and cried, "Help, please help!". *He* was calling to *me*, Doug!' Dorchadas turned again to Douglas, and though the light was dim, Douglas could see the desperation in his face, and could just make out channels of water that were flowing from his eyes down into his beard.

'It broke my heart, it did. I couldn't bear it, Doug,' he said as he now buried his forehead in his hands. 'I'd seen plenty of human pain - all them dreadful things you spoke of back on the seashore just now - but nothing like this.' For a few moments Dorchadas just shook his head and sniffed several times. He wiped his face with his hands, and then looked back out to the valley. 'I could not bear to see the Son in that state - the Son, whose radiance filled the hallways of heaven, whose compassion changed the lives of thousands during His days on earth, whose heart was like no other you have ever known, whose power is the greatest power of all. Yet here, sprawled on that damp earth, He was as busted and broken as any human I've ever seen, and I've seen many, I can tell you.' Dorchadas turned his wet face again to Douglas, 'He finally *knew* your world, Doug. He *felt* it.' Here Dorchadas thumped his heart several times. 'He *felt* it - grief, fear, horror, desolation, anguish. You name it, He felt it, and it was turning his sweat to blood, and it was about to kill him. And I, a great and mighty angel sent to help Him, could not bear to see such a thing. I needed Him strong and mighty, and this was too much to bear.' Dorchadas' face looked stern as he spoke, but then it crumpled with grief.

'Douglas - and you are the first human to know this - I then did a terrible, terrible thing.' His voice turned to a whimper, 'I turned and ran. Can you believe it, Doug? How could I do that to Him? But I ran and ran, and I was back in Paradise in moments, the place that had always felt like home, but not this time, because for the first time in my long angel life I felt terrible shame. I had failed in my duty. I never said as much as one word to help Him.' Dorchadas sobbed briefly, then gathered himself and added in a soft voice, 'Another angel was immediately chosen and sent to do the job. You'd call her female - I don't know how she was able to do it, but she did, and she did a wonderful job so I'm told. She helped Him in an awesome way.

'After that, I knew I could not stay in Paradise, so I resigned there and then. I had failed in my duty to help the very One for whom we exist, and I knew I could no longer serve as one of His angels. I was so relieved my resignation was accepted. One of the angels from the throne came over and touched me here.' He tapped his forehead. 'He told me I would serve as a mortal until the appointed time, and I was told that as a mortal I'd be given a few jobs to do.' He took a deep breath and looked up. 'And so, I have roamed over lands and through the ages, trying to do my bit as a retired angel and a mortal, yet not a mortal that will die - not in your way at any rate.' He paused, looking into the distance.

He then blinked, and he frowned again. 'But now I have been brought back, Doug.' He reached out a shaking hand drenched by his tears and clutched Douglas' hand so tightly that Douglas winced. He turned and looked back at the distant figure writhing on the ground lit by a flickering torch. 'What is happening, Doug? What am I supposed to do? Is this a second chance? Is it punishment? What is it, Doug?'

Douglas had never seen such dread in any face and he had to look away. He felt utterly helpless. His mind was battling with all kinds of impossibilities that were presenting themselves to him and he was completely unable to say a thing. As it happened, he did not need to.

'Dorchadas,' said a female voice with a foreign accent. It came from behind them. Both men turned around and a woman was standing behind them, holding a burning torch.

'Oh, Mary, love,' said Dorchadas, and he got up and greeted her like a long-lost friend. Douglas looked on uncertainly. 'Mary, I didn't know you were here too, you poor, dear soul. This and the terrible afternoon to follow. Surely not?' Dorchadas looked at Douglas and explained, 'Doug - this is Mary. You know, his friend from Magdala.' She smiled kindly at Douglas and then turned back to Dorchadas.

'Dorchadas,' she said. 'What you see is not the actual moment. It is memory, but it is the deep memory and therefore it is alive and it is powerful. Come.' She took the large hand of Dorchadas and turned to Douglas. 'You, Douglas. Will you wait here? We won't be long.' Douglas dutifully sat back on the grass knoll as he watched Dorchadas being led by Mary towards the figure in the distance. Mary looked tiny next to him, yet there was no doubt she was by far the stronger of the two.

Douglas could see Dorchadas stalling every now and then, once even dropping to his knees, but Mary gently picked him up and eventually they made their way to the distant figure, prostrate on the grass. The light was so dim it was hard for Douglas to make out quite what happened next, but it appeared that Dorchadas lay down with the figure, while Mary took several steps back. Quite how long the two figures lay there was hard to tell. Was it minutes? Was it hours? Was it years? Time seemed to no longer have any relevance and Douglas had the strange sensation of being beyond time, or maybe it was upon time. Afterwards he reflected it was his 'once upon a time...', because in many respects this was where a new story began for him.

In those moments, as he looked upon a distant scene of a weeping Christ and a broken angel lying side by side in the grass together, Douglas, for reasons he could never quite make out, felt for the first time in two long years, a genuine sense of peace. Something of his terrible pain was, in this sacred woodland, being utterly understood. It was being held. It was being honoured. It was being lifted. The darkness of the woodland was not a darkness of absence, but became filled with a sense of presence - a beautiful, unnamed presence, a presence that could never be imagined, written about, spoken about, preached about, for it was a presence not for the future, but for the present moment. Wherever this place was, and undoubtedly it was a place of deep suffering, it was also a place of extraordinary glory. It was a blessed place. Douglas knelt in the dusty earth which had become for him holy ground, and the only words that fell from his lips into the silence of those hours were ones he recalled from an ancient psalm: "for the darkness is not darkness to thee..."

There was a touch on his shoulder and Douglas opened his eyes with a start. It was Mary. She helped Douglas stand up, for his knees were stiff from kneeling. 'Let us sit,' she said, and they sat together on the knoll.

'Where's Dorch?' Douglas asked, terribly concerned for his friend. He looked around but there was now no-one to be seen.

Mary smiled. 'Dorchadas is well. He is actually very well. He will be returning as his old self,' and she chuckled 'Yet you will find him changed. You will see him again, but not for a while.' She then took his hand and clasped it in both of hers. She looked up at him and said, 'Your name is Douglas, yes?'

'Yes,' said Douglas, not sure why she was checking his name.

'Why did your parents choose that name?'

'I am not entirely certain,' he said. 'But I think there was a relative with that name, and they liked it.'

'And do you know what the name means?'

'Actually, I don't. I've never really thought to check.'

'Well it means "One who dwells by a dark stream." Your parents must have sensed that one day you would have to dwell near a stream of darkness, and you have done, Douglas. The stream has been very dark these last two years and today it nearly drowned you. But today you made a discovery that there is a darkness that is mysterious and is not harmful, as long as you listen deeply to it. It is a darkness of questions rather than answers, but questions that become luminous in the dark if you stay with them long enough.' She smiled a radiant smile as she said this, and although Douglas was not completely following what she was saying, he felt warmed and reassured by such a kind smile.

She then looked more serious and said, 'And now I must tell you two things before you return. In the dark just now you felt something I think?'

'Yes,' said Douglas. 'I'm not sure I could tell you what it was, but I know it was something very important.'

'Oh, yes,' said Mary with conviction. 'You see a true healing has now started. And it has started because at last you have discovered that He knows. He *knows*.' At this, Mary placed her hand over Douglas' heart. He physically felt something happen within it as she did so. He placed his hand over Mary's in gratitude. 'He knows the dark stream, Douglas. But this is only one darkness,' continued Mary, slowly taking her hand away, 'In the days to come there will be another darkness you will have to face which you must face with great courage. Dorchadas will be with you to help. I cannot tell you more about this now.'

Although the news sounded rather alarming, Douglas was not too bothered because such a deep peace had settled in his soul. They both sat in stillness for a while.

'And the other thing you have to tell me?' enquired Douglas.

Mary looked down at her hands folded on her lap, and then with the kindest smile looked up and said, 'Douglas I have been allowed to see her.'

'To… see my…'

'Yes, your Saoirse…'

Douglas felt the peace within him crack. With a pleading look in his eye he asked, 'Well, if you have seen her, can I…' He felt such an agony of longing and he started to rise, when Mary put a gentle but firm hand on his shoulder.

'Douglas, for you to see her now would not heal you, but she does have a message for you.'

And here Mary breathed in deeply, closed her eyes and started to sing. Douglas knew she was singing in Gaelic, and although he had no understanding of the meaning of the words, he sensed what they were about. Mary held both Douglas' hands in hers as her sweet, lilting voice filled the woodland around. Everything in that dark, yet blessed, world became suffused in the most exquisite love. It had the quality of that love which he had known with Saoirse, and yet it was even more - something he never imagined possible. But in these moments, he knew he was experiencing not just the flow of the love that had been given so liberally to him and Saoirse in those precious years when they were together, but the source of it. And in those sacred moments he knew his Saoirse was near him, and yet he felt no ache of longing, no need to grasp hold of her, nor any fear of losing her. He felt an overwhelming delight that she was alive, and more alive than he believed was possible. And he also knew without any doubt that the curtain between death and life was much thinner than he had ever supposed, and that love could flow through it either way without restraint.

Mary stopped her singing, and yet the song continued, beautifully echoing in the woodland. She lifted her hand to Douglas' cheek and said, 'Be not afeard. Douglas. This world is full of noises, sounds and sweet airs that give delight and hurt not.' Douglas smiled as he recognised the words of Shakespeare that were as a sacred text to him. 'The clouds have dropped their riches on you, Douglas.'

'Yes, yes, they have,' said Douglas. 'I have been given…' He paused for a few moments, then said, 'I have been given sparkling peace.'

Mary smiled again and added, 'Yes, that is the gift, Douglas. Sparkling peace.' She then placed her finger on Douglas' forehead and pronounced, 'Douglas, you are beloved on earth. You are beloved in heaven. Now rest…'

Douglas certainly felt tired, so he lay back, resting his head on the earth that felt to him softer than any pillow he had known. Wherever this place was, he knew that, more than anywhere he had known in the last two years, it was a place of safety, and he felt at peace. The song of the woodland soon ushered him into a blessed sleep that required no dreams.

CHAPTER 22

'He's coming round…' He heard a voice he recognised and some other voices, but they seemed to be part of a different world. He closed his eyes again and tried to find his way back to a forested world he had just discovered. Then a female voice hauled him back saying, 'Douglas, for God's sake, come on back to us, will you.' He recognised a smell… what was it? It was no longer the smell of olive trees… it was the smell of tobacco… 'Come on son, wake yourself up, won't you? Sure, you've been asleep an awful long time now,' said the voice.

He opened his eyes and there in front of him was a teary-eyed Kathleen, with Kevin standing close to her. There was a window next to them, with bright sunlight beaming on them. Douglas was in a room he did not recognise - it was white and sterile looking. He was lying in a bed and there was a tube sticking into his arm. He tried pulling at it.

'Oh no, for God's sake, don't go removing that, Doug. The nurse will kill you, sure she will,' and Kevin's firm hand removed Douglas' from the tube.

'You are in hospital, that you are, son,' said Kathleen. 'Gave us a hell of a shock you did.'

Douglas, who was feeling more alert by the minute, eased himself up on his pillow, asked, 'What happened?'

'God knows what you were up to Douglas', said Kathleen, 'but you decided to go for a dip in the sea would you know it, just when the storm was at its height.'

'Not a grand idea now, Douglas,' chimed in Kevin.

Memories of the stormy seaside returned to Douglas, displacing for a moment the tranquillity with which he awoke.

'Thank God your Dorch's a strong man,' continued Kathleen. 'For reasons I for one will never comprehend, he had planned for you and he to meet down at the shore just when the storm was raging wild, it was. And then a mighty great wave comes in and threatens to swallow the both of you. Well, thank God, Ciaran was there tying his boat down and he charges in, and between him and Dorch they drag you out. But you needed the medics, you did. They did the CPR and mouth to mouth and got you going again, thank God.'

178

'Aye,' said Kevin, 'but you were mighty woozy when they brought you in last night, and you've been murmuring and burbling nonsense until just now.'

'You've both been here?' asked Douglas, feeling deeply weary.

'Oh aye, of course we have.' Douglas felt as if both these two were now his family and he reached out his hand and grasped theirs firmly. 'Thank you,' he whispered as emotion threatened to overwhelm him.

'Where's Dorchadas?' he asked with concern

'Dorch?' said Kevin. 'Oh, once he knew you were safe in the ambulance, he went off and I've not seen him since. He'll be gone a few days now, I shouldn't wonder. That's how it is with Dorch.'

A nurse came in and checked various bits of the machinery around the bed. Kath and Kevin were talking with her, but Douglas eased himself back in the bed and gazed at the ceiling. Somehow or other, in the wild and stormy waters of the Atlantic, while he was perilously close to drowning, he and Dorchadas slipped into another world. As Douglas recalled it all with great accuracy and detail, it seemed he must have been there for several hours, and yet he and Dorch were only in those wild waters a few moments. He knew there was no way he was ever going to understand it, let alone explain it to anyone else, so he closed his eyes and said, 'I think I'll rest a bit now, if that's all right.'

'Yes, that would be a good thing,' said the efficient nurse and a much relieved Kath and Kevin made their way down to the hospital refectory. Douglas slipped back into a gentle sleep and after a further night in hospital he was discharged the next morning.

*

Journal 19 October

I am not going to even try to record what has happened to me in the last couple of days. I will never forget it, and the scene of that woodland and the conversations that took place there will stay with me for always, so no need to write about it. Have all my questions been answered? No, not really. But have all my questions been heard? Yes, most definitely yes, and I have realised that it was more important to me to know my questions were being heard, than their being answered. None of this has brought my Saoirse back and none of it has rid me of my grief, though I do feel quite different in my grief. It somehow feels more manageable, and I can now love my departed Saoirse without yearning to bring her back. And yet I feel a new love has taken hold of my soul, and that love (for want of a better way of putting it) is giving me what I need to get on with life.

And another thing - while I was on my own in that garden I couldn't stop thinking about my meetings with Jacob and Svetlana. It's like - what they said to me somehow got inside of me. I felt in some measure, that I had had my battle with God, not at Jabbok, but on the seashore. In that garden - well, I don't know how to put it, but I knew I was known - through and through. I kept thinking of old Jacob saying, 'and do you know, Douglas, he liked what he saw, and he blessed it.' I had a curious sense that God (yes, maybe he is there after all) looked into all my questions, and rather than rebuking me for them, he actually liked my questioning self. And I really felt blessed - I truly did. And I thought of Svetlana and her account of the rabbi totally accepting and loving her, despite all the rubbish in her life. And in some bizarre way, I saw that rabbi, that Messiah, crumpled and trembling like a fallen leaf in a woodland. It was terrible to see, but the fact that he has been there…. That's what counts. I've got so much to think about.

I've decided I'm not going back to England in the near future. They will all want to know if I have recovered my faith, and I haven't. At least, I haven't recovered the faith I lived and preached up until Saoirse died. Something is coming to life in me, but if feels like a different faith. The faith I now have, I doubt any of them would understand - any, except Mavis, and I'll drop her an email soon. I'll invite her to visit here. She'd love Kathleen. But most of the others will want me back just as I was, and they are never going to get that, so I have just written to Bp Pauline to say that I won't be coming back to serve in the parish. I hope she won't be too disappointed. Sort of feel she'll understand. And one less problem for her to deal with!

I've asked Mrs O'Connell if I can stay another couple of weeks here, just to let things settle in me a bit. It won't be quite the same without old Dorch - I wonder where he's gone? He was so broken when I last saw him, poor soul. But Mary assured me he was well, and I know he survived the storm. I hope he'll be back soon.

Later

I am beginning to think that maybe that crazy old Guinness-slurping guy actually is an angel after all. Well, let's put it this way - one thing I am certain of now is that he genuinely believes he is. He may be highly deluded, but he is certainly not trying to deceive people. I find that a very comforting thought.

When she came to visit me in hospital, Kath bought me an old collection of poems that she had picked up in the charity shop. So sweet of her - Dorch had told her I liked poems. When I opened the book it fell open at George Herbert's 'The Collar'. Not read it for years, but was comforted by the fact that he got pretty angry with God. I love the last lines that come after his rant,

> But as I rav'd and grew more fierce and wilde
> At every word
> Me thought I heard one calling, 'Childe';
> And I reply'd, 'My Lord.'

Somehow feels familiar. I'm not there yet, but at least now I can imagine a day when I might say, 'My Lord.'

Oh, I was having a cup of tea with Mrs O'Connell (she tells me I'm to call her Elsie now). She has a great love for the old Celtic saints like Brigid, Brendan and so on. They don't do a huge amount for me, but she loves them. She told me an old story that I rather liked. There's a big old monastery at a place called Clonmacnoise - it was huge in its time. Well, so the legend goes, one day all the monks were at prayer in the chapel, when a heavenly boat sails overhead drawing its anchor behind it. Then the anchor gets caught on the altar rail. The monks watch with amazement, and then they see one of the sailors climbing down the anchor rope. He struggles to free the anchor from the altar rail. Then the abbot cries out, 'free him!', because the angel - as they assume he is - can't survive in the oxygen of this world. So the monks do free him, and back he goes up to the boat. But then, Elsie said, in some versions of the story, when the angel is back on board, he reports with tears in his eyes that he has been to a most wonderful world, filled with glory. Made me think of Dorch. Yes, he has shown me much to do with the other world. But what really touches me is the way he really does love this world. He says Jesus also saw this world blazing with glory. I'd love to learn to see the world a bit more like that. As Dorch would say, it is how you see things that counts. And I love the thought of heaven and earth... well, just getting on so well together.

I still wish my Saoirse could do something like climbing down a rope to meet me here tonight. I shall never stop missing her. But Mary's song did heal something in me. I'm probably imagining it, but I could swear I heard two voices as she sang - was Saoirse's the other voice? If so, then sing to me again, my sweet. Sing your love through that thin veil. Sing whenever you can, whether I have the ears to hear or not. Sing me through each day of my life, and then one day we will sail the seas of heaven together with such songs on our lips to delight even the angels!

CHAPTER 23

As October drew to a close, the evenings drew in, and the scent of peat fires filled the streets of Dingle. Douglas took to regularly walking around the town and because he had not much else to do, he often passed the time of day with the locals. Usually the conversation turned to Dorchadas, and that always included smiles and laughter. People knew about the seashore incident, but nobody asked him about it, even though some suspected that the grief-filled English priest was trying to put an end to his misery. In a sense, whatever happened in that sea did put an end to the misery. He was much more cheerful, though any mention of his Irish wife still caused the sorrow to show in his eyes, so generally people kept clear of the subject. Most of them were no strangers to grief, and they knew the hard road he had been travelling. The Catholic priest of the town had also been to visit Douglas and showed much kindness, and he noticed that the Englishman appeared once or twice at the back of church at Mass.

Kathleen had raced back from Adare when she heard of Douglas' accident, but later told Douglas that she had had a very good meeting with Peter, who, she said, still looked as beautiful as ever, now with silver hair and stylish beard. He had recovered from their shared trauma, trained as a Psychotherapist and had practiced in Adare for all his working life. He had married a Scottish girl who had died a few years ago. He had become a Quaker, said Kath, but remarked that you wouldn't know it for the quantity of talking he did. Douglas found it hard to believe he was out-talking Kath, but she insisted he did. Seeing Peter was clearly a great help to Kath. As she put it, she could put her demons to bed now. And what's more Peter was going to make his way down to Dingle to make her a visit and, so she said, he was much looking forward to meeting Douglas.

Douglas also had some good conversations with Kevin at the *Angels Rest* and developed a keen interest in Irish politics as a result of their chats. In fact, in time Kevin became his best friend in Dingle which Douglas found an extraordinary and wonderful irony.

He invited Mavis out to Ireland. She was far too nervous to come on her own, so she brought her niece, Alice, with her. Douglas had never met Alice because she had lived in Provence with her French husband, but when the marriage broke down she returned to Sheffield and was currently living with her aunt, with whom she got on much better than her mother. Douglas had a great time driving them around the Dingle Peninsula, and introducing them to his new friends. Mavis was delighted to see Douglas looking so much better.

Douglas decided to spend all his three months in Dingle, and Elsie agreed a very acceptable rate for his lodging for this period of time. Then, one day, he got a phone call out of the blue from an unknown number in England. He was told that he had to attend a meeting that was to be regarded as strictly confidential. It all sounded very cloak and dagger, but he agreed to go to a hotel in Killarney to meet with someone whose name was not given to him. He was to tell nobody, so he just told Elsie that he was having a day out exploring the Ring of Kerry.

He arrived in good time at the hotel and went to the small meeting room as instructed. A coffee was brought in and he waited, reading a paper he had brought with him. At 11am the door opened and a very smartly dressed man came in and greeted Douglas. They both sat at a table near the window. The gentleman pulled out a small folder and placed it in front of him.

He drew out from it a card which he handed to Douglas and said, 'Thank you very much Reverend Romer for seeing me. Don't be alarmed, but I am from British Intelligence. Here are my credentials if you wish to check my identity.' Douglas was very taken aback by finding himself in the company of someone, the like of whom he only ever knew in spy thriller novels and movies. The card he studied gave no name, but showed the photograph of the man across the table from him. It contained some information and official looking signatures.

'Now we have received information about the murder of your deceased wife, Mrs Saoirse Romer,' he said in his very clipped English accent and badly mispronouncing her name, 'but I must insist you keep this information completely confidential. I cannot stress this enough. Before I go on, can I be assured of your confidentiality?'

Douglas nodded. 'Well, I am pleased to let you know,' continued the man, 'that the Kenyan police have apprehended a suspect who has confessed to the murder.'

Douglas felt a cold sweat break out. He had been doing so well these last couple of weeks, but to be taken in to a secret meeting and to be told about the murderer made him feel very unstable again.

The officer ignored the obvious discomfort of Douglas and continued, 'He was detained last week and he is talking. We now have some new and very significant information about the motivation for the attack. And it is not as we were originally led to believe - a terrorist incident. The suspect has indeed worked for terrorist organisations, notably Boko Haram. He is a Congolese national based in Nairobi, and the Kenyan police were watching him but he somehow slipped unnoticed to Cairo. Typical I'm afraid. Now this is perhaps the interesting and disturbing part. We have ascertained that the suspect was recruited not to carry out a random murder of British tourists, but I am afraid to report, he was recruited to single out your wife.'

Douglas was stunned. He gripped the table as he asked, 'Who on earth would want to single out my Saoirse?'

'What we have gleaned thus far,' continued the officer in a voice completely without feeling, 'is that your wife had developed a suspicion about someone in her work or circle of friends.'

'Suspicion?'

'Yes, you see the cause of her... er, demise, is that she had knowledge.'

'Knowledge? Knowledge of what, for goodness sakes?'

'Knowledge of an illegal arms trade.'

'Illegal arms trade?"

'Reverend Romer, may I suggest I just tell you the facts without your repeatedly questioning every sentence?' said the officer curtly. Douglas felt panic rising.

'Your wife - I beg your pardon, your deceased wife - was an extremely intelligent person. As I am sure you know, she was a passionate opponent of the arms trade, both legal and illegal. Well, it is evident that, somehow or other, she came upon some information that led her to believe that a person known to her was engaged in such trade, almost certainly the illegal arms trade. I can only assume she did not tell you until she was sure of her evidence. She was aware there was some risk involved, and you were a public figure.'

'As was she,' added Douglas.

'Quite so. Well, what we are currently surmising is that she challenged this person directly, which if I may say so, was somewhat foolish. She probably had no clue as to how dangerous this was. I imagine that person strenuously denied it, but was clearly panicked by the fact that she was on to him, because our suspect in Nairobi tells us that an unnamed Englishman from Sheffield ordered Mrs Romer's assassination to prevent her from revealing his identity.

'Well, once the man in England heard that Mrs Romer was going to Cairo, the job was relatively easy. Apparently, his normal trade route was with the DRC and he arranged through his contacts for an assassin to be recruited, and this assassin was sent with a nice wad of money to Cairo, and he was told he should make the shooting look like a drive-by terrorist incident so that no-one would have any suspicions about a link with the illegal arms trade. Once the assassin reported he had done the job and escaped back to Nairobi, the Englishman probably assumed the job was complete and the likelihood is that he ceased any contact with the assassin.

Douglas was shaking his head and heard himself muttering something incoherent. He felt he was going to be sick, so he breathed in hard to steady himself.

'Now, the thing is Reverend Romer, it is essential we keep the arrest of the suspect completely confidential. The Kenyan police will keep his arrest a secret, but there will be people in Nairobi starting to ask questions about his whereabouts. It is essential that the suspect in England, whoever he or she is, does not know the assassin is in police custody. At the moment he believes his anonymity is protected. If he knew the assassin was in police hands, he would assume that information could be passed down the line that would soon lead to him. And of course, we are hoping that is exactly what will happen. But we want to get started on the hunt this end in case he should run. So, as you can see,' he continued as he shuffled papers back into the folder, 'it is important that you are aware of this, and we will need to have further highly confidential discussions with you to ascertain from you if you feel there has been any suspicious activity among your circle of friends and associates.'

'Yes… of course,' said Douglas uncertainly.

'And, Reverend Romer. I appreciate this may be difficult for you, but you do need to realise that the suspect we are looking for may actually be a member of your congregation.'

'An illegal arms dealer in my church?' said Douglas indignantly. 'That's certainly not possible.'

'Reverend Romer, when you have been in this job as long as I have, you learn that there is absolutely nobody you can trust. Nobody. You will need to give very careful thought to the members of your flock. Now I hear you are resigning.'

'What? How did you know that?'

'Oh, we are paid to know things. There is very little we do not know about you. But please be assured, it is all highly confidential. As I say, you are resigning and I believe you are currently settling in the Irish Republic, in which case we will come over here to meet with you here. Now, if you will excuse me, I need to be on my way as I have a plane back to London leaving shortly from Cork.'

The man continued with other various instructions to do with security and how he would communicate with Douglas, and then abruptly stood up, gave Douglas a quick shake of the hand, and just before he left he said, 'Please remember you are to tell no mortal soul anything about any of this.'

After the man left, Douglas made straight for the bar and, despite the fact he was driving, ordered a double whisky which helped to steady him. Initially he simply sat at the bar shaking and going over the conversation again and again. But the whisky helped to settle him a little and he felt a surprising calm come over him, and the calmness was in part due to a realisation and a memory.

The realisation was that he actually had one contact who was not mortal - Dorchadas! Once he had tracked down that old friend again, he would have one person to share this with, and so would not have to carry it alone.

The memory was the conversation with Mary Magdalene in the garden, and he could remember her words precisely: 'and there will be another darkness to face which you must face with great courage. Dorchadas will be with you to help. I cannot tell you more about this now.' She had known something, and this news he had just heard had to be the something to which she was referring. The darkness he now had to face was to do with the hideous fact that there was someone in his home city who intentionally sought to murder the most beautiful life he had ever known. This was dark indeed. This was the darkness of evil.

The hotel lounge was buzzing with life, but at the end of the bar there sat a very still English priest who was filled with a surprising peace. Despite the horrifying information he had just received, he nonetheless felt a most unusual calmness. It was a calmness rooted in resolve. He had not been given his recent, intense experience of light in that blessed garden just to sit back and watch darkness prosper. He felt a new power within him, and it was a power of determination - that determination which he saw so clearly in his beloved wife: to champion the things of goodness and light in this world, and to challenge the things of evil.

After draining his glass, he said to no-one in particular, 'And darkness was on the face of the deep, but God said "Let there be light!"'

He then stood up and, much to the surprise of those near him, he said, 'So indeed, let there be light!' With that, he banged the glass on the bar and strode out of the hotel.

NOTES

The quotations from Belden C Lane's *The Solace of Fierce Landscapes* (Oxford University Press 1998) can be found on pages 25, 106 and 184. Reproduced with kind permission of the author.

The quotation on p.2 is from Hebrews 13.2

The Bible stories referenced:
Jacob: Genesis 32.22-31
Svetlana (the woman at the well): John 4.5-32
Annas: John 18.12-24
Gethsemane: Luke 22.43

All the characters in this book are fictional. Much of the action of the book takes place in the beautiful town of Dingle. I have taken some liberties with the geography and plan of this town and surroundings, for which I hope the people of Dingle will forgive me.

The Face of the Deep is part 1 of a trilogy of stories centring around the character of Douglas Romer.

Printed in Great Britain
by Amazon

33534186R00113